CRACKED LINE

AN URBAN FANTASY

ANN GIMPEL

CONTENTS

CRACKED LINE

CATACLYSM SERIES, BOOK THREE

An Urban Fantasy

**By
Ann Gimpel**

Tumble off reality's edge into myth, magic, and Armageddon

Copyright Page

Vampires don't fall in love. Except I did.

Not the best decision of my long life. I definitely cracked an unspoken line, but Ariana trounced me as far as line-crossing went. Very few acts constitute crimes in Vampire circles. Hers was the worst. I fled to the Old Country to buy myself thinking time.

I still loved her, but what she'd done was so vile I couldn't set it aside.

The world is a very different place from when I went into stasis. I woke to wars on every side. Vampires are scarcely strangers to battle. No one's ever accepted us, but they've mostly let us be. It's different this time. Very different. Mortals won't rest until they've wiped out magic.

Normally, their efforts would be laughable, but they've co-opted help from mages. Ones they've imprisoned and systematically stripped of power until the poor sods would agree to anything in exchange for their freedom—and their magic.

We face huge problems, but I'm tackling them one by one. I'll return to Ariana's side, but perhaps only as her comrade-in-arms. Time will tell if we can be more to each other.

Time and circumstances. In a world without magic, Vampires will wither along with every other magic-wielder. I cannot let that happen.

AUTHOR'S NOTE

Part of me can scarcely believe I'm writing this series. Vampires have been the bad guys in my Bitter Harvest series and my Gatekeeper series, and several others. Not so in the Cataclysm books.

Maybe I named the series what I did because turning Vampires into heroes was cataclysmic for me. Mortals are a sketchy lot. When the reality of magical beings got a little too close, they banded together and fought back. Silly of them, huh? Even an army of humans isn't a match for a couple of determined magic-wielders, but they're going to have to figure that out on their own.

Ariana is a great heroine. I'm excited to tell you her story. And Nickolas is emerging as a Vampire I'd love to have next door. You know, for the cleanup work when things get dicey. Conan is perfect. He reminds me of my own wolves: noble, principled, and courageous as hell.

CHAPTER ONE, NICKOLAS

Scottish Highlands

So far, the plastic cards that passed for money in this strange modern world hadn't failed me yet. Someone must be paying the bills back at *Ascent*, a nightclub owned by the woman I love. I truly hope she wasn't underwriting my expenses. One of my Vampire associates from Clan Giovanni is there too. I don't feel much better sticking him with my overhead, but I'm still working things out.

I arrived in Ireland a fortnight ago after crewing on a fishing vessel that was crossing the North Atlantic. I couldn't force myself into an airplane. I can teleport if the distances aren't overly long, but something about the specter of flying makes my skin crawl. I spent time at a couple of airports, and all it did was solidify my uneasiness.

I'm a Vampire. That says everything—or it should. Luckily, the night shift on fishing boats isn't popular. When I made it clear the dark hours were my preferred assignment, I had my choice of crafts. I picked the one that looked the most seaworthy and was shocked how little time it took to cross the choppy Atlantic. My journey from east to west a century before had taken weeks. This trip was over and done with in scarcely a handful of days, spitting me out in Galway.

The captain wanted some electronic something-or-other to transfer my wages, but I insisted on cash. It irked him, but I'd been a hard enough worker, he didn't dismiss me without my money. It wasn't much, but it was enough to rent a room at some point. I had no intention of remaining where I was. Thank all the demons Ireland is perpetually gray, otherwise leaving the ship would have been much more difficult than it was.

I holed up in a squalid pub for what remained of that day. Its allure was it only had one very small window, and it was so dirty not much light filtered inside. The place was empty enough, the proprietor seemed grateful for the brews I purchased. I kept expecting him to insist I buy more, but he never did. Judging from the appearance of his establishment, he was used to patrons who were barely hanging on.

Once it grew dark, I scuttled through the door and hunted for a spot I could teleport from. I wasn't at my best. Fish blood is near the bottom of my list of preferred food. Even obtaining that was a challenge on board the ship because I was rarely by myself.

Tonight, my destination was the Scottish Highlands. My hopes were high I'd find swathes of deserted forest where I could hunt. Because the northernmost lands have always had plentiful game, I aimed for the Northwest Highlands not far from Loch Shin. My spell ran true, and I retained lodgings in a down-at-the-heels boarding house. While far more populated than I remembered, the region met my needs well enough. I'd been born not far from here in a humble shepherd's cottage around five hundred years ago. After cleaning up—I still smelled vaguely of fish—I went hunting. My sense of humor returned after draining a sixth rabbit, and I was able to accept the folly in my expectations naught would have altered during my long absence. The lush forests from my memories had been reduced to not much more than the odd tree here and there, but they were sufficient to meet my needs.

I had no idea what to expect in Castelrotto, Italy, but my plan was to locate my Vampire clan and demand my share of its wealth. It wouldn't go over well, but once I'd been master of the clan. I might have to do battle with the current master, but it could be arranged. I wouldn't stand by and let them fuck me out of what was rightfully mine.

Assuming Clan Giovanni still existed. It could have fallen to ruin in the century since I'd left, with its members dividing the spoils and running for cover.

Throughout my days crossing the United States, and still more on the boat, I'd made up my mind to return to *Ascent* and my friends there. And to repay my debt to Ariana. It was the primary reason I wanted my fair cut of the clan's riches. My other reason for returning was I'd signed on to be a soldier in the supernatural army squaring off against mortals who wanted to crush everyone with magic. I wouldn't welch on my commitment.

I'd been one step up from destitute when I'd left the States; returning with money would ease my way on many fronts. And then, I'd be able to contribute to the war effort with more than my supernatural strength, speed, and affinity for killing.

The part that was still murky as hell was whether or not I'd try to mend things with Ariana beyond apologizing again for trying to kill her. Not that she didn't deserve death—or she would have if the old rules still applied. She'd beheaded Mistral, master of Clan Hawke and her maker. Vampires don't have a whole hell of a lot of rules, but we have clung to that one. For obvious reasons, the punishment for killing a master Vampire is permanent death.

Ariana has gotten away with her crime, probably because everyone assumed a male had murdered Mistral. Centuries had passed, and she'd ended up halfway around the world from where she'd committed her transgression. I'd known something ate at her, and I'd urged her to confide in me. Perhaps if I'd known I'd have kept my mouth shut.

Nah. Knowing would have made it all the worse. The second I found out, my innate vampiric reactions had kicked in, and I tried to end her. I might have succeeded if her dire wolf companion, who was far more than he appeared, hadn't intervened.

Before her revelation, Ariana and I had grown close. Close enough, I'd fallen hard for her. It was why she'd told me about Mistral. Once I was thinking clearly, I understood we could never have developed true intimacy with her guarding a secret like that one.

As usual, when I thought about Ariana, my head grew fuddled. Vampires did not select mates. We didn't "fall in love." Neither did we develop proprietary interests in our sex partners. But she cared about me. And I returned her interest, lust, and affections. That she'd laid aside her longstanding silence about Mistral told me how important I was to her. She'd divulged her secret with full knowledge I'd have every right to demand her execution.

I couldn't think about her for very long without feeling like a rat treading water. I never got any closer to a solution, but I didn't quit trying. I needed to settle on a path before I returned to the nightclub. Even if I vowed I was done hungering for Ariana, I wasn't at all certain I'd be able to follow through and keep my distance.

Every time I shut my eyes, she rose in all her dark-haired glory to tantalize me. Lush curves graced her tall, sinuously muscled body. With her acres of legs and full breasts, she was the stuff wet dreams were made of. And then some. Her eyes were a rich, mysterious blue that shaded from azure to lighter colors depending on her mood.

During my brief sojourn in Scotland, I spent my nights hunting. Days, I retreated to my lodging, thought about Ariana, and brought myself off to a stunning variety of fantasy images. Every evening, I swore I was done, but the following dawn found me with my cock in my hand, dreaming of all the things I wanted to do to pleasure Ariana.

After a week in the Highlands, I'd run out of excuses. My strength had returned. If I was going to go to Castelrotto and hunt for the remnants of my clan, I needed to get on with it. I timed my arrival to coincide with dusk and warded myself because I couldn't think of a single spot it would be safe to wink into view. Turned out to be a wise move on my part. The streets teemed with people, and I ducked into an alcove reeking of piss to drop the spell concealing me from view.

It didn't take long to locate a modest pension that advertised breakfast along with their room rate. Not that food is any kind of draw, but I needed a base to operate out of. I did not want to give the authorities any reason to look too closely at me. Ariana had shown me pictures of Castelrotto on her computer. If she hadn't, I'd have been in shock. The medieval town had altered beyond recognition. Even the ancient buildings had taken on new coloration, new fronts.

I waited until night was well underway to make a trek to the imposing Catholic church on the outskirts of town. Other cathedrals took up part of the town square, but we'd established a clan house beneath the Catholic church's graveyard, taking advantage of multiple crypts. Because the town was so old, excavations to build family tombs were common. We'd simply knocked out the earthen walls between several of them and created a commodious underground catacomb. Mortals had a healthy fear of the dead, so they never ventured into the tombs during nighttime hours. And only rarely visited them even in full daylight.

We made a practice of nabbing the occasional human who entered the crypts during the day. It kept us safe by spreading rumors of ghosts and demons.

And Vampires.

Aye, there was a time when we were feared. Respected, even.

I closed off my thoughts about an era that would never return and merged with chattering crowds cluttering the narrow streets. Why weren't all these people at home, eating their nighttime meal and reading bedtime stories to their children? Music drifted from several cafés along with the smells of everything from roasting meat to decadent sweets.

I can eat if I choose, but there's very little point since I derive zero nutrition from anything that isn't blood. The layout of the streets was the same—tough to alter something as basic as that. The odd person bid me a good evening. I replied in kind as I worked my way past the square and onto darker side streets. Even there, I still felt the press of thousands of mortals, packed into the ancient city like mackerels in crates on the fishing boat I'd just left.

The comparison made me smile. The stark truth was I viewed humans about the same way I viewed fish: not terribly bright and subject to the whims of their companions. If one fish swam into our nets, others were bound to follow it. The lemming effect in action.

I'd passed the worst of the crowds, and I welcomed the darkness as I left the brilliantly lit square. Two more turns and the dark, imposing bulk of the Catholic church came into view. First constructed around 1300, it had been completely rebuilt in the middle of the 1800s. Workmen had been so ubiquitous, we'd had to leave the clan house for several months.

I paused in the shelter of a stone overhang and risked a thin thread of magic. It ran forward unimpeded, and I redirected it to both sides. Not so much as a quiver disturbed my seeking spell. If anyone magical was nearby, they were deeply warded.

I hadn't exactly expected Clan Giovanni to still be in

residence beneath the church graveyard, but I had no idea where to hunt for them, either. Determined to search for clues, I started forward. No one saw me clear the fence around the cemetery. In the years since I'd left, someone had replaced the old wooden staves with chain link that stood taller than my head. Signs suggested entry to the cemetery was controlled by a single gate toward the front.

Graveyards are strange places. I sensed the departed far more strongly here than I had in the realms of the dead. Perhaps many of them had chosen not to cross over. Just like with every other creature, living or dead, there's not much love lost between corpses and Vampires. We have no further use for them, and they hate us because while we're dead—like them—we're still living the life they crave.

I glided to the Giovanni crypt. Our clan name is as common as Smythe or Jones in the U.K. We'd picked that crypt as a joke, but its generous entrance had served us well. Someone had slapped an official-looking proclamation on the door, along with a rusty padlock. The paper was badly weathered, but I could still read enough to get the gist.

Closed to entry—by anyone.

I hit the lock with the flat of my hand; it clattered to the dirt. Apparently, keeping riffraff out had been important once, but wasn't so critical anyone kept up with maintenance. I pushed the door open and ducked inside, pulling the door shut behind me. No one would see the broken lock in the dark, and I may as well maintain the illusion the crypt had been abandoned.

A quick sniff told me there hadn't been Vampires in this place for a long time, perhaps fifty years or more. I dialed in my night vision and strode down the long set of steps into the top level of the tomb. Raised biers lined both sides, like always. Atop them sat a variety of coffins that still stank of embalming fluid.

One more flight of stairs brought me to the stout oaken door that used to provide entry to our clan house. Or the remains of it. The planks bore ax marks, and then someone had nailed crosspieces over them. My earlier caution yielded to anger. I made short work of the cheap plywood sealing the door to what had once been my domain, and kicked it open.

Mortals had dared intrude on Clan Giovanni. I smelled them. Who would have done such a thing? More importantly, why weren't they dead and drained? I hadn't gotten two steps into the clan house when the unmistakable odor of silver burned the inside of my nostrils. I built a hasty ward. Nothing lived down here. I'd checked, and silver couldn't hurt me as long as I limited my exposure and didn't breathe it in. The latter is simple enough since I don't breathe, anyway.

Over the next hour, I searched every last cranny of my former home. My heart grew heavier with each dead Vampire I uncovered. Most were nothing but piles of bones. Why hadn't they teleported out of here? I didn't understand why they'd remained until they died from silver poisoning. Maybe some had escaped. Not everyone was here, but that didn't necessarily mean anything.

Our census could have changed in the years since I'd left.

I punched a wall in sheer frustration and was rewarded with the rumble of unstable dirt ready to cascade onto my head. After that, I latched my fingers together. I did not want to waste scads of magic digging myself out from beneath a cave-in.

How long ago had all this happened?

My first guess was it coincided with the notice tacked to the Giovanni crypt. If it was dated, I'd missed it, but I'd look again. I dragged Vampire remains into the main room. The least I could do was immolate them. My fire burned quick and clean. I crouched off to one side. If I'd still been human, I'd have paid lip service to some kind of prayer, but Vampires don't do things like that. The only deities we believe in are ourselves—and perhaps our makers.

It didn't take much to drag my thoughts back to Ariana. I knew her well enough to understand she must have suffered for her decision to decapitate Mistral. But she hadn't let it get in her way. Maybe when she'd done it, she'd been too young to fully appreciate the ramifications.

A rustle snagged my attention. It might have been the pop and crackle of my dying fire, but I didn't think so. Expecting anything from a nefarious boobytrap to a human with a silver dart gun, I shot to my feet and barked, "Show yourself."

I'd rather feel like an idiot, if no one was there, than have missed a critical clue that spelled my doom.

Shadows thickened, shifted, and reformed. When they quit undulating, Roseann walked out of them. "You're finally back," she said. The Vampire I remembered would have rushed into my arms and given me a hug, but she just stood watching me out of wary eyes.

"Aye. I'm back."

"Naught to return for." She ground out the words. Her flame-red hair had developed rust overtones. Her green eyes were dull. A patched skirt and stained white jacket covered her tall frame.

"What happened?" I asked.

"Pfft. What does it look like?" she countered. "A nosy priest led a mob of Vampire hunters right to us."

"Why didn't you fight back?"

She skinned back her upper lip, fangs on display. "What makes you think we didn't?"

"Because we're better than this." I swung an arm wide. "Since when can a passel of mortals kill so many Vampires?"

The anger that had glistened around her like a prickly cloak broke apart. She shook her head until strands of hair fell in her face.

"Did any of the rest of us survive?" I pressed. I didn't want to pillage her thoughts, but I would if she didn't start talking.

Roseann nodded dully. "Aye. A dozen. We left, obviously."

My fires were out but for glowing coals. "We should too," I told her.

Moving more like a very old woman than a Vampire, she lifted her head until her sad, green eyes bored into me. "I set a snare, so I'd know if anyone disturbed this place. The spell is so old, it shocked me when it chimed today." Pushing her shoulders straighter, she kept talking. "It's best if I leave. The others won't want to see you. They believe your lengthy absence was why we failed. A clan requires a master. If we'd had one, perhaps we'd have known some of our own led a double life."

My mouth fell open. "We were betrayed by our own?"

She nodded. "Fools. We were fools. We didn't pay attention until the poison had already taken hold. 'Twas subtle at first, so faint, we chalked it up to the drugs humans had begun imbibing by truckloads."

"If you deem it wise," I said, "tell the others I am deeply sorry. I was forced into stasis. It never occurred to me the clan wouldn't replace me."

Her eyes narrowed. "What of Clive and Lorenzo?"

"Clive is well. I left him in the northwestern United States. Lorenzo made some bad decisions. Humans killed him with silver darts."

She shrugged. "He always was too impulsive for his own good. Never could tell that boy anything."

I resisted wincing. Her description was accurate enough, yet I still blamed myself for his unfortunate demise. And now I had still more death on my conscience—or whatever passes for one in my kind.

Roseann turned to go.

"Wait. Please."

"Why?" She didn't turn around.

"Did you at least lay claim to our hoard?"

She twisted to face me. "You make us sound like a fucking flight of dragons." Her words might have been harsh, but a ghost of a smile played around her mouth.

"Well?" I raised my eyebrows into question marks.

Roseann spread her hands in front of her, the nails cracked and broken. "We were all sick when we teleported out of here. So weak if we hadn't helped one another, we'd never have escaped." A tear formed in the corner of one eye and rolled down her face. "We did the best we could. Even tried to spirit more of us away, but we knew we were done in." She shook her head. "We had to conserve what little ability we had to shield ourselves from discovery. It took months, maybe a year, before we regained enough strength to make a difference. By then, everyone here was…"

"It's all right." Her tale was almost as painful to hear as it was for her to tell it.

"No." She curled her fingers into fists and punched the air. "This will never be all right. The only good to come out of it was the perfidious scummy mortals killed our two-faced kinsmen."

"Damn. I was hoping to do that."

"They beat you to it." Roseann dropped her hands to her sides. "We'll never be the same, but we're alive, able to feed, and in a safe spot." She stood tall, the first show of spirit I'd seen since she materialized. "You'd asked about our money, our gold. Most of it was in that bank vault. Once the officials knew what we were, we were denied access. One of us tried to use a different name and barely escaped. If he hadn't been ready to teleport out of there, they'd have nabbed him."

I sucked air through my teeth. The bank had been my bright idea. It had seemed modern at the time. So much more civilized than burying gold bars and gemstones and hoping no one dug them up by accident.

"One more thing for me to apologize for," I mumbled.

"Eh, you couldn't have known."

"Same bank, right?" At her nod, I went on, "I'm going to

teleport in there and take what's ours. Where can I leave your share?"

Her faint smile had returned. "Right here, Nickolas. I'll be watching and rooting for you."

"Will you tell me who survived?"

She shook her head. "Better if you don't know."

"Will you tell them you saw me."

"Aye. I will do that."

Before I could list all the things I wanted her to relay from me, magic glistened around her and she was gone. Probably for the best. My days as master of this clan were over. And then some. I raked my hands through my hair. If I'd been here, would it have made a difference? I liked to believe it would have, but I might have been just as clueless as the rest of my clan.

I could dissect this later. My current task was to take back what was rightfully ours from the bunch of bastards who'd stolen it. More than furious enough to kill first and ask questions later, I set a teleport spell in motion, aiming for the basement of the Castelrotto branch of the Bank of Italy.

CHAPTER TWO, NICKOLAS

The brick walls of the lower level of the bank took shape around me. I felt the bite of metal. It made my skin seem one size too small, but I pushed the unpleasant sensation aside. I didn't plan to be here long enough for the iron in the walls and windows and vault to become an issue. A startled gasp told me I wasn't alone.

Before the uniformed man could summon help—or fire the sidearm he was grappling for—I immobilized him. Pouring on mesmerism, I dropped him in his tracks with way more magic than I actually needed. Once he crumpled to the floor, I took stock. The siren call of his jugulars was tough to resist, but I wasn't here to feed. Hell, I wasn't even hungry. A judiciously applied jolt of magic wiped out a chunk of his mind. That way, he wouldn't be able to talk, let alone describe me.

Leaving him sprawled on the fancy gray marble floor, I hustled to the vault. Once upon a time, it had required keys, but the lockset had been replaced by something electronic. Mechanical locks were well within the scope of my magic, but this type stubbornly refused to yield. Crap. What else was new? I feared if I kept chipping away at the damned thing, an alarm would go off, and I'd have to make a run for it. I wasted a moment hoping electronics, beloved brain children of mortals, would end up choking the life out of them.

I stared at the lock standing between me and the Clan Giovanni fortune—assuming no one had stolen our hoard in the intervening years. It sported a glass panel. I felt like an idiot once I understood it required a thumbprint. Heh. Easy enough, so long as the fellow I'd immobilized had access rights. Dirk in hand, I sliced cleanly through his thumb, severing it above the ball of his hand. Blood flowed, smelling heavenly. I gave the wound one quick suck and sprinted back to the lock. The amputated thumb did the trick. The door beeped three times and sprang open.

Better to err on the side of caution, so I shoved a crate into the doorway to keep it from timing out or whatever electronic locks did. Enough metal lined the walls, it might be tough to teleport from inside the vault. I should rob this place blind, but I've always had an honest streak. If my bins were empty, I might reconsider my moral-high-ground stance. No time like now to find out.

The bank might have modernized the lock to get inside this room lined with boxes and bins in assorted sizes, but they hadn't gone to the expense of altering anything else. I'd commissioned two of the largest slide-outs in a bottom row. They still required two keys, but the deadbolts turned obligingly when I jockeyed them with a quick blast of power. If I'd been the breathing type, breath would have whooshed from me.

I tugged one bin out, and then the next, examining them closely. If anyone had pilfered from Clan Giovanni's treasure, it wasn't obvious. Both containers were full to the top with gold bars and soft cloth bags brimming with fine gemstones. At the time I'd set this up, I hadn't bothered with money. Currency changed often enough, it made no sense to squirrel away banknotes that might become worthless when a regime changed.

So far, so good. Now all I had to do was grab the loot and get myself out of here. I started to lift the bins, but then I spied a stack of hefty burlap sacks in a corner and emptied out the contents of the bank boxes into them. All that gold was heavy. It would have defeated a mortal, but not me. Once the bins had been stripped, I shut and relocked them. A quick look around told me I'd done as good a job as I could covering my tracks.

The metal lining the vault was beginning to take its toll. While I could still make good on my escape, I tossed both bags over a shoulder and strode back into the main room, taking a moment to kick the crate back to its spot and allow the main door to swing shut. Nothing more for me to do here, so I summoned the magic I'd need to leave. The guard was just waking up, moaning in pain.

He was damned fortunate I hadn't killed him.

I got the fuck out of there before I changed my mind. I hadn't been hungry before, but I was now. I'd deal with that later. My first stop was the ruins of my clan house—and the remains of my kinsmen. I was bent over the contents of the sacks, dividing the spoils evenly when I felt Roseann's presence.

She knelt across from me, fangs on full display. "Damn if you didn't do it. Did you kill anybody? I smell blood. Please tell me you killed a score of those bastards."

"Nope. No killing. But we can't tarry. I maimed the guard and turned his mind to slurry. Tried to cover my tracks, but you know how it is."

She made a disgusted snorting sound. "Aye. This will be the first place they look. Never mind half a century has passed since they destroyed our lives."

At least that answered one of my questions. How long ago all this had happened. I returned my attention to the stacks of gold bars and bags of gemstones. "You said there were twelve of you. Clive is with me, so I shall take one seventh of what is here."

Rocking back on my heels, I looked at her, half expecting her to protest. Sharing wasn't built into our makeup. "You should take a quarter," she said firmly. "You risked yourself retrieving it, and three quarters will be more than ample to fill our needs."

"Are you certain?" When she nodded, I gathered a stack of gold and took one of the bags of gemstones. At the point when I'd been dividing the gems over a hundred years before, I'd made certain to place more or less equal value in each sack. I wrapped my portion in one of the burlap bags and stood.

Roseann stuffed everything else into the other one. It didn't fit very well, but all she had to do was teleport out of here. "Thank you, Nick." Her hands were full, so she walked close and nuzzled her head into my shoulder. "I chose well when I turned you that long ago night."

Her words warmed me. "I haven't forgotten."

She tilted her head back and looked at me. "I wouldn't think so. We never forget who made us. I won't see you again, will I?"

I shook my head. "Probably not. I'm returning to the States."

"May blood and magic light your path."

"Yours too, Rose." I'd have smiled at one of the few phrases that passed for a blessing among our kind, but something about standing in the wreckage of what had once been a vibrant seethe dragged at my soul.

Nothing remained to say. I waited until she'd gone before I took a final look around and set my own travel spell in motion. Dawn was just breaking when the walls of my small room at the modest inn I'd chosen formed around me. I needed a better way to conceal the gold and gems. Once I figured that part out, I'd begin the trek back to the Seattle area.

I had to wait out the day, anyway, so I took advantage of the time to sew pouches into my garments. My spare pair of trousers provided fabric. When I asked a tired-looking woman at the front desk where a dry goods store might be, she frowned and asked what I needed. Her dirty-blonde hair was going gray, and her blue eyes were bloodshot. The faint reek of alcohol clung to her.

Eh, maybe the term dry goods was outdated, but most women don't expect men to keep up with such things. I rattled off pins and a needle and stout thread and was rewarded with a smile. "You sew?" she sputtered.

"Och, and quite well." I laid on the Scottish brogue I'd been born with. My recent stint in the Highlands had gone a long way toward refreshing it. I avoided speaking Italian because my inflection would reveal I'd spent time in Northern Italy. It was simpler if the proprietor regarded me as a foreigner.

"There's a shop five doors down to the right," she said, "but I keep a kit here. You're welcome to take what you need. My eyes are going, and I can't do fine work any longer."

Her sewing box had been incredibly well-stocked. After I fumbled through it for a few minutes, she'd shoved the whole thing into my hands. "Return it when you're done. No rush."

I'd been planning to chop up the sacrificial pair of pants with my dirk, but her box contained scissors. I spent the rest of the day creating hiding places for the loot. Luckily, the gold bars were on the smallish side. Heavy, but not too difficult to hide. I wove illusion around the pockets in my pants, shirt, and jacket. There was just space in my boots for two thin bars of gold as well.

The day was fading when I trotted the sewing kit back to its owner, thanking her profusely, and giving her a few pound notes from my shipboard wages.

"Now, what am I going to do with those?" She shoved the money my way.

I pushed the notes back. "Take them to a bank. They'll change them to lira for you."

She shook her head. "I hate those places. But thank you for the thought."

I turned to go, and she called after me. "Take your money, Signore Giovanni."

"Apply it to my room rent." I set a brisk pace for my chamber, ignoring her protests that I'd paid in advance, which I had. This establishment had met my needs, and she'd saved me a trip outside in broad daylight. I'd leave as soon as it was full dark, but she didn't need to know that.

This wasn't the type of place that had daily maid service, but when they got around to checking my room—probably not until the week I'd paid for was done—I'd be long gone. I had things to work out, primarily how I'd finesse trip number two across the Atlantic, but the sooner I exited Castelrotto, the better. I didn't need to wait around for the local gendarmes to conduct a search. The more I thought about it, the surer I was the bank probably had those same camera things that were ubiquitous in the States. Digital demons that made it impossible to travel incognito.

One of the urban myths about us is we don't show up in mirrors or on film. It's total bullcrap. Of course we do. It's not as if we're not made of flesh. Dead flesh maybe, but we show up distressingly well on film.

I hadn't killed the guard, but I had maimed him. If they had a likeness of me captured somewhere, I needed to be gone. Now. Spurred into action, I packed my few things into the battered leather valise I'd picked up before leaving the States, and teleported back to the Highlands. I selected the same spot I'd been before. It felt familiar, and the hunting was good.

Usually, feeding improved my spirits, but I couldn't get the wreckage of the clan house out of my mind. At least I'd met one of my goals: figuring out what had happened to Clan Giovanni. Just because I didn't care for the answer didn't make my endeavor less successful, merely less palatable.

Nothing I could do would alter anything.

Picking it to bits mentally wasn't doing me any good.

Vampires don't fall in love, neither do we mourn. But I remembered grief from when I'd been human, and the pain of loss and guilt cut deep. I'd been sunk in stasis when my clan fell apart. The stain of failure would haunt me forever. I should have tried harder to get away from the black Sorcerers out for Vampire blood.

Or selected a far shorter time in stasis.

What in the hell had I been thinking? That I was the second coming of Sleeping Beauty or Snow White? Both those stories are true, by the way. And both involved Vampires, but that part of the old tales was expunged in the latter part of the 1600s.

Two more nights passed. I returned to the same rooming house where I'd stayed before. My cell phone wasn't working any longer. I assumed it required electricity, but the setup I'd gotten with it didn't match up to the wall plugs in my chamber. The village was shy on shops, but I caught a secondhand store at dusk. Luckily, a buxom lassie was working the till. Red curls bounced on her shoulders, and her blue eyes were kind and crinkled at the corners.

Afraid my lack of proper vocabulary would reveal how little I knew about everything, I merely showed her the phone and cord. She understood right away and went digging through a box overflowing with cords and connectors. Handing me one, she said, "This will do it."

I took her word for it, paid her, and skedaddled. Once I'd returned to my room, I plugged in the phone, reassured when a green charging indicator flashed across the display. I didn't need to hunt, but I had things to think about, and my logic improves after I'm adequately fed.

Should I call Ariana?

She was why I was fixing the phone to make it useable. Of course, I could call Clive, but he wasn't whom I wanted to talk with beyond seeing how things were going. If what Ariana said was true—and I had no reason to doubt her—any cell conversations had to be bland. Much like telepathy, anyone could listen in, although the modern term was hacking.

I settled in one of the few remaining groves of trees. This one had governmental warnings tacked on a fence circling it. Ignoring the Keep Out signs, I'd vaulted over the railing and buried myself in thick foliage. Returning to the States wouldn't be as straightforward as leaving. Crewing on a working ship would pose problems, especially given my preferred nighttime hours. No privacy on those types of vessels. Other workers would troll through my things. It meant if I chose that route, I'd have to keep the gold and gems on my person at all times.

Not impossible, but awkward when I was hauling and tossing and shoveling fish onto conveyor belts, the last step before they were flash frozen, swathed in plastic, and dumped into huge freezers. Presumably, I had access to funds to book a berth on a passenger ship, but I'd have to find a way to liquidate a gem or two. Again, not impossible, but I'd have to travel to a city and locate a broker who dealt in such transactions.

Most were scoundrels. The necessity of dealing with them set my teeth on edge. Flying was out of the question. In addition to my distrust of the silver tubes with wings, I'd discovered from the reading I'd done that airports had metal detectors. I'd never make it past them with all that gold strapped to my body.

More than anything, I needed advice. My lack of knowledge about this century was tripping me up. Other Vampire clans had lived in this region. Clan Hawke, for one. Ariana's erstwhile kinsfolk. The only problem with trying to find them is they wouldn't give me the time of day. Not just because I was the master who'd failed his clan—the thought made me wince and twisted my stomach into a sour knot— but because there's no love lost between our clans. I wasn't one of them, so I may as well be mortal or a Sorcerer or a Fae.

I wasn't getting anywhere. I've always hated it when I tossed out ideas and someone yes-butted me. Here I was doing it to myself. I shut my eyes and thought about geography. When I opened them, I had a solution. Something that would actually work.

I'd been so focused on traveling west, I'd ignored the other direction. I could teleport across Europe and Russia in divided jaunts. When I got to Russia's far east, it was the shortest of hops to the string of islands trailing off Alaska. From there, Kirkland and *Ascent* were one more travel spell away.

I buried the drained corpses from my night's feeding session, feeling pleased with myself. I'd wait out the day and leave the following evening. Only one unanswered question remained. Should I let Ariana know I was returning? Simple courtesy dictated a yes to that issue.

I leapt back across the fence after verifying no one was anywhere around and strode through the night toward my room. Roseann perched on the edge of my bed, obviously waiting for me. She'd lost some of the gaunt, desperate look she'd had in the ruined seethe, or maybe I just wanted her to look more relaxed.

I felt the flutter of her magic—thunder and blood—settle around us and faced her squarely. "What is it?"

She held up a finger as she first built and then tested a sound screen. Seemingly satisfied, she replied. "You have to go farther away than this. The bank caught you on camera. It must have taken them a while to determine it was you since they'd have to have relied on old portraits or photographs. If I could find you, so can they."

"How?" I demanded. "You know to track me with magic. Mortals can't do that."

Roseann shook her head. "You slept too long. Everything has changed. We're smack dab in the middle of a war with mortals who are sick of magic. Officials have offered inducements to make apprehending us easier. Some with magic work for them now." She closed a hand around my upper arm. "If I could locate you, so can they. The heist is all over the news."

I patted her hand and then uncurled her fingers from my arm. "Keep talking," I told her and changed into my clothes with the built in pockets, tucking gold and gems away as I went. What little else I had went into my scarred leather valise. I tossed the strap around my body. At least it settled the question about calling Ariana. I had my mostly charged phone in the valise along with both cords, but leaving took priority over everything else. Roseann wouldn't have made a trip to warn me if she weren't convinced my continued existence hinged on immediate action.

"Nothing much more to say," she murmured. "Cover your tracks as best you can. Don't remain too long in one place."

"Got it. Thanks for caring enough to alert me."

She made shooing motions. "Go. Thank me later."

She stopped before adding, *if there is a later*. I pulled power into the start of a journey spell. Before I kindled it, I said, "Your phone number. What is it?"

"No. This must be a clean break. If you call me, they can track your number. Goodbye, Nickolas. Blood and magic."

"May blood and magic light your path," I told her and loosed my casting, aiming for the oldest portion of Prague with its cobblestone streets and narrow alleyways. I felt certain the place must have changed, but it was still dark—barely—so perhaps I had some hopes of escaping detection.

I was warded to the nines. From my spell to my person. Luck was with me; a skinny, overhanging alleyway formed around me, thick with the stench of unwashed bodies and urine. Drunken bums tell no tales, or if they do no one believes them.

I lightened my ward to a don't-look-here spell and shambled to a set of steps leading below pavement level. The door at the bottom was locked, but it wasn't an impediment. Within, I found precisely what I'd hoped for, a storeroom cluttered with shelves and boxes and moldy paper. Prague is damp. Mold of all kinds is a perpetual problem. This was as good a spot as any to wait out the day. Come night, I'd get as far as I could into Russia. Maybe three more nights, and I'd be back at *Ascent*.

Roseann's warning put a damper on things, though. Would I be leading the authorities right to Ariana's doorstep? It decided me. I had to call her. This was her decision as much as mine. The next half hour turned into an exercise in frustration. Apparently, calling from one country to another required something special that I lacked.

By the time I was cycled through to a person—who fixed me up for an additional sum of money—I was ready to pound the phone into the concrete floor. No wonder mortals were such a pack of losers. No one in their right mind set up systems this difficult to navigate.

"Sir. Would you like me to connect you to your party now that we have your international calling plan activated?" the perky bitch on the other end asked.

"Aye. Please."

Ariana picked up on the first ring. "Nick? Is that you?"

"Aye. Who in the bloody hell else would it be?"

"Well, it could be anyone if you'd been captured," she said with a cheery asperity I remembered.

I started to laugh. Once I got hold of myself, she asked, "What's so fucking funny?"

"It would have been a rare kidnapper with the patience to get this infernal bit of plastic and glass to call from another country. It's good to hear your voice, Ariana." I winced. That last had slipped out. I needed to be more careful.

"Thanks," she said softly. "Are you coming home?"

Home. The word was like a gut shot. I wanted where she was to be my home more than I've ever wanted anything. "It depends," I replied and launched into a titrated, could-mean-anything version of my situation.

It was early afternoon, and I was still at *Ascent*. This was one day I hadn't gone home. Workmen were finally installing permanent decorative panels where I'd once had large plate glass windows. Ruby and Percy had told me they'd take care of everything, but I'd wanted to oversee the work.

It's this nasty control streak I have. But better to complain before something is sealed into place than afterward. Cheaper too. So far, it hadn't been too bad. I was swathed up in a hooded cloak, and I'd survived several forays into the bar's main room to oversee the installation. Conan stuck by my side like a wraith. Something had been bothering him since I'd been poisoned with silver on a distant world, but he wasn't ready to talk about it yet.

Enough time had passed, I didn't think he ever would.

"Maybe we can go for a motorcycle ride tonight," I suggested.

His ears flicked toward me as he looked up. *"Can we hunt?"*

I smiled. "Of course."

We hustled into the stockroom in time to hear my phone trill. I snatched it up, saw Nick's name, and almost had a heart attack. A metaphorical one. Vampires don't have cardiac events. Spiraling between delight he'd broken through his outrage at what I'd done—at least enough to reach out—and concern for his situation, I listened as he glossed over events. The glossing part was smart of him in case anyone chose to listen in. Despite the places where he was vague, I was able to fill in most of the blanks.

"I'm sorry about your, erm, guild house," I murmured.

He grunted. It could have meant anything, but my bet was he'd ripped himself a new one for not being there when his clan needed him. "Ariana?" he prodded.

"I'm listening," I reassured him.

"Nay. You're not. I asked you a question."

I sorted through what he'd said before I repeated, "Come home. We'll stand together."

"Are you certain? It might worsen your situation."

"Hard to see how," I mumbled. "A lot has happened."

He made a rude noise. "I'm beginning to hate that phrase. All right. Signing off for now."

Before I could say anything else, the line developed a hollow aspect that told me he'd disconnected. I hustled to the back door and snatched the surveillance devices planted by the paranormal task force. Once I had them in hand, I dropped the bugs and ground them beneath the heel of my boot. The detectives who'd hidden them were dead, and I was sick of pussyfooting around in my own office. If anyone was still monitoring them, they could kiss my ass.

"Past time for that little maneuver." Conan woofed approvingly. "Where's Nick?" he added.

Now that we weren't within earshot of the work crew, he didn't have to use telepathy. Everyone likes to think their dogs talk with them, except my wolf actually does. Because he isn't really a wolf at all, but an ancient magical being. Guardians can take any form they wish, and with a whole hell of a lot less fanfare than normal Shifters. I'd rescued Conan as a scrawny, frightened puppy hundreds of years ago; we'd been together ever since.

"Not sure," I said. "He was evasive. Best I can piece things together, he returned to his clan house and found it ripped apart and most of the Vampires dead. Only a handful survived. Nick broke into the bank where he'd sequestered the clan's wealth, and now the authorities have put out an APB for him."

Conan growled; hackles raised the length of his back. "Means they're looking for him. Right?"

I nodded.

The scents of fur and rain-wet rocks rose, along with the distinct feel of Conan's magic. "Where are you going?" I asked, not expecting an answer.

"To fetch him."

"He said he'd be back here in three days." I frowned. At least I thought that was what he'd meant.

The large wolf shook himself, Black and silver fur flew every which way. "I can bring him back much faster than that."

I dropped a hand on his shoulders. "You forgave him?"

The wolf made a coughing sound that turned into a snarl. "He redeemed himself when he led other guardians to Onyx and rescued us." Conan hesitated before adding. "I couldn't save you. The only reason you are still alive is because of him—and my mother."

It didn't seem like the time to remind him I was dead. Vampirism was a complex topic; not one we ever discussed.

We'd run out of words. When Conan's magic cleared, he was gone.

I made another trip to the main room and ran into Ruby. A Fae even older than I am, she sported multicolored hair. Today, it was done up in shades of silver, blue, and purple. Her eyes had taken on deep-violet matching tones. She wore her usual dark slacks, white shirt, and creased leather vest. Considerably shorter than me, she stood perhaps five feet ten. Her feet were bare, and crimson droplets skimmed the floor from where she'd stepped on construction debris.

I made a slight hissing sound and angled my gaze at her errant blood. None of the workmen had noticed the swirly circles merging with each other, but if they looked this way, the jig would be up. Fae blood is unpredictable and a primary element in spells. If any of the mortals raised an alarm about devil-magic on the loose, Ruby's blood was perfectly capable of shaping itself into a pack of sabers and running the lot of them through.

Ruby's full mouth rounded into an O; a subtle weave of power surrounded her blood, and it arrowed its way back toward her, vanishing on contact. "You can go home if you'd like," she told me. "I've got this—and I promise to put on shoes. In fact, I'll do that right now. I left a pair in the stockroom."

I followed her across the expanse of floor and kicked the door to the back room shut once we were both inside. Before I could gin up a lecture highlighting all the times I'd had to remind her to don footwear, she asked, "Where's Conan?"

"Erm. He went somewhere."

Ruby pushed a hank of glittery hair behind one ear and slid her feet into running shoes, not bothering with the laces. "I figured that part out." Her tone was dry. A whisper of Fae magic settled around me, digging and probing.

Too late to ward my knowledge. "Stop that," I said, indignant at being mined for data.

She shrugged. "You don't seem to be in a talkative mood. I have workarounds for that. Besides, this place is bugged."

"Not anymore, it's not. Beyond that part"—I bristled—"just because you can doesn't mean you should, and—"

"Pfft. Spare me." Her eyes widened; for a moment her glamour dissipated, and I caught a glimpse of golden wings. She rushed forward and hugged me. "Why didn't you tell me you heard from Nick? Where is he? What did he say? Is he coming back? When?"

I disentangled her arms. Vampires aren't exactly the huggy type. Undeterred, Ruby was still chattering a mile a minute. "I told you he'd come back. Remember?"

"Yes. Of course, I do. He ran into a spot of trouble, or I might not have heard from him." In response to Ruby's waggling fingers, I filled in what few details I had.

"He could have gone anywhere," Ruby said after listening for a change, rather than talking.

"Could he?" I furled my brows. "It appears he cooked his goose good in Italy, which means the rest of the continent wouldn't be safe, either."

"Aw hell, there's South America, Australia, Russia. Lots of possibilities." She wound her long fingers around my forearm. "He cares, Ariana. He called to give you a choice because he was worried about causing trouble for you."

I wrenched my arm free. "Damn it, Ruby. He tried to kill me."

"Eh. Lover's spat." She winked lewdly. "Admit it, sweetie. When he was all over you, wasn't there a teensy part of your busy little mind that loved how he felt plastered the length of your body?"

She'd hit uncomfortably close to the mark. If I'd been human, I'd have turned bright red. Not having much of a circulatory system has its perks. Vampires do have blood, but it dries up damned fast if someone chops off our heads. I've always believed it was more for show and to keep our bodies looking human than for its usual purpose, which is moving oxygen and sustenance to every cell.

"We are not going to discuss this." I aimed for as much dignity as I could muster with her leering at me.

"A wee bit too accurate for your taste, huh?" She closed her teeth over her lower lip. "Guess you won't be going home. Not if Nick's arrival is imminent. Is that where Conan went?"

I'm normally an intensely private Vampire. Ruby's relentless spate of Twenty Questions was beginning to feel intrusive, but she meant well. More than a busybody reveling in idle gossip, she truly cared about me. And Conan. And apparently, Nick.

She'd been right about me not going home. All I'd do there would be to pace and fret and worry. And it was stupid. Nickolas was a Vampire, for fuck's sake. And an old one at that. He knew how to take care of himself. A part of me was delighted he'd made off with his clan's treasure. I'd have to ask why he'd trusted it to a bank. Deep in a cave shrouded in spells would have been far safer.

"Ariana?" Ruby elbowed me.

"What?"

"I'm here, sweetie. Talk with me."

"My mind's all over the place. When you poked me, I was wondering why in the hell Nick entrusted his clan's riches to a bank. Crap. If the bank had been in Germany or Austria or Southern Italy or even Switzerland, his hoard would have been commandeered by the bank's officials."

"Perhaps not." Ruby sounded thoughtful. "Mortals fear us. Their antipathy runs so deep, they'd have to be desperate to touch anything that had once been ours."

I tried to muffle a snort, but lost the battle. "The only type of magic that's contagious is vampirism, and we pick and choose carefully. Most mortals aren't worthy of the honor."

It was Ruby's turn to snort. "A few years back, before I got to know you, I'd have said honor and Vampire didn't belong in the same sentence."

"And now?" I cast a sidelong look her way.

"Let's just say I've altered my perceptions."

"I understand how you've come to accept me, but why Nick? Or Clive? You barely know them."

Ruby hesitated; it told me she was considering my question and that I'd receive a sincere response. She hoisted a hip onto the edge of my desk, laced her fingers, and settled her chin atop them. "When I first told my kin at the guild house I was considering working here, they did everything but bury me in spells to dissuade me.

"I got it," she continued. "I'd been raised with the same nasty tales about Vampires as they were. I'd run across a few, mostly in the Old Country, and they always kept to themselves. I'd never totally understood why the rest of dye magical world hated you so much."

I bent a foot around a chair leg and dragged it to where I could sit facing the Fae. Despite working together for a few years, I'd never heard this particular story. "Go on."

She nodded. "I've never been a big believer in doing something because it's the way it's always been done. So I did some digging. Made a trip back to Bavaria and spent days in our largest library reading."

I hated to admit it, but she'd hooked me. I wanted to know what she found. I would have far preferred the condensed version, but I knew better than to try to hurry her. Among their other traits, Fae are born storytellers. Most of the bards of old had more than a spattering of Fae blood.

A staunch knock on my stockroom door shot me to my feet. Ruby reconstructed her slipping glamour, and I opened the door. The crew boss stood there, looking uncomfortable. In his fifties and medium height with close-cropped brown hair, he wore white overalls spattered with paint and dye stains. "Sorry to bother you, Ms. Hawke. Kept waiting for you to make another run through the front, but you didn't."

"It's okay. What's up?"

"We're about done for today. One more day should do it. We've installed the panels. Tomorrow, we'll put a final coat of weather-sealing on them. Were you still wanting a mural on the inside?"

"Yaasss!" Ruby squealed. "We absolutely want a mural." She glided to my side. "Why didn't you tell me that part?"

"Because I was still thinking about it."

"We can have nymphs and satyrs. A regular Bacchanalian display," she gushed.

"Huh?" The crew boss looked mystified.

"Never mind." I spoke up quickly before Ruby launched into graphic sexual imagery.

"Alrighty, then," the man said. "We'll prime the wood facing the nightclub, and then you can hire an artist to paint Bachan—whatever on it."

"Thank you." I aimed a winning smile with a tinge of persuasion his way.

"You're most welcome. Looks as if the original work order will do it. I'll finalize things tomorrow, and you can pay off that as the invoice."

"Works for me," I told him.

His brown eyes skittered from Ruby to me and back. I didn't have to help myself to his thoughts to know he was wondering if we got into a little girl-on-girl action. The idea tantalized him. Before he traveled any further down that particular avenue, I repeated, "Thank you," and added, "See you tomorrow," for good measure.

It worked. He left. I kneed the door closed behind his retreating form.

Ruby was rubbing her hands together, no doubt in anticipation of a mural that would turn us into an X-rated porn hub.

"No," I said sternly.

"No what?" She can be the soul of innocence when she wants.

"Everyone who works here gets a say in the mural, which includes if we have one or not."

If her wings had been on display, they'd have drooped right along with her pointed ears. "But I can draw up a few concepts, right?"

"Sure. But don't put too much time into them."

"Why not."

I wrapped an arm around her shoulders. "Because I know you, and you'll be hurt if no one likes your ideas well enough to blow them up and stare at them every night." I winced. "Sorry. That was a bit blunt, even for me."

"You're probably right, though," she mumbled. "Hey!"

"Hey what?" I girded myself for an end run, but she surprised me.

"Throw a contest. Put a box near the door and have the customers write what they'd like to see on a wall-panel mural. Winner gets, oh I don't know, free booze for a year."

A laugh bubbled from me. "That's a fantastic idea, Ruby. I love it."

"Really?"

I nodded. "Really. All except the free booze for a year part. Maybe free booze for a month, but not for a year."

"Excellent. I'll make it happen. We'll need to publicize it. Maybe I'll drop an ad in the local papers. And online. We can put it on the Facebook and Twitter pages."

"Don't forget Instagram." I was still laughing.

"Social media shit sucks," she said. "But it's still the best way to get the word out." Ruby wagged a finger at me. "You be nice now. No prickles."

I shook my head, confused. "Of course I'll be nice to whomever wins—" I began.

"Not what I meant," she cut in. "Be nice to Nick. Don't chase him away. Again."

I showed her my teeth—and my fangs. "I did not chase him away the first time."

"Details." She flapped a hand my way. "You have another chance."

"So does he," I reminded her.

"Not the way men think," she informed me loftily.

"How would you know?" I demanded, and then sliced a hand downward to nullify my question. "What did you uncover about Vampires that made you willing to take a chance and work with one."

"That is where we were, wasn't it?" she mused.

"Yup. Exactly where we were when the crew boss showed up."

She raked her fingers through her hair. "I have so much to do, now's not the best time, and—"

"Uh-uh." I shook my head. "You can't open a topic like that and run off to your sketch pad. I don't need all the grisly details. Just the Cliffs Notes will do."

"Do they even still have those?" She quirked one dark brow.

"Not the point." I curved two fingers into a come-along motion, certain if I let this drop I'd never drag the story out of her.

Ruby twisted her mouth into a frown. "The first Vampire started out as an arrogant human who pissed off a few gods. Their punishments, piled one on top of another over a period of several transgressions on his part, created the basics."

I nodded. I knew that part. "Yeah. His name was Ambrogio, and Artemis was who did most of the cursing."

"Of course, you'd have been taught your history," she murmured thoughtfully. "Since you didn't know about the guardians, I bet you had no idea they intervened."

I certainly didn't. "Keep talking, sister," I urged.

"It was during a phase when they were experimenting with some of their charges in the realm of the dead. Apparently, they'd selected a few mortals in hopes of bringing them back to life, and—"

"What better way than vampirism," I growled.

"Yup, except no one wanted to cooperate. Not the Vampires, and not the dead mortals—once they discovered what they'd become. Rather than spread the blame equally for their failed endeavor—half on humans and half on Vamps — the guardians assigned the fault squarely to Vampires."

I held up one hand. "Whoa. What about a three-way split? It was their idea, after all. Failure has a whole lot of parents."

Ruby cracked a bitter smile. "You've met them. Do you

honestly believe any of them own their shit—except Conan, of course."

"Probably not. Go on."

"Nothing more to tell. Not in the short version. The guardians believed if you'd tried harder, their pet humans would have signed on and become immortal. It was the start of the current schism between Vampires and guardians."

"How did it play into your decision making?" I pressed for clarification.

She turned her hands palms up. "You got a raw deal. A bum rap. It occurred to me if the guardians had misjudged Vampires, maybe the rest of us had as well. I mean, you are different, being made and not born to your power, but it wasn't necessarily a reason for me to hang on to old prejudices."

I grinned and held out a hand. She shook it and grinned back. "Now can I go draw up mural ideas?"

"I thought we were going to toss it to the customers to decide."

"We are, but they need ideas. Humans are such a bunch of dimwits."

I sucked in an unnecessary breath and blew it out through my teeth. "They are, but it would sure as hell help if some of them questioned the party line."

"You mean the one where the only good mage is a dead one?"

"The same," I ground out.

"One problem at a time," she said and took on a glistening aspect. "I'll return in an hour," she called before teleporting out of *Ascent's* stockroom.

I opened the back door a crack. Dusk was well-established. Soon it would be nighttime. My time. Since I was finally by myself, Nick surged front and center in my thoughts. Despite hundreds of mini-lectures I'd served to myself, I still wanted him with a singlemindedness only another Vampire could understand. Regardless, I had to prepare myself. He might only be returning to pay off his debt to me and take his place in the emerging war. He'd made a commitment, and those were important to us.

After nearly chewing a hole through my lip, I realized my fangs had dropped. The best thing for me would be to feed. It would settle the jagged pit in my soul. The one where I'd substituted my infatuation with Mistral for the same desperate yearning for Nickolas.

Fuck. I was pathetic. Before I fell deeper down the rabbit hole, I set a travel spell in motion, aiming for thick timber replete with enough small game to drown my sorrows in blood.

CHAPTER FOUR, NICKOLAS

Hearing Ariana's voice had been a slice of nirvana. I could have talked with her for hours, but it wasn't in either of our best interests. Calling her at all had been risky. For both of us. If I understood how the whole digital dance worked, turning my phone on—even if I hadn't made a call—would potentially have alerted the authorities and pinpointed my location. I'd shut the phone completely off as soon as I was done, but I still didn't trust the damned thing.

I made a promise to educate myself. I didn't see how anyone could know which Nickolas R. Giovanni my cell phone belonged to. Some of my phony documents, like the driver's license, had my thumbprint, but there shouldn't be anything to match it up to. At the point when I'd gone into stasis, identifying someone from the whorls on their fingers was in its infancy. Databases storing such material wouldn't happen until many years in the future.

Even though linking my phone to the Vampire who'd broken into the bank in Castelrotto seemed remote, I shouldn't take unnecessary chances. If they could locate me, it would be simple enough for them to find Ariana, and I did not want to create any more problems than I already had. Her joy at hearing from me had been genuine. She hadn't tried to be coy or evasive. Her reaction warmed me, gave me hope I hadn't totally alienated her.

Unsettled places remained where she was concerned, though.

Lots of them, but the best I could do would be to take this one step at a time. I'd find a way to convert some of my gold and gems into money and reimburse her for the funds Clive and I had borrowed to cover our identification materials. I'd also have resources to rent a flat and buy a car. Maybe Percy or someone could teach me how to drive. And then I could teach Clive. Regardless of what happened between Ariana and me, I'd do my part in the upcoming war.

Strange how both Ariana and Rose had latched onto the phrase, "a lot has changed." No shit. I shook my head. Modern nomenclature had wormed its way into my thought patterns—and my speech. Hadn't taken long at all.

I'd come to the conclusion I should have picked a much shorter time frame to remain in stasis—or a far longer one. Waking up in the eye of a hurricane meant constantly playing catchup. Dusting off a crate, I plopped it against a wall and made myself a chair. Come evening, I wouldn't bother going back outside. I'd teleport from in here. If luck was with me, I'd make it as far east as Lake Baikal. It was remote enough, I should be able to hunt.

The following night would see me across the Bering Strait and into Alaska.

A light rustle drew my attention to one side. A pair of reddish eyes glared balefully my way. "Well, lookee here," I murmured, "dinner on the hoof."

Prague always had a huge rat problem; apparently, it hadn't gotten better with the passage of years. Since the fat little fellow had chosen to display himself to me, I coaxed him near with a shot of persuasion and made his demise as easy as I could.

I'd just finished draining him when magic flashed around me. Seeking magic. Damn it! Had one of the mortal's pet mages tracked me here? If they had, it would be the last fucking thing they ever did. I leapt to my feet and kicked the crate aside so I could keep my back to the wall. And then I dropped a ward around myself. If someone was looking for me, I wouldn't make their task any simpler.

I learned to fight long before I was turned, but being a Vampire catapulted my skills to a whole other universe. Two could play the seek-and-destroy game, so I baited my own hook and scanned my surroundings.

"Bring it on," I muttered, charged up by the specter of killing someone, particularly a mage who played lackey for human masters. No one like that should be allowed to live. My fangs dropped, ready to deal death. If it turned out to be something I could feed from without poisoning myself, I'd take it. But I'd kill first and figure out the finer points later.

Excitement coursed through me. I'd been keyed up ever since my confrontation with the guard at the bank. Should have sliced him up and been done with it. But maybe if I had, his thumb wouldn't have gotten me into the vault. It seemed remote, but perhaps the scanner had some way of knowing if the owner of an approved thumbprint had died. A grunt shot past my lips. One more thing I didn't understand. How those reader things worked.

Hard to figure out what I didn't know before I came toe-to-toe with it, but I had to accelerate my learning curve.

My first probe came back inconclusive, so I shortened my arc and deepened my magic. Surprise began in my toes and rolled through me. Only one kind of power felt like that. I tossed my ward aside. "Guardian. Show yourself."

The ripple of lupine laughter, whuffly and growly, surrounded me. Not just any guardian. Conan was somewhere close. I dropped my hands to my sides and cut the flow of power crackling from my fingertips. But then I stiffened. No love lost between the dire wolf and me. He'd intervened when I was intent on ending Ariana. And he'd had more than a few choice words he'd aimed at both of us.

Well-deserved choice words, but that was beside the point.

He hadn't tracked me out of curiosity. Nay. He had a definite motive. Probably to tell me to stay the hell away from Ariana. I wasn't certain quite what I'd do in that case, beyond reassure him I only planned to pay her back and do what I could to punt the pesky mortals back into maybe not submission, but acceptance they weren't the only type of living creature who deserved air to breathe.

I chuckled. Not the best metaphor where Vampires were concerned. I was still chuckling when a silver-white gateway formed, admitting Conan to my squalid storage room.

His head was almost even with my shoulders, and he fixed his amber gaze on me. I waited. He'd come to me, not the other way round. Nostrils twitching, he padded to where I'd dropped the drained rat and proceeded to crunch through its furry remains.

I nudged the crate back into place and dropped onto it. I had plenty of time. I could wait the wolf out. Done with the rat, he fluffed his tail and returned his attention to me. "No greetings?" he inquired.

"I saved dinner for you."

He barked. "Scarcely counts since you had no use for the carcass."

Curiosity finally got the better of me, and I asked, "Did Ariana send you?"

He shook his shaggy head from side to side.

Back in wait mode, I met his ruthless eyes. I'd be damned if I'd bow and scrape or apologize again.

"I've come to bring you back to *Ascent*," he said at last.

It got my attention, particularly since Ariana hadn't dispatched him. "Appreciate your concern," I told the wolf, "but I have a plan. So far, it's working."

"I can have you back in minutes, not days," the wolf insisted.

"Why would you want me back in the first place?" I muttered, and then yanked my own chain. "Never mind," I tacked on. "Let's just call this one a draw. I'll finish my journey my own way."

My words earned me another bark, this one with threatening overtones. "Go ahead, be a selfish bastard," the wolf said. "How do you know you won't run into enemies."

"I can fight my way out of most anything," I said stiffly, irritated he was questioning my skill. I might not be guardian-caliber, but I was damned competent.

"Sure you can, but you'll waste a lot of magic. We need everyone front and center now. Not three days from now. Not a week from now, if it takes that long for your power to come back up to snuff."

"What's gone off the rails since I left?"

"Do you really want me to take the time to answer that now?" Conan countered. "The others can fill you in. I'm merely the transport service."

"You're just like all the rest of them," I said.

"How do you mean?"

"You don't like my kind."

Conan growled; hackles sprang up across his shoulders and the length of his back. He slammed a dinnerplate-sized paw on the floor raising clouds of dust. "You dare say that to me, Vampire?"

Before I rose to the challenge and not only dared but added to it, he growled louder. "I have spent my life with a Vampire. Or did you forget that little fact? I respect the hell out of Ariana. I've helped her, supported her, defended her."

I flapped a hand his way. "Aye, I know all those things, but you've done them because it's Ariana. You don't view her as a Vampire."

"You have no idea how I see her. Your point?" This time the wolf snarled at me.

"Fairclaw made it clear guardians have no use for Vampires." I named a guardian who'd been particularly abrupt with me. A silver wolf in his animal form, and a silver-haired mage when he was human, I had a feeling he was a big part of the reason Conan had run from his kinsmen when he was but a mere pup.

"Sins of the fathers?" Conan was still snarling.

"Something like that. Look. I appreciate the thought—and the chat. I'll see you when I return to *Ascent*. I promise not to squander magic unnecessarily, or—"

The scent of guardian magic surrounded me. Fur and rocks after a gentle rain. It was too late to ward myself, and I knew better than to add my own magic to subvert the wolf's transport spell. I could shift us elsewhere, but it would anger Conan. No power I raised would alter the eventual outcome.

Good thing my valise was still strapped around my body. I'd never bothered to untangle myself from it. The hum of ley-lines joined the scent of guardian magic. Had we dropped into the realms of the dead? Or did ley-lines run elsewhere? They augmented Conan's power, and he drew heavily from them.

I considered asking how he'd found me, but he'd have sneered. Rightfully so. It was a stupid question. I could track damn near anything once I had its scent.

Minutes ticked past. Not many before the familiar outlines of *Ascent's* stockroom took shape around us. "Be stubborn with someone else"—Conan was still growling —"not with me."

"We can't talk in here," I switched to telepathy to remind the wolf. He was angry with me, maybe so irritated he'd forgotten about the surveillance thingies.

"Yes we can. Ariana crushed the bugs." With a flick of his tail, he turned to leave.

It cost me, but I called, "Thanks," after his departing form. He didn't so much as twitch an ear in my direction as he stalked through the door leading into the club.

I unclipped the valise straps and set my traveling bag on a chair, transferring the gold bars and bag of gems from my body to the leather sack. It was a huge relief to pry the bars out of my boots. There may have been space for them, but my heels were wretchedly unhappy. Ariana wasn't here. Not just not in the storeroom; she wasn't in the club, either.

I tucked the bag with the loot in the bottom of a green metal filing cabinet and spelled it to invisibility.

Ruby dashed through the door with Percy right behind her. She hugged me. Percy pumped my hand once she'd moved aside. "You're back," she crowed.

"I would have returned under my own steam"—I tried for dignity—"but Conan had other ideas."

"So that's where he went." Ruby nodded knowingly.

"Ready to get back to work?" Percy smiled. It made him appear slightly less intimidating. At better than two meters tall, with a burly build to match his height, he was one imposing Sorcerer. Bald, blue-eyed, and dressed in his usual tartan layered over a cream-colored linen shirt, he looked as if he'd dropped in from an earlier era.

"I sure am." I grinned back. His smile was infectious. "Say"—I looked from one to the other of them—"would either of you know where I could get fair value for gold and gems?"

"Ooooh, gold," Ruby gushed. "Sure, sweetie. Show me what you've got."

Percy started laughing. "Never trust a Fae with gold."

Ruby elbowed him. He swatted her across the back. "Where'd you come by gold and gems?"

The question was harder to answer than I would have expected. For a Vampire who wasn't supposed to have much in the way of an emotional life, mine had shifted into high gear. We were the only ones in the back room, but I lowered my voice anyway.

"My clan house is no more."

"Och, sweetling, I'm so sorry," Ruby murmured.

"What happened?" Percy cut to the heart of things.

"Some of our own poisoned us. They cut a nefarious deal with mortals. I have no idea what they got out of the transaction, beyond maybe their freedom." I licked my dry lips and forged ahead. "I found naught but piles of bones in the underground chambers where we'd once lived. One of my kinswomen showed up. Apparently, she'd set a magical beacon to alert her if anyone entered the seethe."

"At least one of your kin remains," Percy rumbled.

"More than that," I told him. "According to Roseann, a dozen escaped. Anyway, I decided to retrieve the clan's hoard from a bank where I'd stupidly placed it before leaving Italy for the States."

"Answers my question about where the loot came from." Ruby patted my arm. "How come none of your remaining kin collected it long before now?"

"One tried. The bank not only refused to recognize his right to his own funds, they'd have captured my kinsman if he hadn't had a teleport spell at the ready. Vampires—actually all mages—have been relegated to interlopers all through Europe and the U.K."

"That's unconscionable, but Christ! You broke into a bloody bank?" Percy slitted his gaze my way. At my nod, he said, "They have cameras on every post. And scanners."

I shrugged. "I got in and out."

"Did you kill anybody? Please tell me you did." Ruby sounded positively feral.

"Nay, but I wanted to. I relieved the guard of his thumb."

"Oho," Percy cut in. "That's how you got into the vault. Too fucking bad you didn't clean them out."

"He'd have needed a getaway car." Ruby glanced at the Sorcerer.

Another term I wasn't familiar with, but it was simple enough to grasp from the context. "Anyway, I returned to the clan house, met Rose, and split the spoils. Then I started back this way. You never did answer me about how I can convert the gold and gems to cash. Some of it, anyway."

"Rob can help with that," Percy said.

"The one who got me the identification documents?"

The Sorcerer nodded. "The same. He has his fingers in a lot of pies. How soon do you need the money?"

"Whenever." I shrugged. It wasn't critical. I'd been getting by without much cash for a while now, and then I thought about the wages I'd received from the ship. "I have Irish pound notes too."

"Any bank can take care of those for you," Ruby said and drew her black brows together. "Irish, eh? Bet you have a wee bit more of this story to tell."

"It will keep," I retorted. "What's happened since I left?"

"Ariana came back to work a couple of weeks ago," Ruby said.

Before she could go on, I jumped in. "Is she all right?" A month or more was a whole lot of time for a Vampire to recover—from anything. We have cast-iron constitutions. Beyond silver poisoning—or beheading—we bounce back fast.

"She's back now," Percy said firmly. "It's the most important part. Both groups of mages have met several times."

"Both groups? Do you mean—?"

"Aye, the original one that forged alliances near my guild house. And the coalition that was slapped together before they picked *Ascent* as a launch point."

Ruby tapped a foot. She wore soft-sided shoes with undone laces. "We finally got everyone in the same place night before last."

"Long overdue," Percy added.

"Did they arrive at any decisions?" I prodded. In Vampire-dom, the master made all the critical proclamations. Others in the seethe didn't question them. While I remembered many extraneous discussions among Vampires regarding this, that, or the other topic, they were always brief and to the point.

"Ariana stood firm about using stealth and cunning—as opposed to an in-your-face slash-and-burn-your-fields-to-the-ground approach," Percy said.

"The others are coming around," Ruby tossed out.

"Fae, Druids, and Sorcerers are coming around,'" Percy corrected her. "Shifters, Witches, and Sidhe are still on the fence."

"It has to be all one way or all the other," I muttered.

"Allies have to agree on which strategy they'll be employing. If we can't, the balls-out group will make things impossible for everyone else.'"

"Feel free to mention it." Ruby's tone was dry. "The next go-round will be tonight after closing."

I'd planned to be engaged in a heart-to-heart, Vampire-to-Vampire discussion with Ariana then. Disappointment took a chunk out of the reunion I'd been planning. Not that I'd made any assumptions, but I wanted to give both of us an opportunity to clear the air and sketch out future directions.

If there were any.

Maybe she'd been happy to hear from me because she was worried about me. She treated everyone who worked at *Ascent* as if they mattered to her. And I believed they did. Her caring was genuine, not an act.

"Nick?" Ruby nudged me in the ribs.

"Aye. Certainly. Of course, I'll bring it up. Where is this meeting?"

"Right here." Ariana's voice spiked through me like a high-voltage charge.

I'd known she'd show up, but I wasn't ready. To face her. To maybe hear her say she understood my reaction to her confession about Mistral—but still held it against me. We Vamps can be a stubborn lot.

You're who left, I reminded myself.

It did not make things any better.

She must have entered through the front door or one of two side entrances because she strode into the back room, high heels clicking against the floor. Dressed for work, she wore a glittery top in shades of blues and greens, formfitting black slacks, and a jacket made of sheer material. Her dark hair hung loose, curls cascading past her waist.

Ariana rolled to a stop about a meter in front of me and folded her arms beneath her breasts. The motion added definition to the cleavage already showing above the scooped neck of her top. "Cat got your tongue?" she inquired. "Or did Conan relieve you of it when he fetched you back?"

The tongue in question—mine—was glued to the roof of my mouth. Her beauty always hit me like a gut shot, frequently rendering me speechless. She'd bounced back from her near miss with permanent death. The experience had added a translucent quality to her fair skin and an otherworldly aspect to her vampiric charm.

"Good to see you," I finally managed.

She laughed and held out a hand. "Welcome back, Nickolas. Next time don't be gone so long. We need everybody in this war. Everybody includes you."

I lurched toward her outstretched hand and clasped it. The feel of her skin, cool, smooth, but with just the right amount of tension sliding beneath its surface, undid me.

"I'm here as long as you need me," I blurted.

Her gaze developed speculative edges. "Make certain you mean what you say," she cautioned.

I caught the brunt of her blue eyes and gave as good as I got. With a hint of a smile, I nodded my understanding. "Never stretch the truth to a Vampire."

Her laughter deepened. "Never, indeed. We're literal as fuck." Before I could come up with a pithy reply, she clapped her hands together. "Come on, people. We open in an hour."

Something like a key sliding into a lock rammed home. I'd left because I'd had no choice. Perhaps I'd end up leaving again, but for now I was exactly where I belonged. I felt like a total sap. Ariana hadn't breathed anything to indicate I was special—other than as fodder for the war effort—but I'd inhaled her words like blood mist.

Percy beckoned to me; I followed him onto the floor of the club. I knew the drill. We'd walk the perimeter and make certain no one had opened any doors—magical or otherwise —beyond the one we wanted them to come through. I welcomed simple tasks. My mind had turned into a chaotic whirlwind, and I needed all my faculties. Ariana and I would talk, but apparently not for a while.

Control was where I lived, but this was one time I had no choice. Her nightclub. Her game. I unclenched my jaw. If I didn't like it, I could always leave again. Except I wouldn't. Not until she didn't need me any longer.

I'd given her my word.

I scanned the room for Clive, but he wasn't here yet. I needed to let him know what had become of Clan Giovanni. The message was harsh, but he deserved to know.

An Hour Earlier

I'd moved from slaking my hunger to recreational bloodletting when Conan materialized a few feet from me. Without dropping the raccoon glued to my fangs, I motioned at the pile of dead animals. Conan's never been one to stand on ceremony. This time was no exception. Working methodically, he started at the top of the stack and fed quickly.

I waited for a full report. Had he found Nickolas? Was he back at *Ascent?*

"Well?" I finally asked. I'd had enough blood for now. Actually, I'd had enough an hour ago, but I'd kept drinking anyway. Recreational bingeing to manage a gigantic case of nerves. I'd been fine with Nick's original plan. The one where he would have moved east in sprints. Then I figured I had a few days to get my hopes under control.

I'd been flummoxed when Conan said he was going after

Nick, but stopping the wolf would have been as futile as holding back the tides—or any other force of nature.

Conan finished the rat he'd been eating. His muzzle was streaked with blood, and he looked satiated. Not surprising since my considerable collection of carcasses was gone, down to the toenails. He swished his tail and trotted around to face me.

"Your friend is the most irritating Vampire."

Oh-oh.

"Erm. Why? What did he do?" On the tip of my tongue was question number three, which would have been *did you hurt him?* I've known Conan long enough to understand he'd be defensive if he had and wounded to the core if he hadn't. That question never left the safety of my throat.

Breath huffed from the wolf, forming clouds in the chilly air. "First off, he didn't bother to greet me. He'd fed, but he didn't offer me the corpse."

"Since when has that stopped you?" The corners of my mouth twitched, but I schooled myself not to laugh.

"Never. Anyway, once the rat was gone, I told him I'd come to make things easier for him. Do you think I got so much as a thank you? Hell, no. The stupid Vampire insisted on sticking with his plan. *His*, not mine."

I settled my hands on my hips. "Does it mean he's still wherever you found him?" Part of me hoped the answer was yes. Then I'd have my little sliver of time to compose the yearning cutting through my body. To muffle the hunger driving me to wrap my arms around him and never let go.

"Pfft." The wolf growled. "What do you think?"

"I have no idea, or I wouldn't have asked." I tried for neutral, but my reply was pure snark.

"No. He's not still there. I got tired of listening to him and teleported us back to the nightclub. And then I left. Before I said something I'd probably regret later. Particularly if the two of you pair off."

He was looking right through me, as if he expected an answer. I had nothing to say. I was not going to discuss my unrequited longing with Conan. He'd feel sorry for me, and we didn't have the luxury of indulging in soap opera material. Not now with assorted mages all but camping out at *Ascent*.

"I'm going home to change. Then I'll teleport back to the club," I said.

He shook himself from head to tail tip. "I did the right thing," he said stiffly. "Nickolas thanked me. He didn't want to, but he managed to do the right thing too." A whuffly bark rolled from him. "The Vampire is decent. I didn't especially want to respect him, but I do."

I dropped a hand onto Conan's neck, burying my fingers in his luxuriant rough coat. "Thanks for escorting him safely home. See you in a few."

A quick teleport home gave me a chance to change into snazzier clothing. Nothing I wouldn't normally wear to work, but a big step up from jeans and a sweater with holes in it. I warded myself and came out in one of the many alleys not far from my nightclub. Despite being two blocks away, I caught Nickolas's scent and it drew me like a lodestone.

Still, I maintained my ward and glided near enough *Ascent's* back door to listen to him and Percy and Ruby talking. When he described robbing a bank, I was so shocked, my warding almost dissipated. Eh, maybe rob is too strong a term. He was only taking back what was rightfully his. Apparently, the financial institution had refused to let loose of the funds.

It surprised me they hadn't expropriated them. A legend had circulated since the Middle Ages, though, that it wasn't safe to touch anything that had been through Vampire hands for a hundred years. Perhaps they were waiting out the clock.

Regardless, I was happy Nick had retrieved his clan's hoard. And sorry he hadn't taken still more—and done away with the guard. As cool and collected as I was likely to get, I glanced around me. Thank fuck the days when two detectives from the paranormal task force had taken up residence behind my club were over. The alley was empty, so I loosed my ward and trotted to the club's main door. It was locked, as it should be before we were officially open.

Letting myself in, I crossed the expanse of wooden floor and walked into the stockroom. I hung onto the pleasant smile pasted onto my face, but it was soooo flipping hard. Nick was even more profanely gorgeous than I remembered. We're all beautiful, but Nick's coppery hair framed his strong-boned face, setting off his distinct cheekbones and square chin. Joy at seeing me sheeted from him despite obvious efforts to corral it. Twin sparks glinted deep within his green eyes. Today, they reminded me of moss in the Highlands, intense and mysterious.

After exchanging pleasantries, and a muted sparring match where I ragged on him for being gone, we took our usual places readying the club for opening. I may have poked him about taking off for so long, but he could have simply acknowledged the truth in my assessment and moved on. No one had been holding a knife to his throat when he said, "I'm here as long as you need me."

His obvious readiness to protect my back seemed to run deeper than us both being Vampires, but making assumptions was a dangerous game. We'd talk, he and I, but maybe not for several days depending on how the rest of tonight shaped up. A mix of disappointment and relief at the necessary delay merged into a murky brew. Putting things off isn't exactly vintage Vampire. Usually, we lead with our fangs and let the chips fall where they will.

The evening rolled out like most of them—busy but uneventful. I'd asked the collection of mages not to show up until after we closed. The one night they'd outnumbered mortals had been fraught with tension. The humans had no idea why they felt antsy, but many had left early.

Not good when you're an innkeeper. I want everyone to maximize their booze consumption, particularly since I never hopped on the food bandwagon to pad my profit structure. Clan Giovanni wasn't the only one to have a hidden stash of valuables. At the point I'd left my own clan, I'd taken my share of the spoils with me. Over the years, I'd transported it hither, thither, and yon. Cash was pointless. Its value fluctuated wildly as currency came and went. Much like Nickolas, I'd opted for precious metals and gemstones. It was what had given me the wherewithal to purchase *Ascent*, and my current house. In case things went sour here, I had plenty left.

Out of all the things I worried about, money wasn't one

of them. The same was true for all mages except perhaps Druids. I'd never truly understood how they operated. They didn't exactly take vows of poverty, chastity, and obedience, but not far from it, either. Their monastic existence was certainly simple. Back in the day, mortals had left alms for them. That practice had surely gone the way of the Dodo bird. I had no idea how they survived, but it wasn't important.

One of the sideline benefits of living forever is you have plenty of time to accrue resources, so long as you don't go crazy with your spending. Once I no longer had a clan house standing behind me, I'd become downright frugal.

Percy's ten-minute warning prior to closing rang through the club. Since I was thinking about money, I retreated to the stockroom to do a quick-and-dirty tally of the night's take.

Conan lay on the floor next to my desk, head resting on his large paws.

"Back in time for the gathering?" I dropped into my chair and booted up my computer.

The wolf grunted. I took it for a yes.

"Who pissed in your Cheerios?" I muttered.

He pushed to his feet and shook himself. Dense fur flew everywhere. I really should brush him, except he hated it. "Bring up the news on that thing," he said.

As soon as the Microsoft logo was done scrolling, I tapped the shortcut to my favorite news site—the least biased of the bunch as far as I could tell—and stifled a yelp. A headline screamed, *Supernaturals Apprehended.* Desperate for details, I skimmed the piece. If I'd been searching for hard data to support my stealth approach to battling mortals, nothing in this article would help.

"It's a sure bet many here for tonight's meeting will know about this," Conan observed.

"How'd you find out?" I twisted my head and looked his way.

"Read it at the newsstand down the way."

"You must have been warded, right?"

"Why would you think that?" he inquired caustically. "Don't wolves, unnaturally large ones, stand in front of a paper stand staring at the headlines all the time?"

He wasn't expecting an answer, and I didn't supply one. No wonder he'd been looking as if his best friend had tried to pass off rotten meat as a delicacy. I took a little more time with the article.

Apparently, Seattle's paranormal task force—considered one of the best in the nation—had been planning a raid on a New Age supply company for months. The place sold unusual items like hard-to-get crystals, special Tarot decks, herbs, and necessary spell ingredients like dried rattlesnake and eye of newt. Scuttlebutt said they even had dried Leviathan flowers. I hadn't believed it. Those things only grow in Purgatory, and they spring up over Leviathan graves.

In any event, the task force had snatched up Witches, Fae, and Sidhe along with a couple of Shifters unlucky enough to be in the wrong place at the wrong time. Fuck. They'd probably been in the main store, shopping. *Northwest New Age* had a number of branches if I remembered right.

According to the words scrolling down my screen,

seventy-four mages of various persuasions were in custody. Locked down in special cell blocks designed to contain immortals.

"We're going to get them out of there," I said. "And right away. Before they can turn into stood pigeons and sell the rest of us out." An uncomfortable sensation tracked down my spine. The principals for NNA knew about *Ascent*, but not about me specifically. At least I didn't believe they did. It's rarely in a Vampire's best interest to out ourselves.

The wolf's whole demeanor changed. His tail plumed, and his ears pricked toward me. "I was hoping you'd say that. I tried to light a fire under Fairclaw, but he has always drawn a line when it comes to mortals."

"Which is?" I sought clarification.

"If any mage is stupid enough to fall into a mortal-spawned snare, they deserve what they get."

My ungenerous reaction was to hope Fairclaw got hoisted with his own petard. It would be fitting for him to be captured, with no one to save him because they viewed his punishment as richly deserved.

My phone trilled the opening bars of "Fur Elise." Meant it was two a.m. The bar should be empty. We had half an hour before second shift—in this case assorted mages—was due to arrive. I snoozed the computer. I could do my bookkeeping later. Besides, I was more caught up than usual due to my long stint at home.

I got up and started through the door with Conan hugging my heels. After a quick check to make certain all the humans were truly gone, I stuck two fingers in my mouth and whistled shrilly. Everyone stopped what they were doing, which included washing glasses and upending chairs onto tables. I twirled both arms in come-here motions, and my friends surged toward where Conan and I stood.

Making every word count, I sketched out what had happened. Outraged cries and grunts met my announcement.

"The news just broke tonight?" Dee asked. A necromancer and a witch, she favored exotic makeup and jangly jewelry. Black lipstick matched her black hair. Cut geometrically, it framed her stark cheekbones. Olive skin, black eyes, and pronounced bone structure confirmed her Native heritage. Medium height, she was thin with ropy muscles that hinted she might be stronger than she appeared. Tonight she wore a skintight black skirt and her favorite red T-shirt emblazoned with a Witch straddling a broom and the words, "My Other Car Is..."

"Yes." Conan barked to punctuate the word.

Ruby squeezed her eyes tight before opening them. "Ick. Just ick. Means they're watching us even when we don't know it. So glad you deep-sixed the bugs in the stockroom."

"What bothers me the most," Nickolas said, "is not a one of the seventy-something mages picked up on the surveillance."

That fact hadn't escaped me. Either magic was weakening, or the paranormal task force had new tools in their arsenal. I slammed a hand down on the nearest tabletop. "That Witch from Nevada said something about a scanner that detected magic. It was still a prototype, but—"

"No buts about it," Percy cut in. "The task force must have gotten their hands on one. Damn it. I need to rip into one of them. If I can obtain a scanner, I could figure out how it works. Once I know that, I can come up with electronics to counteract it."

"Like chaff?" Christa, another Fae, asked.

"Exactly, like chaff." Percy nodded.

"What is that?" Nick asked.

"A radar countermeasure to confuse the enemy. It was developed in the 1940s," Christa replied. Curly dark hair skimmed her shoulders, and her milk-white eyes identified her as a seer. A black skirt with an uneven hemline was topped by an emerald green tunic blazoned with colorful embroidery. When I looked closely, I recognized runes.

"Let's shelve the history lesson for now," I suggested. "First up is freeing those poor sods sitting in iron-lined cells."

"Aye, high up the list," Clive agreed in his upper crust British accent. "Nick told me about all the turncoats in our ranks. This must be how it begins."

"It is how it begins," Nickolas said firmly. "I refuse to believe any mage would just hang it up and turn into a traitor unless they'd suffered horribly."

Personally, I'd have fought anyone to the death before I'd betray my magical roots. Except no one was doing any fighting. They were sitting in iron cells feeling their power fritter to nothing. It was enough to send anyone over the edge into madness. Enough time in hell took a toll on even the strongest-minded. We had to get those mages out, and sooner rather than later. Who knew what dastardly torture devices the paranormal task force had crafted.

"My thought is we cut the meeting short," I said. "If it

wasn't imminent, I'd cancel it entirely. And then we take what's left of the night and storm the fortress."

"Ambitious," Percy muttered. "We're good, but not good enough to pull this off before dawn."

"How many were you thinking we'd need?" Nick asked.

"Aye, and where are they being held?" Clive spoke up.

"Where are we going to sequester them once they're free?" Dee asked.

"We're not," I replied. "Presumably, once they have full access to their magic again, they'll be smart enough to hide themselves."

"What if some of the others want in on the rescue?" Ruby asked.

"You can bet they'll know what happened," Nick chimed in.

I was chewing my lower lip; it's how I knew my fangs had dropped. "We have to home in on where they are," I replied. "Once we know that, we'll have a better idea how many of us will be needed."

"This is a full-out slaughter, right?" Ruby almost purred.

I wanted to shout, "Hell to the yeah," so bad the words burned in my throat. Instead, I said, "Not exactly. We'll only kill if we have to. Which isn't to say we can't wipe minds right and left."

"Dead. Dead. Dead," Ruby began to chant. Christa took up the refrain.

Before it turned into a full sweep, I shouted, "Stop it! We will do as little harm as possible. Just enough to disable the guards and spring the prisoners."

"What makes you think they're all in the same place?" Nick arched a copper brow.

I glanced at Percy. "Do we still have that map of the prisons mortals built specially for us?" At his nod, I went on, "A while back Conan, Percy, me, and a few others took out several of the cells developed to contain us. Our last foray, we were very nearly apprehended, so we quit."

"I bet if we check the remaining ones, we'll find what we seek." Percy scrunched his forehead into a mass of wrinkles.

"Doesn't seem as if they'd have had time to build anything new," I agreed.

"I'll make the rounds," Conan said. "Shouldn't take me all that long."

"Do you remember where all of them are?" I asked because I certainly didn't.

"I don't have to. All the containment areas looked the same. They were the same depth below ground. I'll look for caged magic. Should go fairly fast."

The drop bar across the main door rattled in its cradle. Before I could spring across the floor to open it, half a dozen Witches oozed through the wall, followed by twice that number of Sorcerers.

Everyone would be here soon. I turned to thank Conan for taking the point on locating the imprisoned mages, but he'd already left.

The newcomers rushed forward. "Have you heard?" a Witch demanded.

I nodded somberly. "Yeah. We know about it."

"We have to do something," she went on.

"Before it happens to us," a Sorcerer added.

Erg. There it was. I felt like I was in the center of a shrinking circle, and it gave me the heebie-jeebies. Meanwhile, more assorted magic-wielders were teleporting into *Ascent*. I opened my mouth to tell them I had the problem in hand—or I thought I did—but Nick glided to my side. "Not much to be gained saying it twenty times," he murmured close to my ear.

"Solid observation," I whispered back. It felt wonderful to have him next to me. When I didn't get lost in the tangle I'd created by telling him about Mistral, we were good together. We thought the same, had similar backgrounds. Someday, he'd ask me why I'd done it, why I'd decapitated my maker. My answer was sure to disappoint him. It wasn't as if Mistral had done anything other than be exactly what he was: a Vampire. My only excuse—that I'd been eaten up with jealousy—was no excuse at all. Not in a clan house.

It had been a waste of energy to stack chairs on tables since the flood of mages were tossing them back onto the floor and plopping into them. By quarter to three, I was convinced everyone had arrived. The din from multiple conversations was deafening, so I did the trick with my fingers in my mouth again.

I whistle damned loud, but I still had to issue three sharp blasts before everyone fell silent. "I'm as outraged as the rest of you," I began. "But getting lost in fury—or fear—plays right into their hands. I have a scout in the field to locate where the *Northwest New Age* mages are being held. Once we know, we'll move to free them."

Cries of, "I want to go," surrounded me. I tried pounding on a table for silence. When it didn't work, I whistled again.

"We have another task, too," I said. "We have to retrieve one of the scanners that identifies magical creatures. Once we have one, Percy thinks he can construct a device to stymie it."

The Witch who'd been from Las Vegas stood creakily, as if the motion cost her. She was slightly built with cropped gray hair and dark eyes. "I already tried," she informed me. "Two ways. When downloading the plans failed, I did my damnedest to sneak into the place they were manufactured."

"What happened?" Nick asked.

She lifted her thin shoulders in a defeated gesture. "The compound has an iron gate. The building is constructed of metal. All the rooms are lined with metal. Teleporting in didn't work. All that steel defeated our journey spells. When we opted for the old-fashioned way—leaping over fences and breaking locks—all of us were so sick before we even got to the main building we retraced our steps. If we'd continued, none of us would have made it out of there."

"We'll have to approach it from the realm of the dead," Dee said firmly. "We'll get the guardians to locate the spot for us. Hopefully, they'll be willing to bend a ley-line to our purposes."

"I'll point it out on a map for you," the Nevada Witch said.

Dee ran lightly to me. "Witches will take over the scanner retrieval."

Cries of, "Yes! Witches!" rose from several places in the big room.

I grinned. "Perfect!"

"Why are you smiling?" Dee asked.

"Don't you see?" I spread my arms to encompass the hundred plus mages ranged through *Ascent.* "This is our first joint project. We're not haggling over inconsequentials like whose magic is better. We're digging in and getting the job done."

A portal formed; Conan shot through. Both happened in less time than it takes to tell about it. "Got a location," the wolf crowed. "Two of them, actually."

"Which spots?" Percy asked.

The wolf fired off coordinates. I translated them into geography and came up with two fortresses, one in the North Cascades and the other west of Tri-Cities. We'd been saving them till last because they were tougher than the cell blocks we'd destroyed.

After a few quick calculations, I said, "We'll need twenty volunteers for each site."

Dee tapped my shoulder. "We're leaving to work on the scanner problem."

"Meet back here," I told her.

"Got it." She hustled to a group of a dozen Witches, and they teleported the fuck out of Dodge. The guardians would either help them—or not. Worst case, they'd come up with a plan B. Or we all would.

Percy had begun vetting volunteers for our get-out-of-jail-free project.

"I'll be in your group," Nick informed me.

"What about Clive?"

"He's pissed, but I've sent him off on another mission. Locating the mages who didn't show up tonight and making certain everyone is fully informed. He can't tolerate daylight, and this operation will probably last well into tomorrow."

"Good call." I winced. Nickolas scarcely needed my permission—or my approval—for how he dealt with his clansman.

"Ariana!" Percy called. "Over here."

"Coming." I ran toward the group he pointed to. Ruby was heading up the second one. Anticipation simmered through my body. Striking those fuckers where they lived was not only right; it was our only alternative. We'd show them they couldn't just drop a net over our heads and get away with it. If we raised enough hell, they'd think twice before doing this again.

Conan stood next to Percy, facing the mages in my group. "We will have to move quickly," the wolf said. "It means killing anyone who stands in our way. Once we're inside, we'll have maybe five minutes before the anti-magic waves weaken us to where we'll be useless."

"What anti-magic waves?" I asked.

Conan snarled. "They're thick inside the places. I checked both. We teleport in as a group, warding ourselves as best we can. Then we kill whoever stands against us and break locks to free the prisoners. We'll have to teleport the mages out of there. Their magic has to be shot full of holes."

Nick addressed his next words to Conan. "How come these anti-magic emanations don't affect the guards? Presumably some of them are mages."

"They must carry charms crafted to protect them," the wolf replied.

"Pity there's not time to make something for us," Nick grumbled, adding, "Everything else sounds straightforward."

Yeah, it did. But things that sounded easy rarely were. Conan had left to deliver his message to the other group.

"We'll adopt the buddy system," I said. "Sometimes we're not the best judge of our own magic, but if you notice your buddy is weakening, it's time to leave."

"What if we haven't freed everyone?" a Sorcerer asked.

"Still time to go," I stressed. "We won't do anyone any good if we end up trapped."

CHAPTER SIX, NICKOLAS

Running off Conan's coordinates, we managed our journey spell so we emerged half a kilometer from our target. A quick walk through dense trees brought us to a rough intersection and the structure's gated entrance. The compound had been built into the face of imposing granite cliffs. Vehicles were parked in a single row off to one side. Only four of them, which suggested a minimal number of staff, although as many as six, or perhaps seven, could have fit into each car.

Seemed unlikely. From what I'd noted, mortals tended to travel alone in their cars in this part of North America. A faint vibration made the ground under my feet feel mushy, unstable. Did it have something to do with the anti-magic waves Conan had described?

An idea took shape, but my lack of knowledge about this era tripped me up. I wasn't certain what types of surveillance this compound had, but I still trusted telepathy more than out-loud speech.

"Hold up," I told the group.

"What?" Ariana shifted her gaze my way.

"Would it be possible to locate the machine emitting anti-magic waves? If we found it—and disabled it—the rest of our job would be simpler."

Percy thwacked me across the back. *"Damned good idea, Vampire. For one thing, it would give us more time inside."*

Conan padded to where we stood. He hadn't traveled with us; at the point we'd left he'd still been talking with Ruby's group. *"I know where it is."*

The rest of us waited, looking at him.

"It's in the same place as the rest of the controls. They take up most of the bottom floor."

How many levels were there? It was impossible to tell from looking at the crisscrossed metal staves that shaped a rolling gate across the entry point. I risked a thin thread of seeking magic. And wished I hadn't. I'd no sooner focused it into a beam when something attempted to wrench it away from me. Cutting the pencil-thin flow should have been simple. It wasn't. I staggered back a few steps to put more distance between me and whatever wanted to extract the marrow from my bones.

"What happened?" Ariana's blue eyes bored into me. Normally, I'd have been delighted by her attention, but not at the moment.

"Not sure," I blurted, and then remembered I should use telepathy. *"So long as magic isn't focused on that"*—I jerked my chin at the entry, which was looking more and more like a trap—*"we can get away with it. All I was doing was trying to determine how deep this building is."*

"And?" Percy prodded.

"The second I opened a channel to explore it, something snatched my probe. If I hadn't been on top of things, it could have sucked me dry."

"Good to know," Ariana mumbled.

"Aye, before we dive inside," another Sorcerer standing next to Percy said.

"Can we go in from beneath?" I asked Conan.

"It's how I figured things out," the wolf said, *"but the pull of the magic-draining engine is strong down there."*

"Can you subvert it with the ley-lines?" Ariana asked him.

A growl rumbled from Conan's throat. *"They're part of the problem. Whoever set this up tapped power from the lines. I'd hoped getting inside would be simpler from up here. Doesn't appear to be the case."*

We had to do something. Standing around looking at each other wouldn't buy us shit. *"Take us to the ley-lines,"* I told Conan.

The wolf snarled, so I tacked, *"Please,"* onto my request.

"But we don't have a plan," Ariana protested.

"We'll wing it," I said, concerned we'd still be milling about undecided an hour from now. We had about two more hours of solid night, perhaps three. My power isn't nearly as robust in the daytime, which meant we needed to get moving.

"The mages inside may be toast," Percy warned us.

"We're nowhere near cell level, and I can feel something insidious dragging at me."

"Maybe incapacitated, but not down for the count," Ariana said. *"It's in mortals' best interests to keep their captives alive. So they can turn them loose to damage the rest of us."*

"Conan?" I walked to the wolf and squatted in front of him. We could flounder about hunting for the lines, but he could take us right to them.

The feel of the wolf's power surrounded me, and presumably the rest of the group. Shimmering light obliterated the clearing, replacing it with the familiar golden glow of ley-lines running through a low-ceilinged channel. I snapped a ward into place; my power operated perfectly.

"We're not precisely beneath the prison," Conan said. "Follow me. Don't ward yourselves until you must."

I loosed mine. Wise not to waste magic. Silence reigned as we followed Conan. He started out trotting along the ley-lines. They augmented his magic, and I felt certain he was topping off his reservoir. I had just begun to sense an eerie pulsing when the wolf leapt nimbly to the dirt beneath the glowing rope. He stopped. So did the rest of us.

"How much farther?" Ariana asked him.

"From our house to the edge of the woods," he replied.

"A tenth of a mile," she translated.

"If you use your psychic senses," the wolf went on, "you'll see a break in the line's energy just ahead. It's where humans rerouted it."

I didn't see how humans could have done something like that. Getting close to this kind of energy should be lethal to them. Apparently, Percy had been reading from the same script because he said, "Not humans. We'll face other immortals within."

I didn't care who we faced, so long as we got this project off the blocks. "Can we redirect the ley-line's magic?" I asked. The question was aimed at Conan, but I wasn't proud. I'd take my answer from any quarter.

The wolf cocked his head to one side, assessing the line. He leapt over it and did the same thing on the other side.

Ariana edged next to me. "If we do that, whoever is inside will know we're here."

"Not much choice. They'll find out eventually."

"That they will. Better to saddle up and get moving."

I nodded agreement. Subtle and Vampire didn't match up very well. We prefer more of an in-your-face, kick-your-ass approach.

Conan was back on our side of the ley-line. "Can you see the spot where the energy has been diverted?" the wolf asked us.

A Witch couldn't, but the rest of us murmured assent.

"I'll work from the far side," Conan said. "Several of you weave your magic together. When I give the word, we'll blast the break."

"How will we know if it worked?" I asked.

"Probably because we'll have immediate company," Percy growled.

I nudged Ariana as a heads-up before I said, "While a group of you work with Conan to sever the line, Ariana and I will prepare a mesmerism spell."

Her eyes widened; her full mouth curved into a grisly

smile. "Perfect," she almost purred. "Worked like a champ on Gamma Four on over fifty Sorcerers. We won't face nearly that number here."

We might, but I didn't mention it. We'd do what we had to.

Conan crossed the line again. The distinct feel of guardian power rose around me, brimming with potential. I'd come to value Conan's brand of magic. I wondered why he hadn't called in reinforcements, but he must have had his reasons.

"On my count of three." Conan was back to telepathy because he was chanting to augment his link to the lines. They'd dance to his call; I felt certain of it. They'd done Fairclaw's bidding in another place when we'd solicited guardian assistance to close a gateway to Earth.

"One. Two. Three, and now!"

Percy headed up a group of another Sorcerer, two Fae, and two Witches. The mix of magic jetting from them was impressive. It married with Conan's enchantment and sliced cleanly through the ley-line. A shudder ran the length of the glimmery golden rope, almost as if it were relieved to be out from under its unnatural burden.

Ariana's magic augured into me. We cobbled our mesmerism casting together in moments, strengthening it as much as we could. Hooking a hand beneath her arm, I guided us in the direction of the severed line. If mages had been monitoring it, they'd approach from that direction, and we'd be ready for them.

"Incoming," Ariana said about the same time I felt a disturbance in the warp and weft of the clean air in the tunnel. At least this part of it had been free from taint. Wise of Conan to bring us in via the back door.

Wary after what had happened with my last seeking spell, I figured I could wait to see what emerged. My power was best employed in conjunction with Ariana's. Killing other immortals is difficult. This way was cleaner. We'd carve through their minds and render them idiots. No reason to blow through scads of power stabbing and choking and draining. Most of their blood was poison, anyway.

A ragged portal glowed, winked out, and formed again. I felt like cheering.

"They're weak." Ariana sounded positively jovial.

"Let's see what we face," I cautioned, even though I shared her assessment.

Conan stood over the lines doing something to the severed ends. Probably making certain they couldn't be reconnected.

The gray-edged portal wavered. "Come on," I urged, wanting to get this over with. We'd wasted scads of time and were nowhere near our objective, which was freeing the mages from the New Age shop.

A Sorcerer and a Witch stumbled through their defective gateway. If they hadn't sold out, become tools for mortals to exploit, I'd have felt sorry for them. Most mages have an inner glow; these two looked as if they'd been rode hard and put away wet.

"Now," I told Ariana.

We loosed our casting. A flowing violet river traveled from our outstretched hands to the two mages, encompassing them. It was major overkill. We could have felled thirty with that amount of enchantment. They crumpled to the rock-strewn dirt floor. The Witch flopped across the ley-line and caught fire.

Without warning, a naked, gnome-like man jumped through the portal and barked a word. A meter tall with gray-green hair and bugeyes, he could have been a blend of damn near anything. Power vibrated around him, but it had a greasy, nasty feel and stank of rot. Not exactly like the dark Sorcerers, but not all that far off, either. The portal winked out, but then it had been clinging to existence by very little. The newcomer traipsed through our casting. It should have felled him, but it didn't have any impact at all.

"What in the hell is he?" Ariana asked me.

"No idea."

Conan was on his feet, growling, snapping, snarling. "Show your true self," he commanded.

"As ye will, guardian."

Black-edged fire burst out of nowhere, surrounding the gnome. A singed, raw-meat smell rolled through the cavern. The ley-lines' humming changed to a throaty hiss. The gnome's body split asunder. Something much larger stepped from it. A demon with a single, baleful eye and one huge leg, he stood taller than Percy.

"Balor." Ariana pronounced the word as if it burned the inside of her mouth.

Once I heard the name, memories rampaged through me. If she was right, this was the Celts' demon god of death. According to legend, he was king of the Fomori, lesser demons who lived in lakes and oceans and preyed on humans.

"Impossible," Percy sputtered. "Balor was murdered by his son, Lug."

"Eh, reports of my death have been a wee bit exaggerated." The lower part of the demon's face split into a maw displaying rows and rows of yellowed teeth.

Conan slapped the dirt with a paw. Balor, who had been hopping forward, stopped. "No farther," the wolf warned.

"Your minions kill mortals." Ariana shook herself. "How is it you've sold out to them?"

"Vampire," Balor cooed. "Come close. Share blood. Ye'll discover all my secrets."

"Ha! I'm picky about my food," Ariana shot back, saving me the trouble of grabbing her arm.

"You will leave this spot and never return." Conan rose on his hind legs and grew as tall as Balor. The scent of fur and wet rocks thickened in the chamber; the ley-lines brightened—and quit hissing.

"And what will ye do if I refuse?" The demon angled his misshapen head.

"Hold a moment." I strode next to Conan and doused the demon in a truth net. "Can you leave?"

Balor shook his head. Watching him was eerie because the single eye didn't appear to move. "Why not?" I turned up the juice on my spell.

"Witches freed me from Purgatory. There were...conditions."

"And they were?" Percy's voice held compulsion and could have cut through glass.

"My aid."

It took all my restraint not to lunge forward and punch

his deformed face. It wouldn't have done any good. Demons are notoriously strong. The white light weaving around Conan grew so bright I shut my eyes. When I opened them, he was in his man's body, dark hair streaming around him. He did what I'd considered and landed a punch square in the middle of Balor's face.

The demon's head jerked back; his nose exploded, and green blood sprayed everything nearby. It stank of the sea and rotting fish.

Conan closed a hand around Balor's shoulder and squeezed until I heard the *thwack* of a bone breaking. "You made a deal to betray mages to mortals. To resurrect your sorry, pathetic freedom."

"I might have," Balor said thickly. A whitish tongue snaked out, licking up drops of blood. "You'd have done the same—"

Conan punched the demon again; one side of his face caved in, and he yowled piteously. "Watch your words, demon," he snarled. "They're an insult. The Fomori will answer to you no longer. Guardians shall see to it. I have abolished the spell that bound you. Begone. If you make me raise magic against you, you will regret it."

"Before you leave"—I jumped in before Conan did something to end the demon—"how many mortals will we face above?"

Balor swung his head from side to side. More green ichor sprayed when he exhaled. "Not enough to bother you."

"Maybe not the right question," Ariana cut in. "How about these? Who are you working with? Only Witches? Or someone else?"

The demon slitted his one eye. "I knew I liked you, Vampire. Come see me sometime. We could have a lot of fun together." The rotting seafood smell intensified by a factor of ten, making me glad I didn't need to breathe. Everyone with me except Conan and Ariana began coughing and gagging.

When the stench finally backed off, the demon was gone.

A hasty examination showed the ley-lines hadn't reconnected. Balor didn't answer my last questions, but so far, so good anyway. I hadn't actually expected he would. My magic was eroding, which meant it wasn't night any longer. At least daylight didn't pose logistical problems underground or in the prison.

Conan wore his wolf's form again.

It was time to accomplish what we'd come for.

"We haven't seen the last of him," Conan said and growled.

Magic glistened around Percy as he constructed a spell to transport all of us. "We'll start on the lowest level," Percy explained. "We'll stop long enough to crush whatever was borrowing juice from the lines. Once it's defunct, we'll free the mages and get the fuck out of here."

"Kill on contact?" a Sorcerer asked.

Percy nodded. "Aye. This mission is now twofold. Let it serve as a lesson to those who believe they can subjugate us. Or that our kind are for sale."

Cheers rose. Percy's words made me aware I'd avoided examining the implications of mages forsaking their vows of loyalty to their own kind. The only reason we'd lasted as long as we had was because internecine warfare had been almost nonexistent. Sure, no one liked Vampires, but those same no ones had known better than to confront us. The same held true for the antipathy between Witches and Fae or Shifters and pretty much everyone else.

Ariana had reeled in our mesmerism casting. She and I were still linked, so I felt the adjustments as she exchanged one spell for another better-suited to active fighting. The burning Witch had been reduced to a pile of bones. Someone had kicked the dark Sorcerer out of the way.

"Given what we've dealt with so far," I said, "we have to assume we'll run into more mages. We can kill humans, but Ariana and I will stick with immobilizing magic-wielders."

"That was diplomatic," she murmured and modified her spell once again.

"Not so much tactful as practical," I told her.

The cavern walls dropped away, replaced by concrete and masses of electronic devices. We must be in the control location Conan had described. The room was empty of people—magical or otherwise. Percy brought a foot down on something, and I heard it smash. How he'd determined it was the magic-annihilator wasn't clear, but I trusted the big Sorcerer.

"Done here," he announced. "Not that they can't rebuild it, but they'll have to start from scratch."

We surged toward the door. It was locked, but locks aren't much of an impediment for the likes of us. No one bothered with warding. Everyone above must know their perimeter had been breached. Hell, they'd known it before the greeting party was dispatched to deal with us.

Turned out the "dealing with" had gone the other way. It

brought a wicked grin to my face. I like to win as much as the next Vampire. The one plus in all of this was I could run wide open, use my power rather than hiding it.

Ariana and I shouldered our way to the front line. "We should be first," I told Percy.

"Got that spell ready to rock?" His dark eyes glittered with anticipation. I hadn't realized Sorcerers were as keen on a good scrap as Vampires.

"More than ready," Ariana assured him.

I looked up and down a cinder block-lined corridor. Lighting came from pallid yellow bulbs set into wire cages in the low ceiling. The sting of metal was uncomfortable, but not terribly debilitating. Not yet. I'd hate to spend much time down here. No wonder the Witch and Sorcerer had looked so rough. How come Balor hadn't appeared sapped? I tried to recall what I knew about demons but couldn't resurrect much.

Ariana had a whole lot of books and scrolls. Some of them probably contained lore. I'd have to ask her about them —once we got out of here.

"The prisoners are one floor up," Conan said. Power crackled around him, and a nearby door creaked open.

We hustled up a long flight with a dogleg in the middle. Before we were halfway up, I heard moans and the sharp bite of commands. "Hurry," I urged. Not sure how I knew, I felt certain whoever was in charge of this place was busy concealing evidence. If they moved the mages—probably via teleporting—we'd have hell's own time locating them a second time.

Nick's power slotted with mine as if we'd been born to work together. I'd never felt that way about Mistral, but then he and I hadn't taken on any mutual enemies. Having the demon show up had been a shock. I'd had a run-in with him once, back when I'd barely been turned. It was the first time I'd ventured beyond Mistral's walls since joining the ranks of the Undead, and I was only outside because I'd snuck out.

Young and full of hubris, I'd felt certain I could control the bloodlust. To be on the safe side, I'd fed and fed well before I slipped away one evening. Mistral was gone on one of his interminable business trips, or I'd never have risked it.

His tempers were legendary. Everyone in the clan house had one whispered tale or another about running up against the rough side of his fury. Since he and I were lovers, I didn't think he'd turn his ire my way, but I hadn't been willing to test my theory.

Everything was new then, so my teleport spell was clumsy. I ended up on the shores of the North Sea smack in the center of a group of water demons. They look a lot like the Mer people with moss-green tangled hair and silvery eyes, except theirs have blood-red centers. And obviously, the demons have legs, not fish tails. Unlike Balor, the Fomori have two. They'd apparently drawn a fishing boat off course. The craft had foundered on sharp rocks not too far offshore, bits of it driven in with the incoming tides.

The Fomori had welcomed me as a long-lost sister and invited me to feed with them. Even if they hadn't, the metal-rich smells of blood roared through me, filling my mind with heat and need. I wouldn't have been able to resist diving on top of an almost dead fisherman, so it's a good thing the demons didn't view me as competition for food they'd killed.

Vampires get high from blood when we're young. It's akin to being drunk or stoned, except we never get to a point where we pass out. The more we drink, the more we want until blood is everywhere. Running down our faces, out our mouths, and coating our hands.

It's glorious. But the splendor is drummed out of new Vampires by the end of their second or third year. While I understood the rationale, I still missed those early times when magic ruled, and I didn't have to ride herd on my impulses.

I have no idea how much blood I'd drunk before something penetrated the lusty haze around my happy place. A quick glance told me the demons had all backed away from our feeding ground. They knelt, heads bowed.

Fuck that crap. Vampires bow to no one.

I did roll to my knees, though, fangs on display as I challenged whoever had intimidated the Fomori to take me on. Balor skimmed the ground, riding a current of magic beneath his single leg. Booming laughter merged with the roar of the sea. The demon stood over me, arms crossed over his hairy chest.

"Stand in my presence, Vampire."

My answer was a snarl. Somewhere along the line, I'd forgotten I was a tolerated guest. These corpses were mine. MINE. A few still had blood. The demon's hand shot out and grabbed my hair as he hauled me to my feet. I didn't wait around to find out what would happen next. Because I was sated, magic jumped to my call, and I teleported the fuck out of there.

I'd had no idea who any of them were—the Fomori or their lord—but I settled in with Mistral's extensive library, educating myself. That had been the beginning of my lifelong fascination with information. Knowledge truly was power.

It didn't appear Balor remembered our brief interlude, which saved a whole lot of explanations. Nick would be the only one who understood any of it, from sneaking out to rolling around in blood like a pig in a trough.

The stairwell had a door at the upper end. I'd heard enough on our brief trip up the steps to understand the prisoners were in bad shape, and their guards were having a hell of a hard time getting them in one spot to teleport everyone elsewhere. Nick had been right when he'd urged us to hustle.

"Ready?" he asked quietly.

"Never readier." I latched onto his green-eyed gaze. Losing myself in him happened whether I wished it or not.

After a quick glance over his shoulder with a thumbs-up sign, he punched the lock with a shot of magic and kicked the door open. We piled through, the mesmerism spell already sheeting off us. If we snared a few mortals, we could kill them later. On the mage front, we'd sort the good from the bad, although we might end up needing help to determine who'd been a prisoner.

If they were out of their cells.

This floor consisted of a narrow center hall with cells lining both sides. Same concrete block construction; same recessed lights in the ceiling. Some of the cells were occupied. "Focus on the aisle," I told Nickolas.

"I count forty-six," he said. "Ten are human."

I hadn't bothered to tally up the tangle of bodies choking the corridor. Presumably, the ones on their feet were guards. No one wore any kind of uniform.

Conan trotted around us. Blue-white crackling magic added a static-like feel to the air. Not for the first time, I marveled at the true extent of his power when he unleashed it. The violet carpet holding our hypnotic magic in place simply flowed around him, as if it understood he was exempt from its pull.

"That's a plus," I muttered.

"Aye, I was concerned about him," Nick agreed.

We were almost at the end of the hall. Only one Sorcerer was still on his feet, but he was wavering. Presumably, behind us, the others were killing mortals and piling the turncoat mages into a handy stack.

The Sorcerer in front of us suddenly tossed off our spell. Or maybe he'd been faking, waiting for us to get closer. Patchy gray hair covered a mottled skull. He was tall and rawboned, garbed in scarred leather garments that had gone out of fashion in the 1600s.

I funneled the mesmerism casting right at him, but he sidestepped its grasp and hurtled toward me. The impact drove me to the ground hard enough to make me wheeze. He smelled rank, musty and acrid like he'd been rolling in a vat of rotten semen.

I landed a few punches as I writhed under his weight trying to lever my way out from under him. I'm strong compared to a human, but those comparisons wither when I'm fighting another immortal.

As quickly as he'd landed on top of me, everything shifted. I'd heard Nick's outraged shout and a solid *thump* as my adversary splatted on the linoleum floor. I understood I was free about the same time I saw Nick straddling the black Sorcerer and stabbing him with the dirk he always carried. The weapon's blade was only about six inches long, but it was serrated and thick.

Blood shot upward from a severed vessel. Nick angled his face to avoid being sprayed. Fucking inconvenient their blood is toxic to us. Such a waste. I quested about for something I could use to bash the Sorcerer's head in. He was bucking and heaving beneath Nick. Clearly, blood loss wasn't having any more impact than our mesmerism spell.

What in the unholy hell was he? My magical antennae read him as a Sorcerer, but he'd borrowed power from somewhere. A lot of power. Back on my feet, I filched a baton from one of the downed mortals. Bats surely identified the dude as one of the collaborators, and a threat to magedom. I could bash his skull in later. Turning, I swung the solid length of wood down across the dark Sorcerer's forehead. It split obligingly under my attack, spraying still more blood all over everything. The white of splintered skull bones and crushed brains showed through; at least the bastard lay still.

Finally.

Nick grunted and heaved himself off the Sorcerer—or whatever the hell he was. I turned and surveyed the rest of the floor. Percy strode toward me, skirting bodies as he went. "We've sorted the prisoners. First batch are on their way back to our guild house. I'll take the rest of them, but there are a few folk where we weren't certain whose side they were on."

"Show us," Nick said. Bending, he cleaned his blade on the shirt of an unconscious Shifter and dropped it back into its sheath.

Percy led the way to four bodies slumped against each other. Nick reached down and separated them. "All Shifters," he muttered.

"My take as well," Percy said and bared his teeth. "Why the fuck weren't the staff wearing uniforms?"

"Because that would have made it too easy for us," I replied and focused a beam of magic to see what I could find.

"Have you scanned the guards you know were traitors to see if their magic felt different?" Nick asked.

"Aye. Of course," Percy said. "First thing we did. A few

were truly deficient in earth-bound power, but it might be long exposure to all the metal in this building."

"Did you check them for charms that would have protected them from the thing you obliterated in the basement?" Nick pressed.

"We did. Nada. My vote is for chips that were implanted. I did a bit of slicing and dicing, but absent knowing where to look, all I did was make a bloody mess."

I glanced from Nick to Percy. "Two choices for these mages. Either we turn their minds to Pablum and call it even, or we rescue them and drop them in a cell until they come around."

"Then we can employ a truth net," Percy muttered.

"Exactly." I nodded. "If Vamps have a motto, it's probably kill first and ask questions later, but in this instance, we need every soldier we can salvage."

"If they were conscripted against their will," Nick said, "they might welcome an opportunity to jump back across the abyss."

"Same thing could be said for everyone." Percy swung an arm wide.

Conan materialized from nowhere. "Next floor up has more. I did what I could, but a dozen got away, some prisoners and some guards."

"Humans?" I asked.

"Pfft. Of course not. I killed them."

"Good man," Nickolas said. "Nothing human walks out of here."

"What do you want to do about these four?" Percy asked again.

"What do you?" I countered.

Breath hissed between the Sorcerer's teeth. "I may regret this, but I say we drag them back to the guild house along with the others. We have a cell in the basement."

His admission regarding a holding tank surprised me, but I didn't inquire what they'd built it for. It was none of my affair. "Fine. Nick and I will finish off whoever's left here once you're gone."

Percy whistled; another Sorcerer, two Shifters, and two Fae came on a run. "Let's get that teleport spell in hand," he said. "We'll bring them too." He nodded at the four ranged nearby.

They must have been expecting Percy's orders because the scents of various magics thickened, almost canceling out the metal stench, but not quite. Once they'd left, Nick and I sprinted from body to body, touching foreheads and frying minds. It doesn't take long to obliterate frontal lobes. Not long at all.

Soon we were traipsing up more stairs after Conan. He'd teleported, but I didn't see why we should use magic when we didn't have to. According to the wolf, beyond dead humans, every mage upstairs was down for the count, courtesy of guardian magic.

The next floor was constructed similarly. Bodies sprawled at odd angles, clogging the space between the cells. "Are there more cell blocks?" I asked Conan.

He twitched his tail. "Yes. Two more floors above this one, but they were empty."

This time, I did count and came up with nineteen

bodies. All still very much alive, but deep in an induced slumber. "Any idea who's who?" I asked Conan.

"I know what they are, but not which side they chose," he replied. "No one was locked up by the time I got here. It made my job simpler because I wasn't threading power through iron bars."

I closed my teeth over my lower lip. My fangs bit into my chin as I contemplated what to do. "Same as with the ones downstairs, we only have two options," I said.

Nick nodded. "Aye. We kill them or transport them to the guild house."

"I don't like the second choice," Conan said. "Importing hostile mages, especially a lot of them, will tax our resources."

"Do you know how many that cell Percy mentioned holds?" Nick asked me.

I shook my head. "First I'd heard about it was a few minutes ago. Frankly, it surprised me. I had no clue Sorcerers needed cells to maintain order."

"Might not be what they use it for. There's a whole lot we don't know about other magic-wielders." Nick cast a pointed glance at Conan.

The wolf growled.

Before the two of them were off and running, I redirected us. "Let's see if we can't thin the herd," I said and knelt next to the nearest body, rifling through his clothes for a wallet with ID in it. "Bingo!" I extracted a leather case with plasticized identification that pinpointed him as a federal employee.

Nick bent over the next body in line.

Conan pawed them, but he'd have needed opposing thumbs to dig through pockets. Our search was quick and thorough. Seven of the mages had been prisoners. We dragged them off to one side, and Conan took out his ire by calling mage fire to reduce the other twelve to cinders.

No one engaged in a discussion about the advisability of salvaging them. They'd made their bed when they sold out to mortals. I hoped we didn't regret our decision to transport the four question marks from one floor down. If they had tracking devices inserted into their bodies, it could turn out to be a major miscalculation.

I kept my worries to myself, but we needed to get moving.

"Done here, right?" I tossed out the question.

"Mostly," Conan snarled.

"What's left?" I asked.

"I'll catch up with you," the wolf said. "I'm going to make certain no one can ever use this place again."

A slow smile lit Nick's face, a Vampire's smile. One we employ when we've cornered prey and the outcome is all over but the crying. He looked wicked, predatory, and so appealing my bones went all melty.

"Need help?" Nick asked.

Conan shook his head.

"I'll take us back. Us and the seven who were inmates." I kept my tone brusque, businesslike as I strode to where we'd piled the prisoners. I couldn't wait to land at the guild house and do a thorough job scanning the cell-bound mages. I wanted to be wrong, but I remembered reading about the Feds marking their key employees with trackers.

Magic leapt to my summons, sweeping Nick, me, and the unconscious mages into its pull. I appreciated him not peppering me with questions. He trusted me; whatever I did next was okay by him.

"Do you think it will slow them down?" Nick asked.

I knew what he was getting at, and I'd have loved to be more positive, but it wasn't smart to nurture fantasies. "No. What we did tonight will scare the pants off the mortals behind this. They assumed they'd won this round. We proved they not only didn't win, but that they're seriously outgunned."

"Frightened enemies make rash decisions," Nick muttered.

"Exactly." The walls of the Sorcerers' guild house great room took shape around us. A few hustled forward and collected the mages we'd retrieved.

"We accomplished a lot," Nick said. "I probably need to run Clive down. Will you be leaving here soon?"

"Fairly soon. I want to doublecheck the mages we weren't certain of. The ones Percy put in cells."

"Why? They can't get away."

Rather than wasting time to give Nick a primer on implantable tracking devices, I raised my mind voice and yelled, *"Percy!"*

"Figured you'd show up." He strode in from a far corner of the cavernous chamber.

"Did you check the ones you tossed in cells?"

"They're not awake yet," he replied.

I shook my head. "Not what I meant. Did you scan for trackers?"

"Fuck!" Twisting, he shot from the room.

I bolted after him with Nick right next to me. "Trackers? What in the hell are you talking about?" he sputtered.

"Same type of thing the detectives embedded in my doorframe at the club," I clarified as we ran through the big house and pelted down a spiral staircase.

"I'm not getting the connection," Nick muttered.

"You will," I told him.

We bottomed out on the stairs and hurried along a corridor lit by sconces on both sides. The floor was wood, and the walls some kind of plasterboard. A small herd of Sorcerers was grouped in a doorway at the far end. "Move," Percy bellowed.

They scattered to both sides.

Power jetted from his outstretched hands, bathing the four prone bodies with sparkly light. I've never been the trusting kind, so I added my own to the mix. Gaelic curses rained from me. This was one instance where I had so not wanted to be right.

Two of the men had trackers in their necks. Percy turned up the dial on his magic, but I shrieked. "Get them out of here before you kill them."

Meanwhile, three of the Sorcerers who'd been clogging the doorway had gotten the picture. Faces screwed into masks of fury and concern, they oozed through the gated enclosure, snatched up the prison guards who could lead their masters right to us, and readied spells.

"Take them off world," Percy instructed, followed by, "I'm coming too."

When the dust settled, Nick and I were standing between the two comatose mages and a bunch of Sorcerers.

"Might give us a simple way to figure out who's who," I said. "Should have thought of this back at the compound. Presumably, they haven't had the prisoners long enough to go to the trouble or expense of implanting them with beacons."

"I feel like a fool," a tall, burly Sorcerer with snow-white hair blunt cut to shoulder level grumbled. Jeans encased his long legs, topped by a plaid flannel shirt.

"You?" another mage countered, hands on her hips. Purple-and-blue hair streamed to mid-back, and she had amber eyes with golden pupils. A pair of black denim overalls was layered over a pale-blue shirt. "We might have to abandon this location. In fact, let's spread the word, so we can be ready to vacate in case we've been compromised."

"No 'in case' about it," the white-haired mage retorted. "If anyone was alive at the switch on the other end, they know where their men were taken, and they're bound to check up on us sooner or later."

"We'll just have to keep them too busy to bother us," the woman shot back and walked quickly down the corridor. The other Sorcerers followed her.

"I need an explanation," Nick said. "Doesn't have to be fancy, but I have to understand more than I do right now."

Of course he did. I nodded and turned toward him. "Sorry. I didn't mean to be abrupt before, but time was critical. It might still be. The men Percy and the other Sorcerers spirited out of here had digital trackers implanted in their necks. Shit like that runs off satellites—I'll get around to what they are later—and tells someone in a distant office precisely where their operatives are. It's quite useful for agents under deep cover in enemy territory. Means their boss knows how to find them if they get into trouble."

Nick's forehead creased as he considered the implications. "So, someone knows where this guild house is now?"

"Maybe. Depends if they had reason to pay attention." If I'd been the breathing type, I'd have exhaled long and slow. "My guess is the guards sounded an alarm as soon as they sensed us in the vicinity of the ley-lines."

"You mean after Conan blew up their connection to the magic-stealing machine."

"Yeah, something like that. Regardless, I'd be amazed if someone wasn't monitoring the situation, which probably means this guild house is no longer viable."

"Appears the Sorcerers have that aspect well in hand," Nick said.

"Indeed. One less thing for us to do. We need to move these two." I jerked my chin at the comatose mages. "No reason to break them out of jail only to have them recaptured."

"Where will we take them?" Nick arched a copper brow.

I scratched my head. "Not to *Ascent*. Not to my house, either."

'Not leaving many choices," Nick muttered.

"Got it." I snapped my fingers. "We'll rustle up whomever is here. They can move these two to an off-world location and wait around until they wake up."

"Once they do, they can cast a truth spell, figure out

which side they're on, and act accordingly." Nick hesitated. "Or we could just kill them. It's a whole lot simpler."

The corners of my mouth twitched into the start of a smile. "No kidding, huh? Let's run down who's here. They can make that decision."

"Perfect. We have a nightclub to open."

We certainly did. Turning, I led the way down the long corridor and up the stairs to the guild house's main floor. Somewhere along the line, we'd need to feed, but we'd figure it out as we went. Before, I'd been concerned I was beginning to view Nick, Conan, and me as a team. While it was warm and fuzzy and comfortable, it was also dangerous ground.

Eh. That ship had already sailed. No matter how the cards shook out, I was in this up to my eyeballs.

Nick came back to me. The soft tone of my usually critical inner voice was unprecedented. Before I traveled too far down that particular road, I reminded myself he might only have returned to make good on his debts, particularly since he'd recovered his clan's gold and gems.

Vampires might be monsters, but we were monsters who paid our bills.

On that wry note, I barreled into the great room amid masses of Sorcerers. We'd deliver our message and beat a track to *Ascent.*

CHAPTER EIGHT, NICKOLAS

Our little chat with the Sorcerers had taken longer than we anticipated. Their primary concern was relocating their guild house. The consensus was to exercise a preemptive strike rather than wait for an ugly confrontation.

In the end, they agreed to move the rescued mages, but it was clear their interests lay elsewhere. And there it was. Never any love lost between the various branches of magedom. If the men in the basement cell had been other Sorcerers—rather than Shifters—it would have been a different story altogether.

It was only after I spouted off with my earlier idea, which had been to kill them and save everyone a lot of trouble, that the Sorcerers came around. I'd have laughed, but it was the wrong tactic. I did find it droll, though, that they didn't have any interest in the rescued mages—until a Vampire casually suggested shunting the question of their fate off the table.

They looked at me as if I were some kind of heartless thug, but it was a small price to pay. I'd manipulated them into doing the right thing. All's well that ends well, and all that Shakespearean rot.

"Nicely done," Ariana murmured as we teleported to *Ascent*. The club was already open by the time we arrived, but everything seemed well enough in hand. The stockroom was empty of anyone but us.

"Breaking those mages out of prison was a lot of trouble." I left it there. No reason to say more, but her compliment pleased me. She'd understood exactly what I was about. Vamps might not like one another all that much, but we were usually on the same page when it came to dealing with roadblocks. Among our other talents, we're masters at persuasion.

"The Sorcerers might have been more generous—if their guild house hadn't suddenly turned into a target," Ariana continued. "My guess is it will be under heavy surveillance soon. If it isn't already."

"They'd have been more charitable if the ones in the basement had been Sorcerers," I retorted. No reason not to call it for what it was.

"Yeah, that too." Ariana smiled wryly.

"Good thing we teleported in and out of there," I muttered and shook my head.

Ariana angled her chin my way. "What aren't you saying?"

"Not sure, exactly. I never thought much about mortals until now—other than as a food source. Or as potential fresh recruits for Clan Giovanni."

"And now?" she prodded.

I skinned my lips back from my teeth. "I hate the rotters. If they'd shown up at the guild house, I'd have gone into full-fang mode—and left a string of drained corpses. What in the fuck is wrong with them? There used to be plenty of resources for everyone. Sure, some humans died, but so did a few mages here and there. It was a dynamic balance."

She shrugged. "Shit changes."

"Aye, you and Roseann keep harping on that."

"Who's she?" Ariana raised a dark brow.

No reason not to tell her, so I replied, "The one who made me."

"You were lovers."

My turn to shrug. "You know how it is."

Ariana chuckled. "Yup. Sure do, except I never joined in the afternoon fuck-fests."

First I'd heard of a master Vampire playing the possessive card with one of his minions, and I didn't care for the implications. "Why, that old bastard." I doubled up a fist.

Before I could drive it into a wall and do some damage, Ariana closed a hand around mine. "It wasn't Mistral. He wouldn't have cared one way or the other. It was me. I only wanted him."

Words clamored for ascendency, but I held them back. She'd just admitted to an almost-unheard-of emotion for our kind. Puzzle pieces slotted together as knowledge rushed through me. "That was why, wasn't it?" I asked after a long enough pause to keep my question short and to the point.

She nodded and trained her blue gaze on me. "He

warned me. Pushed me to take other Vamps into my bed. I figured he'd come around..."

"Except he never did." I finished her sentence.

"Nope. Eventually, after we'd spent a couple of hundred years together, he brought someone else to the clan house. She was all the things I'd once been. Human. Naïve. Besotted with him."

Ariana's eyes pinched at the corners. "I didn't waste time plotting or planning. If I had, I'd surely have lost my nerve. After he led her to his suite of rooms, I headed for the armory, took a blade with enough heft to do the deed, and— And, well, you know the rest. It's a fucking miracle I didn't get caught, but everyone in the seethe assumed I was devastated about Mistral's death. They knew how close we'd been."

"You were devastated," I said softly.

A corner of her beautiful mouth twisted downward. "Yeah, but not for the reasons they thought." She thinned her mouth into a line. "If I'd had any inkling how that single deed would haunt me, shape the remainder of my days..."

"If you'd realized, would you still have done the same thing?" I asked, needing to know.

After a few seconds she said, "Yes," and removed the hand curled around mine. Spreading both of hers in front of her, she went on. "Don't you see? I was damned either way. If I'd remained in the clan house, it would have torn my guts out every time I saw him with a new, younger, prettier—"

"No one could be more stunning than you are," I cut in.

She rolled her eyes. "Pfft. Thanks, but like I was saying. I couldn't remain and watch an endless cavalcade of young perfect bodies file through his bedchamber. I couldn't leave. Vampires didn't leave clan houses in those days. So, I was stuck. I'd tried talking with him, but he did the whole patronizing 'I'm your maker' routine and pushed me to drown my sorrows in someone else's cock."

"Did you at least try that route?" I angled a brow upward.

"Never even considered it."

I rolled the information around, digesting it. "Once I stopped reacting and started thinking about you and Mistral…" I began, but ran out of words. She'd had a very human reaction to a Vampire problem. It hadn't ended well, but she already knew as much without me hammering it into the ground.

"What did you imagine had happened?" she prodded.

"I had no idea. I guess I thought he was forcing you to do things against your will—a whole lot of things. And in a way, I suppose he was. Not that it excuses him," I went on. "He was just being who he was. A master Vampire in charge of a major clan house. I've never known one to take a mate."

I waited, half expecting her to become bristly, defensive. "Neither have I," she agreed, "but there's a first time for everything, eh?" She ran her fingertips down my arm. "Let's get to work. We have a lot facing us, and my ancient history isn't important. I spent centuries running from what I did. It's a relief to have it out in the open."

I started to tell her I forgave her but stilled my tongue. For one thing, it wasn't my place to offer expiation. For another, a small corner of my mind was still revolted by what she'd done. Until I could put that tiny bit of uncertainty to bed, I'd be better off saying nothing. At least now I understood what had happened. It was the Vampire equivalent of a lovers' spat. Or in this instance, perhaps more of a mismatch of needs. If Ariana had been human, she'd have slunk away and cried.

But she was a Vampire, with all the righteous anger we lay claim to.

"After you," I said and followed her into the club. Raucous music pounded my ears, much louder once she opened the adjoining door. It occurred to me Mistral hadn't known Ariana at all despite fucking her probably thousands of times. If he had, he'd have understood what a firestorm he loosed when he brought his next doxy to the clan house.

Poor bastard. His hubris had spelled his end.

I'd functioned as a master vampire for Clan Giovanni, and I don't suppose I was any better attuned to the individual needs of the Vampires in my clan than Mistral had been. Luckily, none of them had decided I needed blotting out. My mind was full as I headed for the main door to take up my post. Percy wasn't there. Probably, he was still dealing with the tracker problem.

A medium-height, rusty-blond Sorcerer I'd never met before nodded briskly. "Are you Nick?"

"I am."

"Loren." The man, garbed in jeans and a leather jacket, stuck out a hand. "Percy told me to stick around until you showed up."

"Thanks for holding down the fort," I said and shook his hand. "Anything I need to know about?"

"Nah. Quiet bunch so far. All human." He made a sigil against evil.

For once I wholeheartedly agreed with the assessment. Mortals had turned out to be far more than the inconvenience I'd always viewed them as. They were dangerous. All the technology they were so fond of had given them an unfortunate edge.

"Are you staying until Percy gets back?" I asked.

Loren shook his head. "Only if you need me."

A quick glance at the clock mounted over the long bar told me it was just shy of nine. The crowd was moderate with more trickling in as Loren and I talked. Depending on how the night rolled out, Percy might not return, but unless things changed substantially, it wasn't a huge problem. "I'll be all right," I said. "Thanks for pitching in."

Loren shrugged. "I wouldn't be much good at the guild house. We were tripping over one another after Percy sounded the alarm."

I recalled the mob scene Ariana and I had walked into. No one had wanted to hear about two unconscious mages. They were far more worried about their home, possessions, extensive library, and personal effects than anything else.

I switched to telepathy. *"You do have that other place. The one where we had that all-mage meeting a while back."*

"Aye, but the gateway will have to be reengineered since it links to the guild house."

I tried for a sympathetic expression, but they don't come easy to Vampires. *"Not very convenient, huh?"* I probed, curious just how difficult it would be to swap out a gateway. For that fact, they didn't require a permanent portal. It meant individuals would have to expend power for every transit, but constructing and maintaining a perpetual gateway required an infusion of magic as well.

Sort of a no-clear-winner choice. Magic has a price. It's lower for me than for most, but that's because I revive quickly with an infusion of blood. Other types of magic-wielders have to rely on time and rest.

"I'll be on my way." With a curt nod, Loren faded out the door. Apparently, he'd done as much sharing with me as he was going to. It was a potent reminder that despite my friendship with Percy, most Sorcerers viewed me as pond scum.

Clive bounded to my side, a drink tray balanced on one shoulder. "There you are, mate. Bet you made those bastards sorry they were ever born."

I grinned. "Your faith in me is touching—and undeserved. We ran into unexpected difficulties, but they're all mostly solved. For now."

Clive drew his fair brows together. *"You did eliminate the problem. Right?"*

"Some escaped our net."

"This is going to be a perpetual thorn in our sides, isn't it?"

I'd opted for honesty when I admitted we'd lost a few. No reason to stop there. No reason for telepathy, either. "You've understated things," I said, keeping my tone neutral. "We can talk after closing."

He nodded and switched the drink tray to his other hand. "Need to deliver these, but so long as I'm here, we have money now, right?"

"Aye. What do you want to spend it on?"

He made a snorting sound. "You know me too well. Obviously, we'll pay Ariana back first, but then might we rent lodgings?"

"Nothing I'd like better," I replied.

"I did a spot of searching after I finished my messenger tasks." He smiled. "Just in case, you know."

He'd been annoyed after I'd barred him from the prison breakout, but apparently he'd gotten over it. "What'd you find?" I asked.

"A second-floor flat about half a kilometer from here. It's not fancy, but it has some furniture."

I'd have clapped him across the back, but I didn't want to dislodge the drink tray. "Good man. Soon as we figure out how to change gold and jewels into money, we'll jump on it."

People were coming through the door, so I turned to my task as doorman and security squad. While I appreciated Clive's resourcefulness—and recognized we needed something beyond the stasis cave—I wanted to move in with Ariana. Part of me did.

Most of me, but until I was certain I could accept what she'd done, I was better off with Clive. At least she'd told me what happened. Without any significant prodding from me, either. As I checked newcomers and collected money, all the while keeping an eye on conversations throughout the bar, I thought about what had unfolded at Clan Hawke.

Mistral probably figured Ariana would get over her infatuation with him. It wasn't unheard of for newly turned female Vampires to be besotted with their maker. He was their only lover—for a span of time. But every Vampire I'd known had gotten over their obsession in a few months. For the best of reasons. Most of us are real dicks. And master Vamps were the absolute worst. Totally lacking in empathy, compassion, or any of the kinder, gentler sentiments, they burned out most of their needier minions. I'd tried my damnedest not to turn into my predecessor at Clan Giovanni.

Some years I'd done better than others. I'd never managed "kind," but I'd aimed for fair. Clan Giovanni had been an egalitarian seethe under my rule, but when the sun set—and our time began—I had the final say. It's how we've always done things. Mistral had told Ariana to back down. Used to absolute compliance, he'd probably assumed she'd lick her wounds and get back on the Vampire horse. During that era, we were still draining humans regularly.

Ariana had been a Vampire long enough, human prey should have been uppermost in her mind. And it should have satisfied all her needs. I shook my head. Mistral had been worse than a dick. He'd been a bloody, fucking fool. Ariana was a catch, a rare find among our people. He must have recognized it, or he'd have booted her from his chamber long before he did.

He wanted her, just not as an exclusive paramour. Accustomed to power and control, he'd snapped his fingers, expecting her to fall into line. Except she hadn't.

One of the conversations I'd been monitoring shot up a few decibels.

Percy was a master at catching things before they grew too heated. I'd learned a lot from him and beckoned Dee to work the door while I hotfooted it to the place trouble was developing. My instincts had been good, but then they usually were. I defused a couple of potential confrontations, offering options. Mostly, it came down to dropping the contentious issue—or taking it outside. Percy didn't care what happened on the far side of our front door. Neither did I.

I saw Conan trot past out of the corner of one eye and hoped he'd left a pile of cinders where that horrible prison designed to corral supernaturals had been. He was warded from humans, but seeing through his camouflage was simple for me. The guardian stopped by the bar, pushing through the swinging door. My guess was he wanted to talk with Ariana.

Back at the front, I thanked Dee and watched her hustle to the station where she mixed drinks. The skin around her eyes was pinched, but she was as heartened about our victory as the rest of us. We were about three-quarters of an hour from closing. The evening had gone quickly. Just as well. I was hungry. Clive and I owed Conan. Maybe tonight would be a good time to return the favor and do the hunting for everyone.

I'd suggest it once we'd shuttered the club for the evening.

I felt Percy's energy before I saw him. The burly Sorcerer padded through the door and plopped on his usual stool. I preferred to stand. Gave me more of an edge if I needed to move quickly. While I'm imposing to look at, I lack Percy's bulk. He's solid enough, people take one look at him and any thoughts of besting him vanish.

"Well?" I furled both brows.

"Taken care of," he said, and then added, "both problems."

"Sorry about the guild house," I began, but he waved me to silence.

"We were all there," he said gruffly. "Any of us could have taken a moment to check. None of us did. It's a good object lesson, though."

"What's that?" I asked.

"Something that rubs our noses in what we should have done."

I tried to muffle it but snorted anyway. Plenty of object lessons peppered my life. Some I'd faced more than once because I'd been too stubborn to pay attention the first time.

"How'd the night go?" Percy asked.

"Compared to cops and Sorcerers from other dimensions, pretty damned quiet."

His nostrils flared as he exhaled. "Quiet is good, but I fear we've edged into the eye of the hurricane."

Even I understood that analogy. "Any idea what happens next?" I kept my voice quiet.

"*Did a spot of hacking,*" he replied. "*There will be a raid on our guild house soon—if they're not there already.*"

"*They won't find anyone—or anything,*" I said.

"*Nay, but they could have. Our vote for stay versus leave was too close for comfort. The officials plan to shutter the house, citing health code violations.*"

"Huh?"

"*It's the only reason beyond obvious structural flaws for a government official to deny habitation.*"

My fangs wanted to drop; I held them in place. *"After we close, what do you say we start at your guild house?"*

"And do what, precisely?"

I met his keen dark eyes. Even without words, he'd understand I was fed up and ready to mow a broad swath through mortals. Upstart fucking humans. Who in the hell did they think they were? They'd tried that trick with tacking a bit of parchment on Ascent's door stating the club was closed. Ariana burned it.

Fuck all this crap. I was ready to burn them. And drain them. Not in that order. Drinking the blood of your enemy is immensely satisfying. Don't ever let anyone tell you any different.

He cupped his hands around his mouth and called, "Ten minutes to closing." When he was done, he slitted his eyes. "Run it past Ariana and Conan," he said. "Ruby and Dee too. If we do this, it's best structured as a stealth operation. Quick in. Quick out. We just might pull it off if we're not tripping over one another."

If my fangs had wanted out before, holding them back now turned into a pitched battle. I could almost taste fresh, sweet mortal blood sluicing down my throat. Before saliva spilled over, I sprinted toward the bar. Ariana would be all over my idea. I felt certain of it. Clive and Ruby too. And Conan and Dee.

The seven of us were more than a match for however many puny humans were pissing in the corners of the Sorcerers' guild house. I raised my mind voice. *"Clive!"*

"Aye, mate."

"Go kill enough for the three of us and Conan."

"*With pleasure. I'll hit you up with a location when I have one.*"

"*Good man.*" I hesitated before adding, "*Be quick. We have places to go tonight.*"

He chuckled. "*I'm a bloody Vampire. We're always quick, mate.*"

CHAPTER NINE, ARIANA

Talking about Mistral—finally after all this time—felt both weird and incredibly freeing. I'd expected Nick to flinch or something because my story read so much like a soap opera. I was watching him closely—really closely—and all I picked up on was interest. More than anyone else around me, he understood the ebb and flow of life in a clan house.

His first assumption was Mistral had forbade me from fucking anyone else. I could have run with it, but the whole purpose of me revealing my long-guarded secret was so I didn't have to lie any longer. About any of it. Besides, if I'd spun a clever tale that cast me in a somewhat more favorable light, Nick would have sniffed out the untruths. Perhaps not today, but eventually.

Vampires have exceptional built-in lie detectors. I'd opened my guarded places so Nick and I might have a chance. It was an all-or-none gambit. No halfways. Because I was curious, I asked what he imagined had happened. His supposition laid all the blame directly on Mistral, which warmed my heart. Mistral's beheading had been his own fault, but I'd ended him for being what he was: a Vampire.

I'd spent the months between the unholy deed and when I left the clan house deliberately not thinking about any of it. For one thing, I didn't want to risk someone picking up a stray vibe from me. But mostly, facing up to my crime would have meant taking a good hard look at what it meant to be one of the Undead.

I'd been turned centuries before, but I still hadn't been ready to stand before a mirror or shine a light into the depths of my non-soul. Any comfort I've developed with what I am came courtesy of Conan. Odd, huh? A creature I didn't have a name for, other than friend, taught me to believe in myself.

After I found the dire wolf—and we had a few years under our belts—I forgot all about trying to blend in with other Vamps. In truth, I went the other direction, avoiding my kind because I didn't like the way they eyed my wolf. Speculation and greed merged into one as they assumed I fed from him. They wanted a taste, and that was never going to happen.

The net effect was Conan and I moved farther and farther from other mages of any persuasion. That didn't change until I bought the club and needed staff. *Ascent's* first couple of years had been sketchy. After hiring better than thirty mortals, and letting them go almost as fast as they signed on, I was at my wit's end. Putting a call out for supernaturals had been a last-ditch effort to make a go of my nightclub.

That hadn't gone particularly well, either. Not once they laid eyes on me and hissed, "Vampires suck," or some variation thereof. It took some soul-searching, spurred by pointed questions from Conan, before I realized my dislike for them was bleeding through. They'd never work their way through their innate distrust of Vampires if I was always in a sour mood and snapped orders right and left.

As if it was a privilege to work for me.

Ha! I needed them way more than they needed me. Keeping that realization front and center had saved my nightclub and been the beginning of interspecies friendships I hadn't believed were possible. Once when I was marveling about it to Conan, he'd lambasted me with his amber gaze and said, "You and I haven't done all that badly."

The memory made me smile. Obviously, he'd understood guardians hated Vampires as much as any other supernatural creature did. Just because I hadn't known what he was for so long was meaningless. Regardless of why, he'd picked me to champion him when he was too small to do much more than hide. With the sharp intuition of his kind, he'd chopped through fluff to the things that mattered. Something about me had enticed him to lay any reservations aside.

Him trusting me had opened the door to an entire universe of possibilities. I hoped I'd given as good as I received, but if he'd found me lacking, Conan would have been gone a long while back. Actions are always more potent than words.

The club was on the verge of closing when he returned from his one-wolf mission to make certain the mages we rescued would be the last ones imprisoned in that horrible place. My skin still tingled from metal residue, and my nostrils felt abraded.

"How'd it go," I asked once he'd slithered behind the bar to where I was mixing libations.

His jaws lolled into an approximation of a wolfish smile. "Better than all right. Several more cars rolled into the clearing just about the time I blew the place sky-high. I widened my casting, and made certain no one walked away."

Crouching in front of him, I buried my hands in his neck ruff. "Excellent work. Any idea how many?"

"At least fifty humans. Some were driving official-looking cars, with writing on them."

I slid my phone out of a pocket and clicked on a news channel.

"I want to see." Conan angled his head.

I scrolled before saying, "Nothing to see. Just like with those detectives you and Nick killed, someone doesn't want this type of thing revealed to the general public."

"Because it would scare the shit out of them. Those hapless bastards should be terrified of us. We're the stuff their nightmares are made of." Ruby had sidled close, her voice a satisfied purr. She scratched behind Conan's ears and added, "I heard everything. Nicely done."

Percy's last call rang through the club. Shortly thereafter, Nick joined us behind the bar. "Who's up for a good scrap?" he inquired archly, a shit-eating grin on his face. For a moment, he looked mischievous and endearing as fuck.

In addition to being profanely gorgeous.

Why profane? Because he was so stunning it almost hurt to look at him.

I rolled my mental eyes. Christ. I had it and I had it bad. I refocused fast, before anyone helped themselves to my thoughts and decided to feel sorry for me. I was fucking fortunate Nick had partially come to terms with what I'd done. If friendship and a genuine respect were the extent we were destined to go, it beat the crap out of him being hellbent on ending me.

And turning me in to every Vampire on this side of the country. If that happened, it was only a matter of time before a pack of them cornered me. I might kill some, but I'd never get the drop on them all.

Even Vamps who hadn't been made when I decapitated Mistral—Nick, for example—knew the story as well as the history of their own clans. My rash act was close to an urban myth in Vampire-dom, and not in a good way.

"Count me in." Excitement underscored Ruby's endorsement, and she dropped her glamour. Wings fluttered in anticipation. A quick glance reassured me everyone was either gone or trudging out the door. Hopefully, my patrons were toasted enough, even if they caught a glimpse of Ruby's wings they'd assume they were hallucinating.

"Me too. I'm always up for a good fight," Dee said.

Conan growled. "I need to eat first."

Surprised his magic needed replenishing, I nodded agreement. "We'll slip off and take care of that," I told him.

"Our turn to cater dinner," Nick said. "Clive's working on it."

The *thunk* of the drop bar falling into its cradle told me Ascent was officially shuttered for the night.

"Where are we going?" Ruby arched a dark brow.

"*Sorcerers' guild house.*" Nick switched to telepathy.

"What will we find there?" I asked. The question was generic enough I didn't waste magic on mind speech.

Percy strode close and leaned across the bar, hands splayed on the polished wood surface. "*I hacked into a few official channels. The cops will be there. Actually a SWAT team from the Seattle PD's Paranormal Task force.*"

A smile formed; my fangs clicked into place. "Great opportunity to kick some ass and take names."

Nick shot a puzzled expression my way.

"It's just a saying," I told him. "Actually, we won't need to take names because those bastards will be deader than dead."

"Maybe," Nick muttered. "What if they have charms like the detectives did?"

"They'd have to have a hell of a lot of them," Dee said. "Witch charms are specific. So unless they have charms to protect them from Witches, Fae, Sorcerers, and Vamps, we'll have an edge."

Conan barked once, sharply.

Dee smiled indulgently. "I didn't forget about you, sweetie. There's no charm made potent enough to shield against guardian magic."

"Did you get one?" Percy asked the necromancer Witch. It took me a moment to remember she and several other Witches had gone in search of a prototype of the magic scanner device.

"Sure did." She grinned fiercely. "It's waiting for you in the back room."

"Good work." Percy clapped her across the back and loped toward the rear of the club.

Nick cocked his head to one side. "Just heard from Clive. Dinner is served," he announced. "Whenever we're ready for it."

Ruby kicked her head back and glanced at the clock. "Let's pick a time. Will three work?"

It was closing on two. I figured an hour would be plenty, so I said, "Sure. Meet you a couple of blocks away, so we can hit it *en masse*."

"There's a vacant lot at the corner of Elm and Meridian," Ruby noted. "Lots of trees. We can use the rear of it as a staging area."

"Perfect." Nick nodded agreement.

The smells of his magic, musk and blood, closed around me.

With his usual understated efficiency, Clive had laid out a veritable feast. We drank until energy coursed through me. Conan crunched through sinew, muscle, bone, and assorted organs. In between carcasses, Nick filled Clive in on what had turned from a raw, unformed idea into an action plan.

"Sometimes the best defense is a solid offense," Clive said and tossed a rabbit Conan's way.

"I wasn't in favor of that approach," I told him, "until earlier tonight. Maybe if we do the whole show of force thing, they'll think twice before they set any more snares for us."

Conan slurped noisily from a nearby creek. When he

was done drinking, he turned and said, "Mortals are hampered by what they do not know. Earlier humans were wise enough to leave some of the mysteries undisturbed—but not this batch."

"They do think they're hot shit," I muttered, thinking about how arrogant Riteway and Hernandez had been. Arrogant and dumb as a box of rocks. We'd twisted them, used them to our purposes. Never mind one had gotten lucky and impaled me with a silver bullet.

No harm done thanks to Nick's quick thinking and Conan's limitless shapeshifting abilities.

"I'm with Nick and Clive on this one," Conan went on. "If humans recognize we'll bite back, hard and swift and without mercy, they'll hesitate before tossing troops into the pit."

We were done feeding, so I built a spell to bring us out in the vicinity of the Sorcerers' guild house. I wasn't certain of the exact location of the vacant lot, but once we were closer, we could find it. Because it was the dark of the moon in an upscale neighborhood, I didn't expect anyone awake at this hour. They didn't disappoint me.

I'd woven a weak ward, not wanting to divert any magic unnecessarily. Once I was satisfied no one was walking their dog or lurking behind a tree, I let the ward go.

"This way." Conan woofed softly and bounded down the street.

I checked my phone. We were ten minutes early. Despite that, Percy, Dee, and Ruby were already in place. "Good news and bad news," Percy said without preamble once we were near enough for his voice to reach us. He wasn't whispering, but neither was he using unnecessary volume.

"Bad first," I said, but then I'm like that. Once I know what could go wrong, I can plan for it.

"Their numbers are manageable," Percy said, ignoring my preferences. "Twenty-two men are wearing SWAT uniforms; two are in street garb. At the point we left off spying on them, they were systematically tossing the house."

"Tossing?" Nick asked.

"Ransacking," Percy supplied in a neutral tone that probably cost him big-time. He loved that old house. Having cops rampaging through it must be killing him.

"That's nothing," Clive sputtered. "We'll be in and out in ten minutes."

"We would," Dee said, "but the SWAT fuckers brought reinforcements."

"Sorcerers." Ruby spat the word. "Dark ones."

Nick doubled up a fist and punched the air. "Excellent. Clive and I have a score to settle."

"We do, indeed," Clive seconded.

"Hear me out." Percy held up a hand. "This won't be nearly as satisfying, but we selected that house because it sits above a juncture of ley-lines. We tapped into their power from time to time. It's why we were able to establish a permanent portal to another world without a constant infusion of our own magic."

"Do it," Conan said.

"Do what?" I asked the wolf, unclear what he meant.

He turned toward me. "Percy's approach is to instruct the lines to unmake the house and everything in it. They're already interconnected."

"Exactly," Percy rumbled in his deep growl of a voice.

"How would it work?" Nick asked. "Sorry, but I'd like to understand."

"The way Percy explained it earlier," Ruby said, "is it's similar to creating a black hole in space." She smiled grimly and nodded as if that should be the end of needed explanations.

"Keep going," Nick urged.

"It's like a vacuum," I told him. "Where the house once stood will be a vacant spot devoid of everything. The molecules—building blocks—of both the house and everyone in it will cease to exist."

"How?" Clive asked.

"Does it mean no bodies to drain?" Nick tossed out. That should have bothered me too, except it didn't. The solution was elegant enough I'd surrender my desire for hand-to-hand combat and buckets of blood. Besides, we'd just fed.

"Sorry about that." Percy gave a small shrug. "The bodies will return to their base elements: carbon, nitrogen, and so on. But then, so will my house."

"If we don't do it that way," Dee broke in, "we risk the dark Sorcerers opening a gateway and doing their damnedest to spirit us through. I heard you lost a few guards and inmates at the prison."

"Aye, sad but true," Nick affirmed.

"Will leveraging the lines' power have the desired

effect?" I asked. "The whole reason for doing this was to teach mortals not to fuck with us."

"It should." Dee sounded positively feral; her dark eyes had turned into smoky holes.

"Someone will know who was dispatched here tonight," Percy said.

"And those same someones will realize there's a big fat fucking problem when none of them return. Not leaving so much as a button or a shoelace has a certain appeal," Ruby agreed.

"We could manage this from here," Percy suggested.

Conan shook his shaggy head; fur flew every which way in a staunch breeze that had blown up. "We'll be more effective from below. The lines will recognize me and respect my dominion over them."

The realm of the dead was starting to feel like my go-to place. Conan's magic, full of fur and thunder and wet rocks, was a balm to my nose—and my spirit.

"Glad he's on our side," Nick said softly.

"Me too." I smiled as the rounded walls of the underworld shimmered into view. The ley-lines had developed an orangish tinge in contrast to their usual soft, golden glow.

The wolf took on a glistening aspect. I wasn't surprised when a man stepped out of the glow and vaulted nimbly to the pulsing lines. After shunning his human form for most of the time I'd known him, Conan had discovered uses for it. "Open your magic to me," he commanded.

I stood between Nick and Clive. Percy took up a spot between Ruby and Dee on the far side of the line.

Instinctively, we'd arranged ourselves to maximize our various magics.

"Do you require aught else from us?" Percy's question was formal.

Conan shook his head until dark hair danced around his naked shoulders. I felt the tug on my magical center and offered everything in me. I trusted Conan. He wouldn't take more than he needed.

The next part happened fast. Pressure built all around us. The ley-lines turned from golden-orange to red as Conan adjured them to give him what he needed. Rolling, crashing, and booming buffeted me from every side. Part of me longed for just one mortal to sink my fangs into. Almost any cop would do at this point, but I'd rather drain one sporting paranormal task force insignia on his uniform.

I did my best to muffle a snort. At least my peacenik phase appeared to be over with. I felt more like myself. More like a Vampire.

The tone and timbre of Conan's chanting escalated. The ley-lines vibrated in concert with his spell. I didn't recognize the language, but it was the one he and his mother had used to save me. I'd been present, sort of, and watching from an out-of-my-body vantage point.

Conan brought his hands down and shouted a series of power words. I'd heard about such things, but never been in a place where a mage chivvied them into play. They shuddered around me, touching every bit of my body from toes to head. Beauty and grandeur and terror wove through those words. The lines trembled; disembodied arms, legs, and heads fell through them and vanished. Next came timber and bricks and glass shards. The stuff the guild house had been made of. Somewhere along the way, the ley-lines had swelled to many times their original size, rather like a snake that had just ingested prey.

As quickly as it had formed, the sensation of something pressing against me let go like an overactive rubber band. One moment it was there, the next, I was panting and feeling naked and exposed.

"It is done," Conan dropped his hands to his sides and morphed back to his usual form.

Dee straightened from where she'd had her arms around a group of ghosts I'd only just noticed. "They were frightened," she explained.

"Probably every shade within a five-mile radius is terrified," Percy said.

News to me. I had no idea the dead felt much of anything. I'd always seen them as kind of like Vampires but without any of the extras that made us special.

"What's left up there?" Clive pointed above his head.

"Hopefully, an expanse of dirt." Conan woofed. "Shall we find out?"

We were all still linked to him, so it was simple to draw us away from the ley-lines and their endless curved tunnel system bisecting the realm of the dead. They were golden once again and their normal size, as if nothing had ever disturbed them.

How in the hell did they manage such a dramatic transformation? It was one of those questions I'd never have an answer for, but it didn't stop me from wondering.

Dawn was breaking as we emerged in a thicket of

hawthorn trees in what had once been the guild house's rear yard. The coming day surprised me. I wouldn't have imagined we'd spent much more than an hour conjuring the lines to do Conan's bidding. The expanse of smooth dirt he'd predicted was, indeed, present. All the excavation for both basement and foundations had vanished.

Shrill voices, riddled with horror, pierced my sensitive ears. Aha! Best of both worlds.

"Dibs!" I shouted and lunged for two officers who looked as if they'd come face to face with their worst nightmares. Their eyes, huge with dilated pupils, reflected madness. Draining them would be my good deed for the year. Not exactly how I roll, but blood is blood.

"Wait! We need to question them," Ruby yelled.

I stopped, hands around one of the cop's shoulders. "Look at them," I told the Fae. "Do they seem like Q and A material to you?"

"They've lost their bloody, fucking minds," Nick said. By now, he had the other cop in thrall, neck bent at the perfect feeding angle. "Come on." He motioned to Clive. "We'll share."

"Me too," I chimed in. "I'll share just as soon as I've had a pint or two."

Conan's snarl told me he expected his share of the spoils. "You got it, bud," I told the wolf. "We'll all hurry."

I felt rather than saw the warding the others draped around us. It was dawn, after all. Some early jogger might see us. I hadn't bothered with mesmerism, so the dude in my grip writhed and shrieked. "Quiet." I added sharp edges to my command. "Vampires are real, and you're a dead man."

Something must have registered because the crazed look lifted long enough for him to wheeze, "Make me like you."

I started to laugh. I was still laughing when I buried my fangs in his neck and drank as fast as I could. The day I when I chose to turn an enemy would be the day pigs flew and lions sat down with lambs—and didn't eat them.

CHAPTER TEN, NICKOLAS

*A*riana was a thing of beauty in full Vampire mode. Watching her feed was nearly as satisfying as getting my fangs into the other cop. Because there were two of us, we drained our fellow fast. Conan snatched the corpse before Clive and I had let go of it.

I got the picture. It wasn't as if any of us were actually hungry, but allowing these two unfortunates to walk away had been out of the question. For one thing, they'd seen us. As things stood, *Ascent* was under suspicion, but no one had actually been able to connect the club to supernatural management.

"Why'd we miss them?" Clive asked and swiped the back of one hand across his mouth, leaving red streaks along one cheek.

"You mean from below?" I angled my head his way.

"Aye, exactly."

"Hard to say," I replied. "Maybe they went out to take a

piss or get something from their cars." Speaking of which, I glanced Ariana's way.

She lifted bloody fangs from the cop's neck. He was still alive. I felt the faint pulse of his heartbeat. "I'm being a pig." Silvery laughter flowed from her.

"No reason to waste resources." Clive hustled to Ariana's side and took over holding the man upright. As we'd done with cop number one, we each glommed onto a side and finished him off in less than a minute. Afterward, Clive retreated to a grove of dense evergreens to shield himself from daylight.

"Should we do something to discombobulate their vehicles?" I asked.

"No," Percy answered. "Best to leave them at odd angles littering the street."

"Eventually, someone will be forced to leak these odd events to the news outlets." Ruby narrowed her eyes to slits.

"Yeah. If a bunch of neighbors see what's out front—and they will—someone is bound to grow suspicious when nothing shows up on any of the major networks," Dee agreed. "I'm heading back to the guild house. See you at work at the usual time."

"Thanks for everything." Ariana hugged her and then smudged a bloody mark with her equally bloody hands. "Damn it. I went and got blood all over you."

Dee burst out laughing. "Not my first rodeo, honey." She was still laughing as her teleport spell snapped her up.

"I'm leaving too," Ruby said.

"Me as well." Percy rolled his shoulders back. "I need to let the rest of us know about our house. Some were hoping we'd be able to return. And I want to spend some time with the scanner Dee delivered."

"Sorry about your house," Conan said.

"Don't be," Percy told the wolf. "I loved the old place too, but we got sloppy. Once we exposed ourselves with those infernal tracking devices, we were done for here."

"Did you have insurance?" Ariana asked.

"You're joking, right?" Percy shot back. "Even if we did, there'd be no way to collect."

"I suppose not." Ariana cracked a grim smile and swept an arm to one side. "Guess this doesn't exactly fit into any of the normal pigeonholes like fires or floods."

"Ya think?" Percy quirked a brow. Ruby was already gone, and he followed her egress.

The day was overcast, but any daylight is uncomfortable after a while. "Clive and I will go to our cave," I said.

"You could wait out the day at my place," Ariana offered.

Clive glanced from her to me. "I'll take the cave," he said. "Tonight I want to stop by that flat I saw advertised. Do you suppose we'll have funds by then to secure it?"

I had no idea.

"I can get hold of Rob," Ariana said. "If anyone can manage it, he can."

"I passed a few pawn shops. They might be good for some of the gems." Clive sounded hopeful.

"Nah, they'll screw you," Ariana told him.

"We'll figure something out," I told Clive. "If you think it would be a good base for us, go ahead and rent it. I'll provide clan funds one way or another."

The muted rumble of an engine drew my gaze to where

Conan had stood. In his place was the large motorcycle shape he favored. *"Get on,"* the wolf said. It wasn't a suggestion.

Clive clapped me across the back. "See you soon, mate." Power shimmered around him as he fashioned teleport magic.

"Can you carry both of us," Ariana asked the wolf.

"I could carry ten of you."

For a moment, the motorcycle grew, expanding to twice its usual size.

"We need helmets." She scrubbed blood from her face. "Last thing we want is some random cop making a routine traffic stop and taking a good hard look at the motorcycle."

She had one back at the club. I'd seen it.

"How about this?" I suggested. "There's at least one helmet at *Ascent*. My portion of the Clan Giovanni resources are there too, and—"

"Fine. We'll teleport to the club and leave from there." Without bothering to shapeshift first, the motorcycle disappeared.

"I might have an extra helmet," Ariana told me. "Beyond that, moving your stash is important. I had no idea you'd left it at the nightclub."

"When would I have had a chance to relocate it?" I countered. "Plus, I'm not certain the cave is any safer."

She nodded. "The sooner we transition some of it into a usable form, the better."

The storeroom took shape around us. Ariana tugged out her phone and tapped on its display. I still wasn't used to cell phones. They did a whole lot more than I'd imagined, like miniature versions of the computers everyone hunkered around.

"I hope Rob's there," Ariana mumbled.

I did too. The odds weren't great since his guild house had just gotten sucked into the void. His small office was in a different location; at least it meant he'd have a spot to sleep without teleporting off world. From the small amount of time I'd spent with Rob while he made my phony identification documents, I'd been impressed by his quiet competence. He got the job done without any wasted effort. He was definitely a Sorcerer of few words. He'd asked me what he needed to know; the remainder of my time with him had passed in silence.

I hadn't minded. Idle chatter is a human convention. The rest of us don't require constant moral support.

"Yeah, Ariana, what's up this time?" a gruff voice blasted out of her phone. She must have set the speaker function so I could hear too.

Rather than answering, she responded with a question of her own. "Are you all right, Rob?"

A bitter laugh reverberated from the tinny speaker. "Oh hell, yeah. Fine. Couldn't be better. Peachy keen. What do you need?"

"Gold and gemstones turned into cash."

The laughter stopped cold. Apparently, Rob hadn't been expecting that answer. "What'd you do?" he inquired archly. "Hold up First Vampire Savings and Loan?"

"Very funny," Ariana carped back. "Look. I'm really sorry about your guild house. If this is a bad time, you can find me after shit settles out."

"Shit will never settle out," he retorted. "This is the leading edge of the new normal. None of us have a clue what it will look like, but we're fighting for everything near and dear to us. If we lose, magic will die out of all worlds."

"And humans will be fucked right along with us," Ariana agreed.

A silence might have mirrored surprise. "You get it?" Rob's question clinched my impression.

"Of course I fucking get it," Ariana snarled. "The ones who don't are mortals. They're still under the misguided impression they're superior. What a bunch of dicks."

"Stupid, ignorant dicks," Rob tossed out, followed by, "Yeah, I can fence some shit for you. Not too much at a time. Maybe ten grand worth."

I tried for calculations, but I was missing a few critical items. "How much is gold worth?" I asked.

"It closed at $1500/ounce today," Rob replied.

I was surprised he had a figure at the tip of his tongue. It proved he followed such things. Probably, computers made it far simpler.

"How much do you have?" Ariana asked me.

"In gold? Three kilos, perhaps a bit more."

A long, low whistle swooshed through the phone. "Holy fuck. I had no idea Vampires were loaded."

"Aye, we're chockful of surprises," I muttered.

"Bring me about seven ounces of gold," Rob said, "and a handful of gems. I'll get top dollar for all of them."

Ariana arched a dark brow my way. I understood what she was asking. "The gold is in quarter kilo bars," I told her.

"I can work with that," Rob spoke up. "That's slightly

over half a pound."

"How much was seven ounces?" I asked, unsure of the conversion.

"Half a pound is eight," Ariana explained.

"What's the purity of the gold?" Rob asked.

I didn't understand his question. "It's real," I said.

"Yeah, but is it eighteen karat? Twenty-four karat?"

I shrugged. "I don't know, but I bet you will."

This time, the Sorcerer's laugh held warmth. "Indeed I shall. I'm in the same spot, and I'll wait for you if you won't be too long."

"We'll be there soon," Ariana told him and disconnected.

"Where's Conan?" I asked and walked to the filing cabinet where I'd stored the gold and gems, dismantling my concealment spell.

"Not sure," Ariana said. "He might have gone home. I hope he didn't stay in the bike's form. A riderless motorcycle is bound to attract attention."

"He's smarter than that," I said and sorted one of the gold bars from the leather sack. Fishing through it, I selected a ruby and a large uncut yellow diamond.

"Probably not that one," Ariana said. "It's worth a small fortune, and Rob will have a tough time offing it."

I looked askance at her. "You seem to have some experience with this type of thing."

"Yeah. I do. Rob fences shit for me from time to time. I've never trusted banks. Only reason I have a bank account now is to facilitate payroll and supplies for the club."

I dropped the diamond into the bag and extracted an emerald. "This one okay?"

"Should be—" Her head whipped around.

I stared the same direction and felt the distinctive bite of guardian magic with its scents of fur and wet rocks. Conan oozed through from wherever he'd been. Back in wolf form, he gripped the straps for a helmet between his jaws.

"Thank you so much." I hurried toward him understanding he'd somehow come up with the item I needed to ride him.

"Where in the hell did you find that?" Ariana asked.

"You don't want to know," the wolf replied and shifted into a motorcycle.

"We're going to Rob's first," Ariana cautioned him.

"*I know the way.*" Conan punctuated his statement with a muted, "Vroom-vroom."

I returned the leather bag to its hiding place and resurrected the spell keeping it safe. The fastenings of the helmet were simple to negotiate. Ariana offered to help, but I managed nicely on my own.

We were in and out of Rob's in short order. Or I was. All I did was run up four flights of stairs to his grotto tucked beneath the eaves of an older house and give him the gold and two gemstones.

He motioned me inside and shut the door. As usual, he was all business. Magic flickered from his fingertips as he assessed the lump of gold. "Mmph. Pure all right," he muttered and then turned to the gems. "I can get you at least eleven grand for all of this," he told me, "maybe more. You good with that?"

"Aye, any amount would be appreciated since Clive and I have no resources. Thank you."

"I'll be in touch."

"I'm sorry about your guild house—" I began.

He made a shooing motion with one hand. "Something like this was bound to happen sooner or later. I've been advocating wiping humans out for the last hundred years. Maybe not all of them, but enough so they know their place again."

"No one listened, eh?" I angled a glance his way.

"Pfft. No one ever does."

This wasn't the time for a lengthy conversation, or really any conversation at all. I nodded and let myself out. Ariana waited until I was settled behind her on the motorcycle's seat. "Everything okay?" she asked.

"Fine. He'll find me once he's done whatever it is he does."

"Rob is trustworthy."

I laughed.

"What's so funny?" she asked.

"No one double-deals a Vampire. Not more than once."

"Ain't that the truth." Ariana laughed along with me, the silvery peals welcome after the night we'd just had.

Conan's wheels began to turn. I settled my feet on the pegs and reached around Ariana to grip the handlebars like she'd showed me. Riding on the motorcycle was exhilarating, even if it wasn't a real one. I figured the wind against me would feel the same whether I rode the dire wolf or a machine powered by petrol rather than magic.

Aside from the motorized cycle, the press of Ariana's body sitting between my legs was delicious. She had to feel the jut of my erection against her back, but I couldn't help myself. Having her this close was spine-tingling, and a whole lot of other things tingled too.

I did my level best to keep a lid on my lust. Vampires are far from squeamish about public sex, but Conan's presence held a mitigating effect. We had a slender window of time. We should use it plotting our next steps. Mortals would strike back quick and hard. Fear has a way of lighting a fire under everyone, no matter who they are.

The helmet shielded me from the emergent day. My head, anyway. The backs of my hands would be burned, but it was a small price. I'd heal quickly enough. "Do you expect backlash from tonight?" I asked, following up on my thoughts from a moment before.

"Yup. Heavy backlash," Ariana turned her head and spoke next to my ear. I suppose we could have used telepathy, but this worked.

"*What we did at that prison was bad enough.*" Conan joined the conversation. "*But then I went back and demolished it.*"

"*Along with the next batch of mortals who came to bail the place out,*" Ariana reminded him.

"*I've scarcely forgotten,*" the wolf said stiffly.

"This was a good night for our side," I said. "The rout at the guild house was icing on the cake, but everything was almost too easy. If this is all mortals have to fight with, the war won't last long."

"I'd love for that to be true," Ariana said thoughtfully. When she twisted like she was doing, her head fit nicely into the hollow between my neck and shoulder. I snugged an arm around her midsection just below her breasts. It wasn't as if I needed to steer Conan. Anything I did with the controls was for show.

"It's not," Conan growled.

"Figured as much," I said over the roar of the wind.

We covered the remaining distance to Ariana's in silence. I had no idea what the others were thinking about. I could have tapped into Ariana's mind, but Conan's would be closed to me no matter how I went about spying. I took advantage of the conversational gap to consider our problems.

And take a shot at prioritizing them.

Conan slowed once we left paved roads, and we bumped along what was starting to feel like a familiar path to Ariana's place. The motorcycle skidded to a halt in her gravel driveway. Before I could dismount, the wolf slithered from between our legs.

I unbuckled my helmet and followed Ariana through her stout door into welcome shelter from muted sunlight. My body still vibrated with a slow, sweet longing from how close she'd been to me.

"I'll brew us some tea," she said, "and then we need to take stock of where we are." Her tone was brisk, all business. If she shared my yearning for more closeness, she hid it well. Probably for the best. I didn't want five stolen moments with her. Five years wouldn't come close to slaking the heat and need that had me in its grip. Much as I like to control everything, this was one instance where I needed to trust we'd find a way to one another when the time was right.

"The consortium of mages—some of them, anyway— showed up right before we launched our rescue effort. Has anything else happened with them since I left?" I asked once Ariana had brought mugs of steaming, fragrant tea.

Conan had stretched full length in front of the hearth, head on his paws. "Not much. They're still hashing things out," he said.

"Aye, but do we have any idea what they've come up with?" I pressed.

Ariana shook her head and took a sip of tea. "Not really. That whole mess with Northwest New Age was our first real test, and frankly I was delighted the way everyone pitched in."

"But I was gone for weeks," I protested. "Surely, long enough for something definitive to have happened."

"They're still feeling one another out," Conan clarified. "After millennia of suspicion, crafting alliances takes time. But I agree with Ariana. Everyone pulled together during our rescue effort."

"To answer your question and catch you up"—Ariana angled a gaze my way—"the Witches from Nevada lost their guild house, and the magic detector moved from prototype to the real deal. You already know that because Dee stole one. From what I hear, though, the groups are doing lots of talking with very little actual planning."

"Has anyone actually talked with any of the mages we rescued?" I asked.

"Probably, by now," Ariana replied. "Why?"

"They had to have had a weak link in their organization," Conan said, punctuating his words with a growl.

Same thing I'd been thinking. "Seems to me our problems run along two tracks," I muttered.

"Only two? How so?" Ariana arched a brow. It was tough not to stop and worship in the face of her beauty. Her ivory skin held a rose tint from our long motorcycle ride and the heat in her kitchen. It set off the elegant bone structure of her cheeks.

"Humans are one issue," I said slowly, "but then they've always been an annoyance. They wouldn't be much more than an inconvenience if it weren't for them teaming up with black mages, fallen mages, off-world mages." I shrugged. "Who would have guessed a mage from any locale would toss their hat into the ring and do anything a mortal requested?"

Conan drew his lips back from his teeth and snarled. I felt like joining him. "We can fight what's in front of us"—I frowned—"but if we do that, we'll always be reacting, and we'll never do aught except hold our own."

Ariana nodded. "Every rock we've turned over lately has had a nasty creepy-crawly beneath it. While the surprise factor holds some allure, I want to develop an overarching strategy that actually buys us something."

"Feel like a discussion with a few guardians?" Conan rose to his feet and shook his fur out.

"Sure, but what makes you think they'll want to talk with us?" I countered, remembering their antipathy toward Vampires.

"They won't, but they agreed to be part of a joint effort at that meeting in the place beyond the Sorcerers' guild house. We invaded their domain when we leveraged the ley-lines earlier. I've heard their talk on a channel in the back of my mind, and—"

"Is that something new?" Ariana demanded.

"Yes and no," Conan told her. His head whipped around.

A veritable deluge of guardian magic cascaded through Ariana's living room. I stared at Conan. "You knew they were about to descend on us."

"Of course, I knew."

"So the question about how we felt wasn't much of a question after all," Ariana sniped.

"No. I guess not," the wolf said and turned to face a silver portal that exploded out of nowhere, its edges pulsing with power.

I got to my feet, fingers still laced around my mug. It wasn't a sign of respect, more one of apprehension. I didn't trust the guardians as far as I could see them. There had to be something they wanted to use us for, and I wondered how obtuse their reasoning would be.

And how pervasive their incentives to do as they wished.

If they just came out and ordered us to follow their lead, it would be one thing. I could refuse orders. But they were canny and well able to manipulate other mages into dancing to their desires.

I forced my mind to stillness and warded my thoughts. Whatever this was, I'd find out soon enough. I caught Ariana's eye. She nodded my way, clearly as cynical as I was about the guardians' impromptu visit. They wouldn't remain long. They never did.

Not when staying extended their contact with those like me.

CHAPTER ELEVEN, ARIANA

I was high on blood. Human blood. It's the best. Every time I imbibe, it reminds me how much I'm missing when I drain animals. But I was high from Nickolas's arms around me too. My back pressed against his front was delicious. The unmistakable bulge of his erection jutted into my spine, whispering promises of red-hot, nonstop fucking.

No combination quite like blood and sex, but we had a war to choreograph. Unfortunately, it took precedence. Over everything.

Good thing Conan provided a mitigating presence, something to concentrate on beyond the lust heating my core. He was my friend, my companion. We believed in each other, and it had carried us through. He didn't have to remind me we'd backed mortals into a corner. We'd taken a stand and couldn't stop now. Never mind, they hadn't given us much choice. Leaving all those mages from the New Age supply company to wither and turn into slaves never would have flown.

The very thought of any of us—no matter how much they loathed Vampires—turning tricks for mortals made me physically ill. Where was their pride? If I'd been captured, I'd have gone down swinging. There wasn't any torture device in any world potent enough to force me to kneel to a human and do their bidding.

Nope. Once it was clear I'd killed as many as I could, I'd have sunk into stasis. At some point, when my lack of responsiveness infuriated whoever had been assigned to waken me, I'd have been beheaded. It beat turning into a serf hands down.

We didn't talk much on the ride from Rob's place to my house. It was fine. Some moments don't require words. The wind rustling against me and Nick's arms around my body made me happy. Odd, but during my years in the clan house, I'd never considered human motivators like happiness. It was only after I left there that I began growing, merging who I'd been as a human with the creature I'd turned into as a Vampire.

Conan had a great deal to do with it. When he was small, he'd brought out my motherly side. If I'd realized he wasn't anywhere near as helpless as he appeared, I might not have been so protective. Actually, I suppose I did recognize it on some level, but Conan projected a perfect combination of innocence and neediness. In retrospect, he'd manipulated the hell out of me, but I hadn't cared. Not then, and not now, either. Vampires are quite self-serving, and self-indulgent.

We rarely do anything that doesn't push our singular agendas forward.

If there wasn't blood in it for me. Or sex with Mistral, I wasn't interested. I'd lived that way for centuries. That I'd been able to break loose, back off, and regain any perspective at all was miraculous. I owed most of it to Conan. Nick had said I was different. So was he. Perhaps Clan Giovanni hadn't played by the same rules as the other Vampire clans. His insistence Clive wasn't his minion suggested as much.

I willed the ride to last forever. My bare hands were taking it up the shorts, the backs burned from exposure to daylight. I should have grabbed a pair of gloves before we left the club, but I'd been so wrapped up in Nick's money exchange it hadn't occurred to me. Mostly, I rode Conan at night, so I wasn't used to donning gloves as part of my cycle-riding gear. Despite my throbbing hands, I could have ridden through the day and on into the next night. There wouldn't be too many moments like these, ones where Nick was quite this close. He still harbored doubts about me killing Mistral. I saw them in his occasional sidelong glances. He cared about me, longed for me, but he hadn't passed the point of no return. The one where he could look at me and not see "treason" stenciled across my forehead.

Him coming to terms with my faux pas wasn't something I could hurry along. I'd done all the explaining I planned to. Either he accepted it. Or he didn't.

Meanwhile, we'd thrown down the gauntlet.

Despite my earlier misgivings, I was mostly okay with coming out with all our guns blazing. Maybe, if we struck fast and hard and didn't let up, mortals would think twice.

Yeah, there were bazillions of them, but most were civilian-grade, not warriors. People who'd be horrified mages walked among them, Sorcerers who could off them with a casual snap of the fingers or an errant thought. Witches who could turn them into toads.

Truth be told, I'd realized my cushy little existence running *Ascent* wouldn't last forever, but I'd hoped for at least another twenty years or so before my obvious lack of aging forced me to adopt a new identity. I'd done it before. Many, many times.

Like I said, the only constant in my life has been Conan.

Eh, many moons ago, I'd assumed I'd live out my years in the Clan Hawke seethe. That hadn't exactly panned out, either. My life post Mistral had been better in so many ways it would take days to write them all down. I hadn't realized how confining a master Vampire's strictures were—until I was free.

I wasn't surprised clan houses had fallen out of fashion. They'd been linked to an earlier time, one when we were feared and the stuff of legends. When we didn't skulk in shadows and make do with any blood that came our way. I still shuddered at the crap I'd pilfered from local morgues and slaughterhouses.

Because I hadn't been paying attention, I was surprised when the crunch of gravel under Conan's wheels told me we'd arrived. He shifted in the blink of an eye, and the three of us went inside. I'd no sooner gotten tea together than guardians showed up.

Christ on a crutch. I'd been looking forward to a personal little war council with Conan and Nick where we brainstormed a few ideas we could present to other mages. They wouldn't all agree on an overarching strategy, but most of us respected democratic process. The idea with the most votes would be our first shot out of the box.

The guardians' unexpected appearance changed all that. Or put it off for a little bit. Probably not a big deal since I hadn't planned to venture out much before dusk.

The main problem with the guardians was they'd present a plan and expect the rest of us to hop to. Judging from how Percy had bowed and scraped when Fairclaw and his companions had shown up a while back, it wasn't an unrealistic assumption.

But it rubbed me the wrong way. Vampires bowed to no one, and the only orders we followed came from the head of our clan house. The occasional rebellion spoke to how tenuous most master's holds were on their respective clans. As I considered things, we could use more Vampires in our war against mortals. I wished I had an easy way to get hold of a group I was pretty sure was still in Southern California. Before, I'd have jumped in my car, but if the scanners to detect magic were well on their way to becoming a staple on major highways, long car trips were out of the question. We could teleport, of course, but it wasn't ideal. It would get us to California, but then we'd still need a car to snoop around.

Every teleport expended magic. It would alert our enemies to our location. Maybe not the first journey spell, but with each subsequent one, our risk would grow. Maybe Percy would come up with something to stymie the scanners. It was the simplest solution, but he was overloaded right now.

My mind raced in several directions as I waited for the portal that had taken shape in a corner of my living room to disgorge guardians. I still knew less than nothing about them, a lack that wasn't about to be remedied anytime soon—or ever.

Fairclaw, Conan's mother, and three other guardians jumped gracefully through the gateway before it sputtered and vanished. I took the bull by the horns and glided in front of them. "Welcome to my home. If I'd known you were coming..." I let my words trail off on purpose to get the point across it was a wee bit on the rude side to simply drop in.

"So long as you're here," I continued smoothly, "you know my name and Nick's, but other than Fairclaw, we haven't been introduced." I didn't bother mentioning the only reason I knew Fairclaw's name was because Conan had used it to address him.

"We are not in the habit of offering our names." Fairclaw focused his amber eyes on me, wolf's eyes if ever there were a pair. His long, silver hair had been braided out of the way.

I shrugged. "My home. My rules. We all understand names hold power, but if you don't trust us to know yours, you have no place in my house." I held eye contact with him. It wasn't easy. Not much intimidates me, but the latent power oozing from Fairclaw like a creek swollen from snowmelt gave me pause.

Nick glided to my side and inclined his head. "Nickolas Giovanni. Pleased to make your acquaintance."

The corners of my mouth twitched. Nick's traditional words of introduction presented an opening. Would the guardians accept the invitation to establish a level playing field? At the end of the day, their knowledge of who we were, while withholding similar information about themselves, was nothing but a big fat power play.

"This is ridiculous." Conan's mother stepped in front of Fairclaw. "I am Moonglow." Like all guardians, she was naked in her human form and had amber eyes. Pure-white hair spilled around her almost to foot level, and a large blue gemstone was suspended around her neck on a slender golden chain.

"Thank you," I told her and meant it. She'd saved my life when I'd inhaled silver fumes. I'd never forget her kindness or underestimate what it had cost her to tend to one like me.

"'Tis a small enough request," she said and turned her keen gaze on the other three guardians. Magic crackled, changing the air until it fairly sparkled with incandescent motes of light.

The other guardians—two men and a woman—avoided looking at Fairclaw. The woman aimed her amber gaze my way. "I am Earthtime." Violet hair shimmered around her in shades from pastel to the deep purple of a winter sunset.

"Pleased to meet you and Moonglow." Nick offered an engaging smile and bowed low. Damn Vampires can be charming as fuck when we want to be, but I was probably prejudiced where Nick was concerned.

I looked expectantly at the two yet-to-be-named guardians. Both had black hair shot with silvery strands that fell to midback. Built much like Fairclaw and Conan, they were tall and broad but not overly muscular. More lithe and graceful than burly.

"We are seers," the man on the right said. "I am called Future."

"And I am called Past," the other guardian said. "Clearly, our true names are far more complicated, but these will do. Every guardian will know who you mean if you mention either of us."

Fairclaw smirked my way as if to ask if I were satisfied, but since he didn't voice the question I ginned up a noncommittal smile.

"We are here to tell you what will happen next—" Fairclaw began.

"Not how it works," I cut in.

"But I have seen the future clearly," Future said.

Still in wolf form, Conan growled. "So have the Witch seers and the Fae seers and every other brand of seer. Have you checked to see if your future-seeing matches up with theirs?"

Future shifted to wolf form quicker than I could follow. Coal black, he stood nose-to-nose with Conan, growling. "I remember you from when you were a pup. You didn't listen then, either."

Hackles at half-mast, Conan ignored the barb. "I take it, your answer is no. Guardians never check anything with anyone beyond our immediate circles. Why start now?"

"Excellent question." Fairclaw crouched next to the snarling wolves. "Future's visions always come to pass. He told us you would run, but Moonglow didn't believe him. She's never made that mistake again. Her inattention cost her dearly."

I glanced Conan's mother. Probably should have kept my

mouth shut, but a few words escaped anyway. "Do you have other children?"

She shook her head. "We are only allowed one."

I backed up a step to cover my surprise, and to forestall the dozens of questions her statement had spawned. Uppermost was who Conan's father had been, but he'd have told me if he wanted me to know.

A quick refocus was in order. My curiosity wasn't important. "Stop it!" I aimed my words at the wolves who looked as if they were a nanosecond from ripping one another's throat's out.

"Not your affair." Conan snarled louder.

"You're my dearest friend," I told him, "but in this instance I disagree. Let's hear them out, and then we can do a compare and contrast with seers from other branches of magedom."

"We already know some of their predictions," Nickolas spoke up. "The part about gathering darkness and magic leaving Earth entirely."

I nodded grimly. We did, indeed. "The part we don't know," I said, "is if our actions at the prison and torching the Sorcerers' guild house changed anything."

Fairclaw slitted his eyes my way. Before he opened his mouth and said something that would really piss me off about him never viewing Vampires as mental giants, I added, "A simple yes or no will do."

"Yes." He narrowed his eyes further.

Conan left the Mexican standoff with Future and padded to my side. His hackles were still activated; it made me wonder how much bad water flowed under the bridge between him and Future. My guess was quite a bit.

I looked from Fairclaw to Moonglow. I'd been so used to thinking of her as "Conan's mother," it seemed strange to have a name assigned to her.

Future shifted back to his human form and raised his hands, index fingers extended as he drew pictures in the air. His fingertips left silvery strokes that held a soft glow. A series of concentric circles took shape; each had a jagged break in it. Some of the circles appeared to slot into others, while a few remained stubbornly off to one side. He barked a few words, and the circles took on coloration.

"Red is Witches," Future said in a tone that reminded me of a college professor. "Blue is Fae. Green is Sidhe. Violet is Sorcerers. Pink is Shifters. Those are the primary branches of magery."

"We didn't make the cut?" I asked acidly, furious to be left out as usual. No one counted Vampires despite how strong our magic was.

"'Fraid not," Future said. His tone could have meant anything, so I chose to interpret is as a suck-it-up-buttercup speech.

"Why are the green circles bundled off to one side?" Nick asked.

"Because you can't trust them," Fairclaw grunted. "They led the charge to help mortals by sharing magic. Their acts are forbidden outside our circles."

"There was a black Witch at the front end of the current mess," I said.

"Aye, and a passel of black Sorcerers," Nickolas tossed out.

"I didn't say they were the only ones," Fairclaw was quick to clarify, "merely that they were the leading edge. And it's not all the Sidhe. The defection began in the dark court. I'm not certain if it ever spread to the light side of Faery."

"Not yet," Future said, "but everyone in Oberon's court is biding their time to see which horse to jump on."

I didn't see how he could sound so certain, but he did. From what I'd observed, scrying the future was a hit-or-miss proposition.

"The problem is deeper than culling Sidhe out of the action," Moonglow said in her steady voice. "Not all of them have been corrupted, and their magic provides a necessary element."

"Without it, you will not win," Future chimed in. His sanctimonious tone was getting on my nerves.

"How does this work?" Nick asked him.

"What do you mean?" The seer drew his thick black brows together.

"Do you see various possibilities?"

He nodded. "Aye. In this instance, I scryed the same bit of future over and over until nothing new emerged. Three primary timelines showed themselves to me. In the first, mortals won. It takes centuries, but their alliance with the Sidhe gave them sufficient ammunition to defeat the rest of us."

"Do we leave Earth?" I asked.

"Aye, those of us who are left. At that point, it isn't

many." Breath rattled through the guardian's teeth. "Vision two is a draw, but it is meaningless because the damage done to Earth rendered it uninhabitable."

"So neither side wins?" Nick arched a blond brow.

"True enough, but the carnage extends for untold millennia. Time when magic should have been focused on salvaging a damaged world."

"Pfft." I flapped a hand. "If humans don't care about their planet, why should we?"

"No particular reason"—Future leveled his gaze my way —"other than many of us reside here too."

"What did door number three look like?" I asked.

"Huh?" Future looked confused.

"It's an expression." Conan mimicked Future's patronizing tone. It didn't sound any better coming from him.

"If you're inquiring about the third leg of my scrying, it's more promising. We win, and the planet limps along—at least as far out as I focused my lens."

I narrowed my eyes. "There's a 'but' hanging around. What is it?"

"Nothing comes without cost—" Fairclaw began.

"Spare me the sermon," I interrupted him, not caring it was rude. "What do we have to do to win?"

Conan growled. "I don't like this," he muttered.

I didn't, either. If it were straightforward, Future—or Fairclaw—would come out with the goods. They were being cagey, and it made me uncomfortable.

"No allies," Future said.

"What do you mean?" Nick asked.

"This war will be fought by guardians," Fairclaw clarified. "We will plan it, execute it, and deal with any fallout."

"While the rest of us sit on our thumbs?" I demanded, followed by, "Go fuck yourselves."

"I understand it's not the message you'd have preferred," Moonglow spoke up, "but if any of the rest of you join in, we will be back to either of the first two scenarios."

"Why should we take your word for this?" Conan sounded different. When I glanced his way, he'd shifted to his human form. Maybe he was trying for equal footing with his erstwhile kinsmen.

"Why would we lie to you?" Moonglow asked.

He shrugged. "You did it before, so—"

"You were a child," she protested. "I did it to keep you safe. If I'd had any idea—"

"Aye. You'd have done things differently." Conan sounded tired. I understood him well enough to recognize this was a topic he'd played back and forth in his mind too many times to count.

"What do you want to do?" Nick addressed the question to me.

"What we are going to do"—I turned so I faced the guardians—"is discuss your information with everyone. Fae. Sidhe. Witches. Shifters. Druids. Everybody. Hell, I might even try to scare up a few more Vampires."

"We will take your beliefs under advisement," Conan said.

"But there is no guarantee we will follow them." I

wanted to make certain that point came through loud and clear.

"You have little choice." Fairclaw tried for neutral, but anger bled through the tight lines of his shoulders and neck.

"We only suffer the loss of choices once we select a direction," Nickolas said. I could have hugged him.

"If your future seeing is in agreement with other seers, we may well step aside," Conan said.

"And if it's not?" Future arched his gray brows.

"Then we shall select the path that appears to meet our needs," Conan told him.

"Will you inform us?" Moonglow asked softly.

I hesitated, considering. Before I could reply, she went on, "When you tapped the power of the ley-lines to absorb the Sorcerers' guild house and everyone in it, you altered much. It is done. There is no going back."

"I understood the risks," Conan answered.

"They will be...unpredictable for a bit," his mother murmured.

"Unpredictable, hell. They were never meant for such an undertaking. Beyond that, you levied their power twice in quick succession." Fairclaw's flat tone rose as fury shuttled to the fore.

"They responded readily to my call." Conan spoke over him. "Recognized me for who I am."

My eyes may have widened. What in the fuck did he mean by that?

"We should leave," Moonglow said. "We have overstayed our welcome here."

I opened my mouth to tell her she'd never been welcome,

merely tolerated, but even I'm not quite that crusty. The guardians didn't bother with a portal. The air shimmered, glistened, and developed scents of wet rock and fur. When it cleared, they were gone.

Conan stared at the spot they'd vanished through. "Do you feel like talking?" I asked him.

"Not particularly," he replied and walked through the nearest wall and out into the day.

CHAPTER TWELVE, NICKOLAS

I picked up my now-cold tea and slugged it back. "That could have gone better," I said once I'd drained the mug.

Ariana looked askance at me. "Ya think?" she inquired acidly and blew out a totally unnecessary breath. "Fuck. Tough to know who to believe."

"Do you think they were lying?" That hadn't occurred to me.

"Maybe not so much an in-our-faces-lie, but definitely an attempt to control us, force us to step aside."

"It's quite different from their position at that initial gathering," I replied. "The one where all of us agreed to work together to defeat mortals."

Ariana headed for the kitchen end of her home and put the kettle back over a burner. After rummaging through some cannisters, she refilled the tea strainer with fresh herbs and dropped it into the kettle.

"Do you think Conan will be back?" I asked.

"Yeah. He'll come back. A bigger question is whether he'll pony up information."

I handed over my mug for a refill. "When you asked if he felt like talking, he left. Doesn't bode especially well for answers. How about your collection of books and scrolls? Might we find something useful within them?"

"They're mostly lore and history directly related to Vampires and Celtic legends. I never knew much at all about guardians. Never cared about them, either."

"That could be said about any of the other types of mages." I blew on the tea to cool it. "Vampires aren't even team players amongst ourselves."

"Ha. Ain't it the truth. So long as we're on this topic," she went on, "what would you think about adding more Vampires to our ranks?"

I thought about the question and could build arguments on either side of the road. "Maybe we should check in with Christa and the Witch seers first," I suggested. "If their latest scrying syncs with what Future told us, we might not want to add more incendiary material to the mix."

Ariana laughed softly. "We're not the easiest bunch to get along with, are we?"

"No. We won't find any Vamps from either of our clan houses in the States. What's left of Clan Giovanni is scattered through Eastern Europe, and it sounds as if Clan Hawke never left the British Isles."

"If they did, I didn't hear about it," Ariana concurred.

"That would leave Clan Ravnos and Clan Tremere," I said. "Ravnos, in particular, are a bunch of bastards."

"Tell me about it. I ran into them when I went to New Orleans many years ago. I'd heard Vamps were thick in that area, but they made it abundantly clear either I signed on with their clan or I needed to leave."

"Not so different from how we operated in the Old County," I reminded her.

"I remember," she replied. "For some oddball reason, I'd thought maybe time and distance and modernity might have changed things, but none of it made any difference at all."

Ariana's rich, melodic voice drew me in. Watching her, listening to her delighted me. Fascinated me. Memories of the kisses we'd shared blasted through my head, and my errant member shot to attention. We were alone—for now. My next moves were pure instinct, not thought out at all. Her energy attracted me, sang to me, made me long for the press of her lips on mine, for the sweet tang of her blood in my mouth. I set my cup down and moved close, placing my hands on her shoulders.

Reaching up, she covered my hands with her own and looked at me with her intense blue-eyed gaze. Today, silvery flecks floated around the irises. "Someday," she murmured, "we may have time to indulge. You're not five-minute-quickie material."

"We found time once," I reminded her. "It wasn't nearly enough, but—"

Ariana shook her head. "That was before my big confession. You're not sure about me, and you have to be before we go down that road again."

Desire surged, so heady it was all-encompassing. Sex with mortals was bland, boring. Nothing like fucking my own kind. I tangled my fingers in strands of her hair. "I've never wanted any woman as much as I long for you."

She leaned close enough her lips almost brushed mine and said, "I want you too, but I learned from what happened with Mistral. I can't separate sex from loving—unless it's a roll in the hay with a mortal. So you have to be certain you can look past my sins, accept all of me." The air around us thickened, turned musky with copper, blood-tinged edges, as we released pheromones.

Evidence she ached for me with the same singlemindedness I longed for her was intoxicating. I slid my hands down the graceful curves of her back until I grasped the high, firm globes of her ass and drew her against me. My harder-than-hard cock pressed into her belly. She grabbed handfuls of my shirt, and the peaks of her nipples grazed my chest.

If we'd been human, we'd have been panting.

My mind glazed over, oblivious to everything but a driving need to plunge my cock into her and never ever leave the heat of her body. It was stupid, ill-advised. With all the other problems facing us, we should be setting up meetings with Ruby and Dee and Christa. With Dahlia and Percy.

I couldn't make myself care about any of it.

The woman in my arms was all that mattered.

As quickly as she'd taken hold of my shirt, she let go and slithered out of my arms. "Damn it, you're enticing as fuck," she said and backed partway across the kitchen. "But you harbor doubts about me."

I could have floated a partial truth, but she was too precious to try to manipulate her into my bed. My body hummed with lust; wanting her felt good, right, perfect. "I do have reservations," I agreed. "But only a few. They're diminishing by the moment."

"Only because you're caught up in heat and hunger." Her lips curved into a soft smile. "Come on. I need your other brain, so we can map out a game plan and run with it."

I laughed. "My other brain, eh? Never thought about it in quite those terms."

Ariana moved to the living room and picked up an electronic device that was smaller than a computer but significantly bigger than a cell phone. For scant moments, I considered bolting after her, wrapping her in my arms and kissing her. My body screamed at me to brand her, make her mine. It was the Vampire way.

I held back. My connection with her was too vital to ruin because my blood ran thick with desire. For now, it was enough to know she was waiting for me to find a way to pigeonhole her rebellion. She wouldn't wait forever, but maybe I wouldn't need forever. I'd come a long way from the day I tried to end her over her indiscretion. Then I'd been reacting out of pure, blind fury. No Vampire got away with such an act.

Except she had. Retribution should have come hundreds of years ago. That it hadn't didn't make it my place to mete it out. The realization was sobering. Worse, Clive had realized as much off the bat. He wouldn't have cared if she'd decapitated the first Vampire, let alone a bit player like Mistral.

"Nick?" Ariana called from one of the couches. A scroll

sat on a table in front of her, and the electronic gadget was in her lap.

"Coming."

The front door clanged open and Conan trotted through, his muzzle streaked with dried blood. "Drowned your frustration in a hunt, did you?" I inquired.

He growled.

"Be nice," Ariana said. "You're who left."

"What are you doing?" Conan swiped blood away with his tongue and glanced over Ariana's shoulder.

She angled her head and stared him down. "You could make my life a whole lot easier by telling me what you know."

"What makes you think I know anything?" Conan raised his snout to her shoulder level.

"For starters," I spoke up, "what are the odds this Future fellow was telling the truth?"

Conan's attention shifted to me. "He cannot lie, which means he relayed what he saw in his visions."

"How about the interpretation?" Ariana pressed. "I've spent enough time around Christa to know there's more than one way to decipher future seeing."

"Why would they want to get rid of the rest of us?" I asked. "What's in it for them?"

"Not the rest of you so much as me," Conan clarified.

Ariana narrowed her eyes. "I don't get it. You're their long-lost brother. They were pushing hard to lure you back into the fold."

"Where they can control my every move," Conan growled.

I moved closer and asked, "What is it they're afraid you'll do if you're not under their thumb?"

Conan's tongue lolled. I was no expert on reading lupine body signals, but damn if he didn't appear pleased with himself. "The same thing I did with the lines. They're especially attuned to my magic."

"Why?" Ariana let the question hang between us.

Conan tossed his head. "I should be the one in charge. It was my birthright, but I didn't care for the terms. So I left."

"What were they?" Ariana asked before I could get the same question out.

"Doesn't matter. Even as a youngster, I understood they'd hamstring me. Better to be free." He reared back and placed his front paws on top of the scroll. "It's not dissimilar to the decision you made when you left the seethe."

"But I had to leave," Ariana said softly.

"So did I," Conan told her. "Now can we talk about something important?"

"Certainly," I said. "Which item would you like to address first?"

"Not so fast," Ariana broke in. "I need a quick and dirty primer about guardians. Why were they in such an all-fired rush to clear the playing field? A couple of weeks ago, they sang a different tune."

The wolf cocked his head to one side. The vellum crinkled beneath his big paws, developing a few rents. "A couple of weeks ago, I hadn't let my magic run wide open. Fairclaw is worried about losing control."

"You have to say more than that," Ariana urged. "If you were the heir apparent, why would it matter?"

"How does that work?" I added a question to the mix. "Is it like royalty where the mantle is passed from father to son?"

"Mother to son," Conan said.

"Was Fairclaw your father?" Ariana asked. I'd wanted to know much the same but hadn't been bold enough to inquire.

The wolf snorted and snuffled. If he'd been in his human form, he'd have been laughing.

"I take it that's a no." Ariana reached across the table and buried a hand in his ruff.

"More than no," Conan said. "Mother has far better sense than to link herself to that insufferable prig."

A likely scenario was emerging, so I took a chance and floated it. "Fairclaw schemed to get rid of you from the moment of your birth. Your mother offered what protection she could, and—"

"He couldn't get rid of me," Conan cut me off. "Mother wouldn't let him, and even then my power outshone his. Besides, it would have looked bad. We'd never had issues with succession of leadership before. Fairclaw is sly. He drafted new laws. They fit his brand of magic perfectly, but I would have run up against them every time I cast the smallest spell. Meanwhile, factions had formed. One on his side, the other on mine. It wasn't the first time guardian stood against guardian, but this time was worse than any other according to Mother."

Conan pivoted, returning his front paws to the floor, and shook himself from head to tail tip. His claws made clicking noises on the wooden floor. "Mother told me to act more like a puppy to not attract the wrong kind of attention."

"And did you?" Ariana asked.

"What do you think?" he replied. "I wasn't about to be anything other than what I was, but the reason I left was because I caught wind of plans to imprison me."

"What?" I was outraged. "You were their prince. How could they have done something like that?"

"Easily, since it was under the guise of preparing me for my future duties. Fairclaw set up a school on another world. I'd be transported there, and I would have been unable to leave. Guardians would have shown up regularly with supplies."

He shook himself again, more vigorously this time. "I didn't wait around to see what would happen. Mother said she'd protect me, but I didn't want to put her in the position of alienating herself from other guardians."

"Why'd you pick Earth?" I asked.

"It's the most densely inhabited world. I figured it would be easier to hide myself. I understood Fairclaw and his contingent wouldn't just let me go. Much as he'd want to dust his hands together and say something like, 'Oh well,' I was the heir apparent. It meant he had to at least put up a show of hunting for me."

"I take it Future was on Fairclaw's side back then?" I eyed Conan.

The wolf bobbed his head. "You heard him say I'd been naught but trouble from the gate, eh?"

"Why'd you pick me?" Ariana's question was soft, but it thrummed with emotion.

"Are you certain you wish to know?"

"Yes." Ariana nodded briskly.

"As you will. Guardians hate Vampires. It was the last place they'd look for me."

I was watching Ariana and saw her flinch. Clearly, it hadn't been the answer she'd hoped for. Truth burned in the wolf's words. It was impossible to fault him; he'd offered her a chance to withdraw her query.

Conan trained his liquid amber gaze on Ariana. "Initially, my choice was self-serving, but I quickly grew to respect you. Over time, my respect expanded to love, and you became my sister in every regard except blood."

"Thank you for adding that last," she said.

He shook his head. "Far more than an afterthought. It's true. We've been together long enough, you must already know as much. I should be thanking you. Hiding in your shadow shielded me from discovery. The Sorcerer you hunted down and mesmerized helped as well. He inadvertently taught me different ways to ward myself. Eventually, my kin gave up and went away."

Ariana's eyes widened. "Guardians got close to us?"

"Many times, but they never looked beyond what you were. They didn't know enough about Vampires to understand how unusual it was for one to keep a pet."

"Thanks be for small favors," she muttered.

"Indeed," I chimed in. While it was gratifying to know more about Conan and the guardians, we hadn't made any progress with the myriad problems facing us. I aimed my next words at Conan. "What Future said about the rest of us stepping aside. Was it true?"

"As far as it went, yes. As I said, he cannot lie. Neither can Past. They are bound by laws that govern us."

"Is the interpretation of their prophecy flawed?" I pressed.

"I've asked Christa how looking into her mirror works," Ariana said. "Although sometimes she uses water. What she told me is this. The past is simple. It presents as it rolled out. For future-seeking, she sees a series of images. Sometimes one at a time; sometimes superimposed. One of the rules in her guild house is that all scrying must be presented and discussed in a group format."

"Is that because it's so difficult for one seer to come up with the correct analysis?" I asked.

"I always assumed so," Ariana replied. "So in this case, Future gave Fairclaw data and he massaged it to meet his needs, one of which was making certain Conan wasn't around to muck things up."

"How could you do that?" I stared at the wolf.

"By showing my power to be superior to his, which it is," Conan replied somewhat smugly. "There was a time when we were more evenly matched, but he is very old, and millennia have taken a toll on his ability."

"Strange," I murmured.

"Yeah," Ariana agreed. "It's the opposite for Vampires. The older we are, the stronger we get."

"That is because your magic derives from a ritual. Newly made Vampires are weak and have little control," Conan tossed out. "Some don't make it past their first year."

How in the hell did Conan know so much about Vampires? Probably, he'd made a point to learn about us after hooking up with Ariana. "Our clan house always waited at least two years before we gave up and destroyed one of our own," I mentioned as a point of clarification.

"Ha!" Ariana sputtered. "Mistral was done after six months."

"But you see," I said, "Clan Giovanni made certain our new Vampires wanted the transformation. Even with that precaution, we had a few washouts. Not many, mind you."

"Clan Hawke had lots," Ariana mumbled as if the dropout rate offended her.

"We need to feed," I said.

"I hunted," Conan informed us. "I will talk with Christa and Dahlia to see if their prophecies have altered. We can meet at *Ascent* later today."

"Between four and four thirty," Ariana told the wolf.

"I will make a point of locating representatives from the various mage groups," he said.

"Perfect," she replied. "We can have a short get together before the club opens."

"If it opens," Conan said. "It's possible we'll have more important work tonight." This time, he left through the front door. Magic is where I live, but seeing him ooze through walls is somewhat unnerving.

My guess was it had edged into afternoon. "Is there a way to see if Rob has money for me?" I asked Ariana.

Nodding, she snatched up the tablet she'd been working on before Conan returned and tapped its glass top. Lights flickered across its surface. Ariana smiled. "He found a buyer for the gold. You're rich!"

I laughed. "So long as it means I have enough so Clive can rent that flat, all is well."

"Oh, there will be plenty for that," she reassured me and closed a leather cover over the tablet.

"Good. Then I can repay my debts to you and start fresh."

She stood and hooked a hand beneath my arm. "Feeding isn't all that essential, but I'd like to get out for a bit before we're stuck in a meeting where no one is likely to agree on much of anything."

A glance told me the backs of my hands had healed from their earlier burns. "Come on." I started toward the door.

She retrieved her hand and rolled the scroll, placing it in an empty spot on a nearby shelf. "All right. I'm ready."

I wasn't sure how to phrase what I wanted to ask, so I kept it as neutral as I could. "Are you relieved to know more about Conan's background?"

"Relieved isn't quite the proper word. I'm pleased he finally said as much as he did. And I'm furious at Fairclaw and the rest of them. How dare they mistreat one of their own so badly?"

"You're thinking with your human mind," I said gently. "Vampires pull rank all the time. Guardians probably do much the same. In truth, there's no such thing as an egalitarian governmental structure anywhere in the magical world."

"Thanks for the philosophy lesson, Signore Giovanni."

"Anytime." I grinned and draped an arm around her shoulders. "Anytime at all, *cara.*"

"You must have liked Italy," she said as we walked out the door.

"Not at first. It was a big change after Scotland, but I grew used to it..."

I wasn't in the habit of talking about my likes and dislikes and feelings, but I wanted to kick the gates open. No secrets from Ariana. None at all. Somewhere along the way, maybe my openness would be the key to sweeping away the last of my reservations and paving a way for her and me to be together.

CHAPTER THIRTEEN, ARIANA

scent was crowded with Sorcerers, Fae, Witches, Shifters, Druids, and Sidhe. I remembered the guardians' warning about the Sidhe, but the ones here were acting totally appropriately. I'd even taken the added step of subtly screening their thoughts to test for traitors.

Didn't find any.

Conan had done a bang-up job gathering everyone. He'd relayed the guardians' warning. Conversation ran thick through the large room with people talking over one another. Everyone was as certain they were right as the guardians had been. Or maybe they'd only been pretending. Didn't matter. The net result was stubborn running head-on into more stubborn.

About the only area they agreed on was that the guardians' future-seeing was badly flawed.

No one seemed inclined to give an inch. We were about twenty minutes from when I'd normally open the club. It had worked last time, so I leapt on top of a table, stuck a finger in my mouth, and whistled shrilly.

The unexpected noise had the desired effect. I jumped into the momentary silence and projected my voice. "Action, not philosophy. We don't need to plan out the next ten years, folks."

"But we don't want to make any mistakes, either," a Witch called from the back of the room.

"We'll make dozens, perhaps hundreds, of mistakes," I retorted. "More important is how we recover from them. Mortals will fuck up too. Their last couple of gambits didn't fare so well."

Nick walked to the table I was perched on. "First off," he posed a query to the group, "do we go on the offensive? If we choose not to do that, we'll end up waiting to see what mortals cook up next and be scrambling to react."

"Rinse, recycle, repeat," I added to pound his point home.

A grumble rippled through the room. Apparently, being at the mercy of humans stuck in everyone's craw. I'd been expecting another police raid ever since Riteway and Hernandez went down. Conan killed them, but it hadn't obliterated their case notes. Other cops had also been here the afternoon I'd been sucked through a vortex into what turned out to be the guardians' original world.

I'd never heard so much as a peep from them about that day, either.

Normally, law enforcement was quick to alert business owners about problems, particularly ones that cost the PD money and personnel. Nick was still tossing ideas out. I focused on what he was saying.

"The way I see things," he went on, "we either concentrate on taking down as many key humans as we can as fast as we can. Or we target the dark mages who've crafted charms and offered magic to mortals." He rolled his shoulders back. "This won't go over well, but Guardians tell us Sidhe are behind much of the diverted magic."

A slender girl who looked about twelve but was probably several hundred years old flowed to her feet. Ruby wings were folded behind her; fair hair cascaded to her knees. Rings adorned every finger including her thumbs, and she wore ragged jeans and a pink sweatshirt. "Much as it pains me to admit this," she said in a high, clear voice, "it's true. This isn't much of an excuse, but the dark court has fallen to temptation, not the rest of us."

"What could possibly tempt them?" I asked.

She shrugged. "What else? Gold. The Fae aren't the only ones perpetually hunting for rainbows."

"Speak for yourself," Ruby said tartly from where she stood behind the bar.

I muffled a smile. Ruby was like a truffle-sniffing pig whenever the topic of anything money-related popped up. Nose to the ground, she wouldn't give up unless I flexed some muscle and told her to stop.

So long as I was thinking about money, we'd stopped by Rob's earlier and collected a big fat briefcase bursting with cash. There'd be more as soon as he found buyers for the gemstones.

Clive had wanted to grab a handful of bills and go look at

an apartment. I'd convinced him to use one of the credit cards Rob had obtained for him. Tomorrow, we'd open several bank accounts split between Nick and Clive. That way there wouldn't be so much in any one of them as to attract attention.

The childlike Sidhe had raised her hands in front of her. All her rings glittered, lit from within by magic of their own. At least I understood why she wore them; like as not they were keyed to her particular energy.

"I wasn't wanting to intensify the bad blood between our people," she told Ruby. "Mostly, I was confirming what the Vampire said about the dark court being to blame for many of our current problems."

"Has the light court done aught to address this?" Percy asked. He stood in his usual spot near the front door wearing his customary tartan over a linen shirt. Sandals laced up his legs, and his arms were crossed over his burly chest. Strain had carved lines deep into his forehead and around his eyes.

She shook her head and switched to Gaelic. "Nay. We live separately and havena spoken in close to a millennia."

Great. Made it our problem. I'd much rather the Sidhe would have ridden herd on their own.

"I like the idea of selecting mortal targets," I said. "We can deal with whatever twisted mages pop up as we run into them. It's what we've been doing since the beginning of all this, anyway."

"Where do you see us starting?" Dahlia asked. Her raven, More Than Never, perched on her shoulder. The mistress of the local Witches' guild house looked as unkempt as ever with her spiky red hair, green eyes, and sharply cut features. Tall, gaunt, and to the point, she didn't pull any punches.

I appreciated her straightforward approach, so I matched it with directness of my own. "Seattle's paranormal task force is a worthy goal. If we could take them out, it would be quite the coup."

A rippled, "Oooohhh," surged through the room. I didn't have to say much more for everyone to get it. They all understood Seattle's PTF was preeminent in the country. If we were successful gutting it, it was bound to take a bite out of the opposition.

"It will only work," I cautioned, "if we have targets number two and three lined up and ready to hit immediately thereafter."

"San Francisco's PTF would be my second choice," Ruby said. "They're a bunch of prime bastards, who are convinced they're indestructible."

I arched my brows her way. "There's more to that tale," I said.

"Aye, but you'll not hear it from me."

I knew better than to press.

"The Seattle operation will be a litmus test," Percy said.

"What does that mean?" Nick called out.

"We'll find out if we have the ability to pull it off," Percy clarified. "Earlier, Ariana mentioned we'd make a bunch of mistakes. We will. By the time we move on to the San Francisco task force, we'll be smoother—and smarter."

The club should have opened five minutes ago. "We have to wrap this up," I told the group.

"I'll take a few Witches and identify weak spots in Seattle's operation," Dahlia said.

"Be careful," I cautioned her.

She grinned, but without a trace of warmth. "That job is partially complete. One of my Witches works in that unit. We planned it that way to keep an eye on them."

Nick broke out laughing and sputtered, "If they're so dense they never figured it out, we'll be fine."

"Don't underestimate them," Dahlia said. The raven squawked agreement. "Zoe has maintained a very low profile."

"What does she do for them?" Ruby asked.

"Dispatcher."

My mouth rounded into an approving O. "Excellent. Means she'll know whenever calls come through."

"So long as it's her shift," Dahlia warned. "She's one of half a dozen, and they rotate."

"We'll want to do this soon," Percy said. "The story about last night blew up all over every major network. Complete with footage of the abandoned cop cars and the missing mansion."

"I saw." Ruby rolled her golden eyes. "Every psychic and ghost hunter for leagues around is either already there or headed that way. They'll blunder into one another for weeks chasing down dead ends."

"Some of those psychics were hired by Seattle's PTF," Dahlia told her.

"Goddess knows who else they've employed," Percy rumbled in his deep voice. "Which is why we need to move quickly."

"Before they get even more organized," I added.

Knocks sounded on *Ascent's* door. Percy pushed it open, and I heard him inform whoever was out there we'd be open by seven thirty. Once the heavy door slammed shut, I glanced around. "Other than the prison break, most of us have never fought together before. That will be as big a challenge as anything."

"Everyone needs to select a specific role," Nickolas said. "It was how we managed back in my days as a knight. Oftentimes, we'd field men who'd never worked as a unit. Some efforts went more smoothly than others."

"First, we'll select our targets," I spoke slowly, gathering my thoughts. "Once we know who we're taking out, we can assign two or three of us to one of them."

"Isn't that kind of overkill?" Dee asked.

"Might be," I agreed, "but we won't know until we're in the thick of things. I'd rather be over-manned than under."

"Are you thinking we'll strike simultaneously?" Percy inquired.

I nodded. "It's the only way. If we don't knock them all out at the same time, word will go out, and whoever we've missed will go to ground. We'll still be able to find them, but it will expose us for longer. Much longer."

"How many are there?" Nick aimed his question at Dahlia.

She screwed her face into a sour expression. "Seventy-eight at last count."

Nick whistled long and low. "Christ! Must cost them a bloody fortune to outfit all those men."

"Some are women," Dahlia corrected him. "But yeah, it's very pricey."

I squeezed my eyes shut for a moment considering the logistics. "Some of them will be off-duty."

"Of course," Dahlia said, "but Zoe can get us their addresses."

"Assuming they're home," Ruby said, "and not out getting it on with some hooker they busted."

"We'll meet back here after closing tonight," I told everyone. "Dahlia will have a list of the officers, and we can firm up the rest of our plans."

"Will we move tonight?" Conan asked.

The wolf had been uncharacteristically silent. "You asked for a reason," I replied. "What was it?"

Conan paced back and forth across the front of the bar. When he turned to everyone, he flowed into his human form and ran his gaze over the assemblage. "Guardians will not approve of our plans. Do not delude yourselves they won't find out. The quicker we make this happen, the less time they'll have to sabotage our efforts."

"Would they actually do that?" Percy sounded mildly horrified.

"Aye. They don't appreciate being crossed."

"But we never agreed with their edict," I protested.

"Doesn't matter," Conan said.

"Are they in cahoots with the dark court?" the youthful-appearing Sidhe asked.

Conan frowned, dark brows nearly touching in the middle of his forehead. "I don't know. Anything is possible, but the thing I can't figure out is why they would be. What's in it for them?"

"Guess we'll find out," I muttered and made shooing motions.

Teleport spells blossomed all around me. When they cleared, the only mages left were my usual contingent of workers. Percy opened the door, and patrons filed in. From the looks of things, it would be a good evening.

Clive bounded from the back room. He looked pleased, so I assumed he'd rented the flat. I was glad he and Nick would have a place to call home, except I wanted Nick's home to be with me.

We'd had a moment before leaving my house to hunt. Many moments, actually, where he'd been so close the scent of his need kindled my own. If I concentrated—and not all that hard—I could still feel his hands squeezing my ass and the hot, hard length of him against my belly. I'd been strong, resisted temptation, but there'd come a time when I'd rip his clothes to shreds and climb up his body.

If it happened before he'd come to terms with what I'd done, nothing but trouble would follow. Once I'd had more than a small taste of Nick, I'd jump in with both feet and label him mine. I already kind of viewed us as a permanent arrangement, but I could live with us being special friends—kind of like Conan and me.

Once Nick and I had fucked one another's brains out, my special-friend fallback position would fly straight out the window. Mistral had blown me off. If Nick did, I refused to be responsible for what happened.

I was cataloguing all the ways Nick and Mistral were

different when Clive hustled to where we stood, brimming with enthusiasm. "You'll like it," he told Nickolas. "We each have our own bedroom, and there's a living area and a kitchen and endless hot water in the bathroom. The last tenant left all their furniture. It's not great, but it will get us by." He extracted a key from a pocket and handed it to Nick.

"Thanks." Nick took the key. "Not looking as if we'll be spending much time there for a while, but I appreciate you doing the footwork to make it happen."

"We'll still have the cave in case things go sour, but this will be much better. I paid two months' rent plus a deposit. The bloke was most insistent about no pets. Kept telling him it wouldn't be a problem. Damn! It was tough to keep a straight face."

"Vampires and pets don't belong in the same sentence," I agreed.

A growl told me Conan was back in his wolf form. "We fooled a whole lot of people for a very long time," he reminded me.

I ruffled his thick coat. "Indeed, we did. And we still are." Riteway and Hernandez had believed Conan was my oversized dog. Considering they viewed themselves as experts in all things paranormal, they'd been one step up from the Three Stooges.

"Do you want the address?" Clive asked Nick.

He started to laugh. "Do you think I need it?"

Clive laughed too, and his pale skin developed a rosier tint. "Heh. Probably not. The day you can't track me would be—"

"The day you'd be obliged to end me," Nickolas finished

for him.

It was a potent reminder how different we are from humans. Vampires live and die by a set of ironclad rules. Much like pack leaders, if we miss our kill, we're replaced. No judge. No jury. Just action to set the world right again. We were about to bring Seattle's PTF to justice the Vampire way. No need to mention that to the other mages, though. It would only make them uncomfortable.

"Where do you want me to work tonight?" Clive asked.

"Same as always," I told him.

"I'll work with Percy," Nick murmured and faded toward the front of the club.

True to my prediction, the night went well. We earned a lot of money, which always makes me happy, particularly in light of perhaps not being open for a short time in the immediate future. In my few spare moments, I made lists on my computer in the stockroom. We'd probably have enough soldiers to assign three mages to each of the seventy-eight cops. But we'd also need a team to hit their headquarters and obliterate their electronics. I wanted to erase everything down to the gunnels, so they had no data trail left. No record of any of their activities back to the day they'd formed their task force.

I'd been looking forward to sinking my fangs into Seattle's PTF, but I'd probably get stuck with the electronics end of things.

No blood. No fun, but necessary. I was more computer

savvy than most of us, but we'd take stock and work with the talent we had.

Nick had stopped by several times through the evening. Sometimes, all he did was drop a hand onto my shoulder. It was enough. It told me he was thinking about me. Since I wanted to be the center of his universe, evidence of his caring was especially sweet.

I was still laughing to myself at my very unVampirelike neediness when the club closed. Our impromptu army must have been waiting in the wings because gateways formed as soon as the mortals had left.

"We discussed this," Dahlia said without preamble, "and we're all in agreement our groups of three should include two similar mages with the third offering complementary magic."

The meaning behind her words sank in. I was beyond thrilled the group had moved the gathering elsewhere and continued to hammer out the fine points of our mission. Apparently, with far greater success achieving consensus.

"Did you assign everyone?" I asked her.

"Not everyone," the coven mistress said.

"Good. Because we need a team to take out all their electronics and digitized records."

More Than Never left Dahlia's shoulder and flew around the room cawing. I took it to mean the bird agreed with me.

"I'll volunteer for that," Percy said. "Who's with me?"

No one spoke up, so I flapped an arm around. "I'll help."

"Clive and I will guard your rear," Nick said.

"Are you certain?" I asked. "Killing would be far more satisfying."

"How do you know there won't be something to kill where we're going?" Clive angled his head to one side in a combination of feral and engaging. It was a typical expression on a Vampire. On anyone else, it would have been confusing as fuck.

"I don't," I told him.

"Their primary bank of computer equipment is in an underground bunker next to the Seattle Police's main building downtown on Fifth Avenue," Dahlia told us.

Another Witch sidled forward. Dark hair in a butch cut, she wore a PD uniform. "I'm Zoe. The main issue you're going to run up against is metal. It lines two of the four walls, but the ceiling and floor are clear."

"Can you tolerate being down there?" Percy asked.

"Barely." Zoe made a face and unhooked a plasticized card from around her neck. "You'll need this to get inside. Once you use it, though, I'm finished working there. I'll have to go to ground."

"Maybe not," Ruby spoke up. "Things will be pretty nuts. How about if you give this a couple of hours and call in and report your ID was stolen?"

"Might work," Zoe said. "My last shift was Tuesday night. My next one is tomorrow morning. I could tell them I was getting my gear together and my badge was MIA." She bit her lower lip until her teeth made creases and went on, "If I play it right, am really hysterical, I can probably pin it on someone taking it when I was working out at the police gym and my shit was in a locker."

"Sounds good to me," Dahlia said. Taking the ID badge from Zoe, she handed it to me.

I glanced around the room. "Everyone has their assigned target?"

"We do," rose in unison. Damn if they didn't sound stoked.

"They're ready. Excellent." Nick breathed the words near my ear.

I hoped everyone was as enthusiastic when morning rolled around. "Some things are bound to go sideways," I cautioned everyone.

"We have backup plans," Dahlia said. "Everyone knows who they'll be working with except the staff here." She rattled off assignments for Ruby, Dee, and the rest of my workforce. I was pleased to see most of my people had been tapped to work together.

"What will you be doing?" I asked Conan.

"I will be the rear guard," he said. "First, I'll pay a visit to my kin. I'll take my time and play dumb and assume they'll want to help. If I'm subtle enough, maybe one of them will offer up clues why they were so insistent it had to be them or no one."

Worry beat a track through me. "Be careful," I told him.

His tongue lolled in a grim approximation of a lupine smile. "Not much they can do to me. Not anymore."

Before I could offer further motherly admonitions, he was gone. I hoped his assessment was correct.

"He'll be fine," Nick told me.

"Probably."

Nick turned me to face him, nailing me with his intense

green eyes. "Conan gave them the slip when he was barely a youth. Means he's quicker and smarter. We'll catch up with him once you've smashed the computers."

"We don't have to do anything that Draconian," I told him. "Eradicating data is quick and easy."

"Hope so." Percy joined us. "I'll have to hack into their system. Bet it has fail-safes."

"One step at a time," I told the Sorcerer. "Is there a way you can get into their database remotely?"

"Maybe. Already thought of that, but we will definitely try it that way first."

The feel of his magic surrounded the four of us. Whiskey, wildflowers, and heather ticked my nostrils. When it cleared, we were at Rob's crowded studio.

"A bit of warning would have been nice," Rob muttered.

"We won't be here long," Percy told him. "I need your computer."

"Figured as much." Rob heaved to his feet and pattered across the room to a refrigerator.

"I have to be very stealthy," Percy told us. "If this doesn't work, last thing I want to do is alert them anyone is interested in their mainframe."

"Here you go, mate." Rob dropped an open bottle of Guinness next to Percy, but the other Sorcerer was so deep into what he was doing he didn't even look up.

"*Do you know what he's doing?*" I switched to telepathy so as not to disturb Percy.

"*Not exactly,*" Ariana replied in kind.

Percy's big fingers flew over the keyboard to the accompaniment of clicks, clacks, bells, and chimes. "Fuck!" was followed by a spate of Gaelic and equally frantic typing.

Clive started to ask a question, but Ariana shushed him. Sweat beaded on Percy's forehead. When he finally pushed his chair back, he muttered, "I don't think they caught me."

"What happened?" Ariana asked.

Percy huffed out a breath. "On the good news front, I have a better idea how their file system is organized. And I'm confident I can make it through their firewall, but we need to do it on-site."

"They had sentinels set up, huh?" Ariana said.

I understood what a sentinel was, but in my world they

were men on patrol. In this instance, it had to be some kind of electronics that kept the watch.

"Really sophisticated ones," Percy answered her. "I tried several different strategies. Hell, one even got me into the CIA's database a few months back, but no dice."

I wanted to ask what the CIA was, but it wasn't important right now.

"Best of luck," Rob said. "Do you need me to ride shotgun?"

"Thanks for the offer," Percy said, "but in this case too many cooks might not help. We could end up tripping over one another."

The feel of his magic wrapped around us again. "Ward yourselves," he cautioned. "I'll do my damnedest to make us undetectable, but duplicate magic won't be a bad thing." He addressed his next words to Clive and me. "Your job is to clear the decks for us to hit the computers quick and hard."

"We'll kill anything that so much as twitches," I reassured him.

Ariana handed him the card she'd gotten from Zoe.

"Not sure we'll need this," Percy said. "I'm aiming for inside the bunker, and this probably doubles as an electronic key card. Besides, if I can avoid using it to defeat a lock, her story about it being lost, or maybe stolen, will go over better."

He pocketed it, and the scents of his magic thickened. I warded myself and extended my fortifications to Ariana and Clive. Not that they needed anything extra. I felt their own protective magic grow around them, prickly and impressive. The click of fangs dropping into place made me proud of what I was.

No matter who was guarding the computers, we'd take them out. "Nothing fancy," I said. "Kill clean, quick, and smooth."

"When the day comes we need instructions in killing—" Clive began.

"Sorry." I cut him off. Whatever passes for adrenaline in Vampires was pumping through my body. I couldn't wait to dig my fangs into scores of mortals. Hundreds. Bloodlust wasn't useful. I dialed it back a few notches until my mind was crystal clear.

"Get ready," Percy's telepathic command held terse edges.

A room constructed of concrete blocks took shape around us. Filled with banks of blinking lights, humming machinery, and dozens of monitors, it reminded me how much I'd missed out on during my years in stasis. I felt the zing of metal immediately. Whoever had built the place must have embedded it into the concrete. It wasn't debilitating, just annoying—over the short haul. This wasn't a place I could remain for more than a few hours without consequences to my magic.

Half a dozen people were spread through the good-sized room. Many wore some type of headset over their ears. By rights, they shouldn't have any advance warning we'd arrived. All but one were oblivious, but the sixth person, a woman with close-cropped red hair, whipped her head around. She had to have magic of her own, or she'd never have realized she had company.

I didn't care what the fuck she was. Before she could screech a warning, I aimed straight for her, leaping on her and breaking her neck. Vampires can move with the speed of a vengeful storm when we want to. My bet was she was dead before she knew what killed her. My strike ruined her neck vessels. They broke open, showering everything in the vicinity with blood; no magic in the world could have brought her back. She was losing blood faster than she could heal herself.

It's the only way to kill an immortal.

A taste of her blood confirmed she was Sidhe. Maybe the guardians had been onto something after all. Meanwhile all hell had broken loose. The other five people yelled terse orders and opened fire with sidearms.

"Do not let them summon aid," Ariana shouted and slashed her fangs through a man's neck.

Firing willy-nilly was a stupid move on their part. Bullets ricocheted all over the place, bouncing back to kill two of their own. Once I ascertained the shells hadn't been spiked with silver powder, I relaxed and attacked the next mortal. The tang of their fear added spice to their blood, but I wasn't here to feed.

Clive and I made certain everyone was well and truly dead. Ariana and Percy hustled to a bank of blinking lights. I wished I could do more. Speed was our friend. I didn't think anyone had sounded a warning, but they might have.

"Hurry," Ariana urged, mirroring my concerns.

"Going as fast as I know how." Percy's ham-sized hands pounded a keyboard so hard, I expected the plastic keys to go flying. The screen in front of him flashed red. He yelled, "Finally." A long list of something scrolled past, vanishing as soon as it appeared, only to be replaced by another.

He fist-pumped the air. "My work here is done. There's no way to undo this auto-destruct sequence."

I sensed more than heard mortals approaching. Lots of them. Despite not hearing an alarm, someone must have set one off. I missed the days of bells and shouts for reinforcements. Bolting toward Percy and Ariana, I motioned Clive to stick close.

"We have to get out of here. Now," I said.

"Yeah. Someone must have triggered a panic button." Ariana confirmed my suspicions. Power spilled from her as she constructed a journey spell.

The door at the far end of the room rattled alarmingly. "Why are we still here?" Percy asked Ariana.

"I'm trying." Her forehead creased from effort. "It's the fucking metal in the walls. It slows everything down."

"Because we're trying to punch through it," I said. We needed time, something we were unlikely to have handed to us. "Switch gears," I told Ariana. "Let's mesmerize the batch about to pour through the door. Then we'll leave."

"Good call." Her trust in my assessment and instincts pleased me; she could just as easily have told me to fuck off. She refocused her casting. Clive and I poured our own skill into it. A violet river poured from us, rolling along the floor. For once, our timing couldn't have been better.

The door snapped open, clunking against its stops. A couple of dozen mortals stormed through and then stopped dead, crumpling to the floor as our mass hypnosis spell curled around them. The two men in the lead managed to snap off bursts of automatic weapon fire before their rifles clattered to the ground.

Percy must have anticipated they'd show up with their guns blazing because he'd constructed shielding around us. Good thing. These bullets stank of silver. It made me gag and burned the lining of my nose and mouth.

"Switch it up," Percy instructed tersely. "We bought a few minutes before the next wave converges on us. Lend me your magic, and I'll get us out of here."

Bodies were still falling atop other bodies, reminding me of a stack of dominoes when the fucking room finally, finally shimmered to motes of light. "Who were all those men and women?" I asked.

"Aye, why aren't they dead?" Clive tossed out.

"If any of them are part of the paranormal task force, they soon will be," Ariana replied smartly.

"We could have killed them." In stark contrast to his choirboy good looks, Clive sounded vicious. It made me proud to call him clansman. "In fact," he continued, "we could return and—"

"Nay." I cut him off.

"Why not?" Clive pressed.

The walls of *Ascent's* stockroom clicked into place around us. "Because they weren't our assignment," I explained.

"What difference would it have made? Dead one way is just as good as dead another."

"No. It's not," Ariana spoke up. "The teams assigned to each of those dudes would show up and waste time hunting for someone who was already off the board. They'd put themselves at risk for nothing."

"Hadn't thought of it in quite that light." Clive nodded curtly.

"We need to plot out the bones of our next attack," Percy said. "Ariana. Have you been to San Francisco within the last ten years, give or take?"

She shook her head. "We can still locate their HQ on a map and consider how to best approach it."

"Did Kelpies or Mer-people make it to the New World?" Clive asked.

If they had, it was news to me. "I don't think Kelpies can leave the British Isles," I said.

"They can," Percy corrected me, "but their power isn't as robust in other places. Travel would be a challenge because of how far they'd have to swim."

"But they can appear as men," I reminded him.

"I know, but they can't hold that form for very long. It drains their power damned quick." Percy turned to Clive. "Why'd you ask after them?"

Clive raked curved fingers through his disheveled blond hair and shrugged. "They might be willing to help. After all, mortals are out to get all of us."

Ariana had moved to her desk; her monitor flickered to life. A map formed, followed by a closer view. "San Francisco PD's main offices are here." She moved a pointer around on her screen. "On Bryant and Sixth Street."

"I bet their paranormal division is elsewhere," Percy said.

"Any particular reason?" Ariana asked.

He offered a noncommittal expression. "Call it a hunch. If I were them, I'd want to be stationed in a spot I was more readily mobile. Traffic in the center of San Francisco is so bad, it would impede their ability to respond to much of anything."

"We're making this too hard." Ariana pulled out her phone, tapping on its front.

"What are you doing?" Percy asked.

"Texting Zoe."

"Be careful," the Sorcerer cautioned.

Ariana angled the phone so he could see. I crowded in; so did Clive. One side of the tiny screen was Ariana. The other was presumably Zoe responding.

ARIANA: YOU OFF SHIFT YET?

ZOE: HEY THERE! NOT MY NIGHT TO GO IN. BESIDES, LOST MY BADGE—OR SOMEONE KIPED IT.

ARIANA: COOL! YOU'RE NOT WORKING. ERK. DID I WAKE YOU?

ZOE: NOPE. I WORK NIGHTS, SO MY OFF DAYS ARE ACTUALLY OFF NIGHTS

ARIANA: WHEW. GLAD I DIDN'T DISTURB YOU. SAY, IF YOU HAVE A MINUTE, I COULD USE A HAND WITH SOMETHING AT THE CLUB.

ZOE: BE THERE IN A FEW.

Ariana plopped the phone on her desk. "When she gets here, we'll just ask her where the SF headquarters are. She'll know. Meanwhile, do we want to do the same thing there?"

"Wouldn't we need to know how well it worked out here first?" I asked.

Ariana rolled her eyes. "Duh. Yeah, I'm not exactly a tactician, am I?" She glanced across at Percy. "Guess we're kind of dead in the water until the teams start reporting in."

The Sorcerer had been busy with his phone. When he

looked up, he said, "According to public record, the San Francisco PTF covers the entire Bay Area, including nine counties, a hundred cities, over seven million people, and something like 7000 square miles."

I whistled, long and low. Those figures were almost unimaginable. "Must be over a thousand officers. Perhaps we shouldn't aim quite so high."

"Think of the impact," Ariana argued.

"If we get the logistics right," I argued back. "Otherwise, we'll lose valuable ground. The initial battles of any war are critical. If we nail them, we'll have an easier time down the road."

"Exactly." Percy screwed his features into a frown.

"News of tonight will travel like wildfire," I went on. "It would argue we should try a totally different tactic. Mer-folk can't leave the sea, but us showing up with an army of Kelpies would give even a seasoned officer pause."

"No one who doesn't hail from the Isles believes they exist," Clive said, and then added, "I've never seen one."

"You're the wrong sex," Ariana informed him.

"For their human guise, sure." He nodded. "I'm scarcely a child or a maiden ripe for the plucking, but I've never seen them in the lochs or seas, either."

"They don't just pluck." Percy screwed his face into a disgusted moue. "They devour their prey once they've had their way with them."

"Jeez. On a scale of one to ten, that makes them worse than us." Ariana smirked.

I wasn't sure of that. Some of our victims died, but we turned others into monsters—exactly like us. "Kelpies are an unknown—for now," I said. "Even if they're around, I've never heard even a single tale of them joining forces with other mages."

"Good point," Clive said. "I'll keep my trap shut."

"Don't," Ariana replied. "We need all the ideas we can get."

The distinctive scent of dried mint and rosemary presaged Zoe's arrival. Her dark hair stuck up in spikes, and circles edged her lower lids. I hadn't noticed her eyes before, but they were hazel. "Sorry for the delay," she said and shoved her hands into the pockets of a denim jacket. She'd changed out of her uniform into black pants, a red wool sweater, and the black jacket.

Percy handed her ID card back. "We didn't use this," he said.

Zoe snatched it. "Great! I'll tell them right away that I misplaced it. Hang on." She dredged out a phone and typed a message.

I had a long way to go to get used to how ubiquitous cell phones were. Everyone not only had one, they used them constantly.

Once she was done, Percy asked, "Are you sure you weren't followed."

"Yeah. It's what took me so long. I went two other places first and waited to make certain. I protected my teleport spell, but it's not always ironclad. Some of the guys in the PTF have had charms made to circumvent pretty much all types of warding."

I winced. It wasn't welcome news.

"Where's the headquarters for San Francisco's

operation?" Ariana asked. "That's actually the only thing I need to know, and I didn't trust texting."

"I wondered what you wanted." Zoe offered a weak smile. "Figured it had to be something you couldn't ask directly. They're stationed in the Berkeley Hills. Everything hubs out of that location."

"How many men?" Percy furled his bushy brows.

Zoe closed her teeth over her lower lip. "A lot. Something like twelve hundred officers and half that number of support people."

"Is there any way you could scare up a list of names?" I asked.

"Maybe. It would have been simpler if you'd requested that before the computers went down. Any digging I do on my own at this point will be suspect."

"So long as I'm only trolling for data," Percy said, "and not trying to initiate an auto-destruct sequence, I might be able to download their personnel records."

Zoe's phone dinged; she glanced at it. "My supervisor is relieved I located my ID."

"That's it?" I asked. "No shockwaves from the attack?"

"It's not the kind of thing they'd let us know piecemeal," she said. "We'll hear something, especially in dispatch because we won't have anyone left to deploy. But the brass won't say anything until they've developed a polished, politically correct press release."

Her phone dinged again. Not that there was anyone to bother me with anything, but I'd set my device to silent shortly after getting it. Never saw any reason to alter that. I'd be damned if some rectangular blob of plastic and glass would slip a noose around my mind.

After typing a response, Zoe smiled grimly and looked at us. "The rumor mill is taking off like wildfire," she said. "That was one of my coworkers telling me about officers being slaughtered and the computer database going up in flames."

"Permanently," Percy said. "They can rebuild, but they'll never resurrect that baby."

"I shouldn't stay any longer," Zoe said. "Erm. If anyone asks what I was doing here—and yeah, they know where I am most of the time—I'll tell them you'd asked if I could fill in for Dee's shift and needed to show me a few things before I reported for work two nights hence."

"Got it," Ariana said. "Although, *Ascent* might be shut for a few days."

Zoe shrugged. "Those decisions are above my paygrade. I'll keep Dahlia apprised of the party line that emerges from the brass about tonight. I'm sure she'll fill you in. Best of luck with the Bay Area. It's far more challenging than this unit—and not only on account of employing so many more people."

"Why would you say that?" I asked.

"Magic has a solid toehold in San Francisco. Always has. The old parts of the city have been a haven for mages for well over a hundred years." She blew out a breath. "The basic play goes something like this. An officer identifies a mage and watches them long enough to figure out what drives them. It could be a business or a loved one. Even children aren't off limits. At some point, the task force threatens whatever the mage values in such a way it's at risk of eradication."

"And then they offer a choice," I said bitterly.

"Pretty much right on." Zoe made a sour face. "Cooperate or you'll never see your kids again. Or your grandmother. Or we'll wreck your livelihood. Expose you as a mage. The possibilities are endless."

"Why don't they fight back?" Ariana sounded outraged.

"Some do," Zoe said. "It rarely goes well because of how much magic the PTF already has in hand to toss about. I really do need to run. Be in touch if I can."

"Be careful," Ariana told her.

"Oh, I am. They've suspected me forever, but they can never actually pin anything on me. Once the machine that scans for magic arrives, I'm toast. I have to leave before then, so I've been keeping a close eye on the tracking data."

"Fuck!" Percy sputtered. "They already ordered one?"

"That they did," Zoe told him. "The scanners are active in perhaps ten percent of jurisdictions around the country. Ours shipped two days ago, which is why I'm following its course. By the end of the month, they'll be everywhere, and they're close to 100 percent accurate. Denying you're what the machine says you are is pointless."

Percy rattled off a number. Zoe understood it was for her and tapped it into her phone. "Send me the tracking info," Percy said.

"You got it."

"I have one of the scanners," Percy told her. "I can probably come up with something to scramble its sensors, but for that I'll need a solid block of time. Hasn't happened yet."

Zoe leveled her gaze his way. "If you could prioritize it, you just might save my bacon. Otherwise, forwarding the tracking data might be one of the last ways I can help."

"You've done a lot. Above and beyond." Ariana crossed the floor between them and hugged the Witch. After stiffening for a moment, Zoe hugged her back. When Ariana let go, the Witch turned and strode out the back door and into the rapidly vanishing night.

"Where do you want to wait out the day?" Clive asked.

Ariana twitched heavy curtains over the stockroom's single window. "We should stay here until people start reporting in. If things went well, we'll firm up how we deal with San Francisco."

"I'll be back in a bit," Percy said. "Going to take stock of how many Sorcerers we can field for our next gig. And have a quick peek at that scanner."

"Nice work, tonight," I told him.

"Thanks. After my near miss with the Death Star at Rob's, I was delighted to pull it off."

Once he was gone, I turned to Ariana. "Death Star?"

"A fictional space station from a movie, *Star Wars*."

It told me less than nothing, but I recognized one of those loose ends that wasn't worth pursuing.

"I'm going to take the next hour before it's fully light and troll for Kelpies," Clive said. "I still think they could be useful."

"Be sure not to miss your timing," I warned. "You'll be seriously injured if—"

He waved me to silence and switched to Gaelic, "Aye, Da. Doona worry overmuch about your wee bairn."

I laughed, wished him Godspeed—a very unusual gesture from a Vampire—and said, "See you either here or at our new flat."

He wasn't quite gone when the *vroom-vroom* of Conan's motorcycle reverberated off the stockroom walls. *"Come for a ride,"* the wolf said. More order than invitation, it suggested he needed us away from here.

"All right, but we have to return to meet everyone fairly soon," Ariana told him.

After grabbing her helmet, she tossed me one. I had no idea how they'd gotten here. Last I'd seen them had been at her house. She propped the back door open. The bike rolled through with me walking behind it. After locking up, Ariana tossed a leg over the rumbling machine. I'd been so immersed in strategies and plans, it didn't register until I clambered on behind her that we'd be smushed against each other in the delicious, lust-inducing position that had addled my brain and kindled my body last time.

"Where are we headed?" Ariana asked the wolf.

He didn't answer, but we rolled through dark streets. Clearly, Conan had a distinct destination in mind. We'd find out soon enough what it was. Meanwhile, I stretched my arms around Ariana and luxuriated in the press of her spine and butt against my chest, belly, and lower still.

She twisted around and grinned. "We have to stop meeting like this."

"Here I was thinking we needed more, not less," I shot back.

Both of us laughed as wind tore at our bodies and pressed her even tighter against me. She fit perfectly, as if we'd been made for one another. With its usual disregard for timing or propriety, my cock swelled until every bump in the road turned into an erotic delight.

"Someday." Ariana breathed the word into my ear.

"Don't make promises you can't keep," I told her.

"This particular ball is in your court," she informed me archly. "You already know where I stand."

I felt the press of her breasts against the insides of my arms, and I hungered to fill my hands with them, rubbing her stiff nipples into even harder peaks. I did know where she stood. No idle sex play. If we got to the clothes-off, bodies-straining-against-each-other part, with my cock buried to the hilt inside her glorious body, there'd be no, "That was grand, darling. See you around." Nay. Once we coupled, we'd be as good as mated.

Just like Shifters, a corner of my mind piped up.

I shushed it. I was almost, almost there. Times like this with her so close her scent drove me mad, it was easy to overlook Mistral. I didn't have to forget about him, but I needed to bury the past—and be damned good and sure it would remain ten leagues under.

CHAPTER FIFTEEN, ARIANA

I considered asking Conan again where we were going in such an all-fired rush. Although, if he'd wanted a speedier approach, we'd have teleported and been done with it. Nick's hard-muscled body behind me and his arms holding me in place drove everything but the moment from my mind.

I should be feverishly working on logistics, but all I could think about was how much I yearned for the Vampire crushed against me. I'd thought after Mistral, I'd never love anyone again. Yeah, it was a stupid, schoolgirl-crush kind of conclusion, but I'd done damned well at making it reality.

Until Nick.

He was far from the first Vampire who'd crossed my tracks, so him being like me wasn't the driving factor. Nope. It was him. His to-die-for body, his quick mind, his courage. The package deal was irresistible. What I'd felt for Mistral had been a pale imitation of how much I longed for

Nickolas. I'd been truly young then. Mistral had been my first lover. He'd known it, the old bastard, and capitalized on it to keep me close at hand.

Until he tired of me and moved the next Vampire-in-waiting into position.

Others in the clan house had whispered how unusual it was he'd spent hundreds of years focused on me. I'd gotten the distinct impression most of his flings didn't last a decade, let alone centuries, but I'd been naïve enough to assume he was so smitten, our liaison would go the distance.

Silly me.

At least, this time round I knew myself better. I reminded Nickolas his decisions would either make or break us—and left it at that. No reason to belabor the point. With everything facing us, whether Nick and I had a future together shouldn't take center stage.

But it did.

Nothing I could do about it but accept it and move on. Vampires didn't fall in love, except I had. And I felt certain of Nick's caring for me. Whether it had moved to the level of can't-walk-away-even-if-he-wanted-to remained to be seen.

Conan took a hard left turn onto a curvy road that hugged Lake Washington's shoreline. We were well north of Kirkland, but we'd passed the turnoff to my house. Another left turn took us past a closed sign and to a deserted parking lot with a public park and a beach beyond it. The edges of the sky were developing a pearlescent gray that told me dawn was near.

The motorcycle rolled to a stop and turned into Conan faster than ever before. He took off at a nimble trot for the beach. Nick and I dropped our helmets beneath a bush and fell in behind him. Whatever Conan had on his mind, I'd hear about it soon enough.

"Look." The wolf angled his snout at the spot where sky met water.

"What am I supposed to see?" I asked, confused. Other than the coming dawn, nothing appeared out of place.

An uncharacteristic intake of an unneeded breath suggested Nick was quicker on the uptake than me. "What is that?" he demanded.

I squinted. "What's what? I still don't see anything noteworthy."

"Switch to your psychic vision," Nick suggested.

I made a face, annoyed to be reminded of something so elemental. Narrowing my eyes further still, I tried to interpret what was spread before me. "I see an...edge." I stumbled for want of a more descriptive term.

"It's a rip in the firmament, isn't it?" Nickolas directed his question at Conan.

"Yes. To be more precise, in the layers of atmosphere surrounding Earth. What does that mean to you?" Conan woofed.

"There's an old legend," Nick spoke slowly. "I haven't heard anything about it since I was first turned and learning about the history of various magics."

I turned my gaze on him. I'd never stumbled onto something even close to an urban myth about holes in Earth's atmospheric layers. "I don't remember anything like that at all, and I spent gobs of time in Mistral's library to pass the days when I couldn't go outside."

Nick clasped his hands behind his back. "It doesn't relate to Vampires, so you probably wouldn't have come across it. We were the only clan who taught other than strictly Vampire history, otherwise this particular story wouldn't have been part of my education, either."

Mistral's library had been deep, but he'd tended toward bloody history, like the Crusades or Roman gladiators. Philosophy bored him, as did anything that smacked of storytelling. "Go on," I urged.

"I'm trying to reconstruct it," Nick said. "Perhaps it would be better if Conan just told us."

The wolf shook his head. "I want to know if other variations exist. Try to remember."

"All right. This lore was tied to Norse mythology and the One Tree. So long as men revered the gods, they'd care for the tree. When that reverence failed, the tree's roots would begin to rot from the bottom. Once the rot was complete, the tree would list to one side or the other, punching holes in the firmament. When that happened, Earth would enter its latter days.

"The demise of magic would become inevitable. Everyone who can leave does. Once the last mage is gone, Earth will be destroyed. The precise mechanism wasn't sketched out, but my sense was it would be something cataclysmic. Fires. Floods. Volcanic eruptions."

"Not so different from all the Armageddon fables," I murmured.

"Which is why I paid it scant heed," Nick said. "I'm surprised I recall it as well as I do after all this time."

"The difference"—Conan stepped into the conversation

—"is this isn't myth but foreseeing. It originated from a conclave held between guardians and the Norse gods. It's why Future's depiction is accurate as far as it goes. The guardians see the answer—if there is one—in patching up Yggdrasil, not in engaging mortals in combat."

I rolled it around in my mind. "They interpret what we're doing as a waste of time?"

"Worse than that," the wolf replied. "What we did earlier tonight expended magic, lots of it. The more extraneous power floating around, the tougher it will be to convince Yggdrasil not to give up."

I was still having a problem with the stupid tree being real. I'd always relegated it to the realm of a fairytale. "Not sure I agree with their assessment," I muttered. "Wouldn't a magical tree be thrilled by evidence of a magical world?"

Conan barked. I took it as a who-the-fuck-knows?

"I still don't understand why they wouldn't want our assistance," Nick said.

The wolf shimmered into a man. "You don't, eh? We don't have much of a track record as team players."

"Get on board or get out of the way," I grunted.

"Nah. It's just get out of the way," Nick corrected me. "Unless I missed something, we weren't invited on board anything."

"So, they want us to leave?" I furled my brows Conan's way.

"Look at it from their viewpoint," he replied. "They believe this world has turned into a lost cause, a ticking timebomb with only a single way out. The way they figure it, you'll have to leave anyway. Sooner rather than later simplifies their efforts."

"Not how I read things at all," I retorted. "If this mythical tree—"

"It's real," Conan cut in.

"Fine. If this tree isn't so far gone nothing can save it, seems to me the guardians could use a magical assist from the rest of us. If us tossing power about to kill mortals gums up the works, we could redirect our efforts along whatever lines the guardians thought might be more beneficial." I peered at the thing I'd labeled an edge. It was fading with the approaching day, but still visible. "How much worse will that rift get?" I jerked my chin at the horizon.

"I don't know," Conan replied. "I brought you here because it's not visible everywhere. For all I know, it could have looked like this for a very long while. To hear Fairclaw tell it, the sky is falling, but I don't trust him."

"Is it possible this whole tree thing is smoke and mirrors?" I tugged a hood over my head to shield myself from daylight.

"They could be hiding something," Conan admitted. "I spent a chunk of tonight dragging information out of my kin bit by bit. When I walked away, I wasn't satisfied I'd heard the whole story."

I was grasping at straws when I said, "Are the ley-lines connected to the tree?"

"They'd almost have to be." Nick sent an approving look my way. "Both of them being bones of the Earth and all that."

Conan's amber eyes widened. "You may be onto

something." The scents of fur and wet rocks wafted from him.

"Hold up." I waved a hand in front of his face. "Where are we going?"

"To the lines. Where else? That could be why my kinsmen didn't want me tapping their energy. They need it to salvage the tree. Or there might have been other reasons."

"Yeah, like so you wouldn't find out they're a lying pack of shitheads," I growled.

He curled a hand around my shoulder. "Hush. We need allies, not enemies." Lights flickered as he transitioned back to his preferred form; the hand turned to a paw along the way.

"Where are you?" Ruby's gravelly voice sounded in my head.

Rather than answering, I asked, *"Is everyone back?"*

"More or less."

"I'll join you soon," I told her.

I looked from Nick to Conan. "I need to go to the club to hear how tonight went."

"I'll go with you," Nick said. "I picked up on Ruby's sending."

"And I'll join you presently," Conan was gone almost before he was done talking.

I hurried back to where we'd left the helmets and set the start of a teleport spell in motion.

"Do you suppose our side prevailed?" Nick asked as my casting hit terminal velocity and swept us into its path.

"No idea. Ruby never says much in mind speech. I don't blame her. It isn't safe." Switching gears, I turned my head toward Nick. "What did you think about Conan's information?"

"A lot of it makes no sense. Do I know about the One Tree? Certainly. Have I ever believed it had aught to do with anything? Of course not, and—"

"Yup. Me too," I cut in without waiting for him to finish. "If Earth is in its death throes, it's because of shit mortals have done to it."

"Not because of a legendary tree with rotten roots?" Nick grinned.

It made him look about twenty, dangerous and desirable as fuck. If the walls of *Ascent's* main room weren't popping into view around us, I'd have tossed my arms around him and kissed his gorgeous mouth.

"There you are," Dahlia rushed forward, More Than Never riding on her shoulder.

"Sorry," I said and added quickly, "The computer part of things went off without a hitch."

"We know," the coven mistress said. "Percy's here."

The dregs of my spell dissipated, and I scanned the bar's occupants. Too many of us for me to determine if we were all present and accounted for, but the crowded room spoke to few casualties among our ranks.

Ruby trotted over. "We did pretty well."

"Define pretty well," Nick said.

"Three got away." She made a fist and punched the air, her golden eyes blazing with fury. "Unfortunately, one of the three was mine. I turned his mind to mush before he slithered out of my net. I still don't quite understand how he managed it."

"Witch charms." Dahlia sounded bitter. More Than Never squawked his (her?) disgust with the situation. "I'd apologize, but I have no control over renegade Witches cooking up charms and selling them to the highest bidder."

"Is that what's happening?" I asked.

"More or less." Dee joined us. "We shook down a couple of Witches skulking on the sidelines and encouraged them to talk."

A smile played around my lips. Torture is right up my alley.

"I assume they're permanently silenced?" Nick turned his intense green gaze on Dee.

"You'd be correct." The Witch skinned her lips back from her teeth.

"We did more than that." Dahlia stepped in. "Word has gone out to every Coven, er guild house, to check each of their members for unusual activity starting with their bank accounts. Any Witch who received sums of money not readily accounted for by employment or other 'normal' streams of income will be considered suspect."

"And kicked out and stripped of their power." Dee's words held grim edges.

"What about the ones who hid cash in a coffee can or a shed or a cave?" I asked.

"No system is perfect," Dahlia agreed, "but at least this is a start. Because it will soon become public knowledge among Witches, they'll think twice before selling so much as a hangnail to the highest bidder."

"Zoe told us it wasn't so much a matter of money as threats to their families," Nick said.

Dahlia dusted her hands together. "Not much we can do about that. If a Witch is threatened and comes to her coven mistress, we can help her. If she chooses to suffer in silence and deal with the situation on her own, there's not much that can be done."

"Treason aside, we killed seventy-five cops tonight?" I sought verification.

"We did, indeed," Percy said.

"Has anyone checked the news?" I asked.

The Sorcerer nodded. "It's there but watered down to almost nothing."

"We don't see how that's going to go over." Ruby's wings fluttered. "Most of the task force had families. Surely, they'll compare notes and figure out the PD is going all out to quash the truth."

"Not our problem," I said.

"The more confusion in their ranks, the better," Nick spoke up. "If they're chasing their tails, they won't be focused on us."

"Is San Francisco still a go?" Percy slitted his gaze my way.

"Whole lotta maybes to that question," I told him and launched into an abbreviated version of what Conan had shown us."

"I know that bit of prophecy." Christa strode from behind the bar. "Learned it when I was barely twenty, but I never paid it much heed."

"So, do we keep on keeping on?" I scanned the group. "Or do we pack up and look for new homes?"

"We already have one," Percy reminded me, "but the

consensus in the guild house is to find another rambling old mansion and set up shop again." After a pause, he added, "Here. On Earth."

"Talk among yourselves for a bit," I suggested, "but first I want to let you know what we found out about San Fran's PTF."

"I already filled them in on the scope of the project and how large the task force is," Percy said.

"We don't know if we have enough mages, even spread among all our disciplines, to manage such an ambitious undertaking," a Shifter called from where he stood toward the far end of the bar.

"How'd it work with three assigned to each cop?" Nick asked.

"In some cases, it was overkill," Ruby said. "In others, like mine for example, it obviously wasn't enough."

"Could we get by with two?" Nick pressed.

"Probably." Ruby knitted her brows in thought. "But that's still something like 2500 mages. We couldn't identify more than about 900, and we counted everybody we could think of."

"Seems like the primary decision is whether we thumb our noses at the guardians and keep on slugging," Percy said. "Once we cross that bridge, we can plot out our next moves."

"You all did great," I told everyone.

"In sheer numbers, yeah," Dahlia agreed, "but two of the targets can identify us."

I'd have sucked in a breath, if I'd been the breathing type. It wasn't especially good news.

"We need to find them," Nick said, "and finish the job."

"Already tried," Dahlia said. "They've gone to ground and covered their tracks."

Nick offered her one of his ten-million-watt smiles. "You're not a Vampire. Tell me who escaped, and I'll make certain they don't have an opportunity to spread the word."

"Whose cover is blown?" I asked.

Two Fae, two Shifters, and a Sorcerer shuffled forward.

"Where's the sixth mage?" I asked.

"She was really rattled and left for one of the other worlds," Dahlia explained.

Alrighty then... Evidence of cowardice has never sat well with me. "Congrats to the rest of you for manning up and not running," I told the others. "From now on, employ a glamour. Pick something simple that's not a huge power hog and stick with it until we get this problem under control."

"It will never be 'under control,'" one of the Shifters said. "By now, they'll have APBs out for the lot of us."

"What's that?" Nick asked.

I shook my head. "Never mind. I'll explain later."

"I can take care of the computer end of any APB shit," Percy said. "In fact, if Ariana doesn't mind me using her machine, I'll clean up that little problem right now. Shouldn't take long. After all that floundering around I did, I understand their data system and how it's constructed."

"Be my guest." I waved a hand at the stockroom.

"Thanks. Back soon." He strode away

Over the next few minutes, Nick and I absorbed data on the two cops. Most critical was their scent. It still clung to the mages who'd tried to take them down. Vampires are exceptional trackers. It's one skill where we leave other magic-wielders in the proverbial dust.

"We'll find them." Nick sounded resolute.

The other spot where Vampires excel is mind-control. Once we located the two hapless fucks, they were toast.

Percy bolted out of the back room. "My part's done. Go get 'em!"

Dahlia bustled forward. "We took a vote while you were nailing down details on the mages."

"Yeah?" I turned to face her and tried for an encouraging expression. Not sure I pulled it off. I'd already made my decision. I'd stick it out and kill every fucking mortal who so much as looked cross-eyed at me.

Until either they backed off, or Earth imploded. Whichever came first.

"We're 100 percent for staying and kicking some serious ass," Dahlia said. A raucous cacophony of "Hell yeah," and "Hell to the yes," roared through the bar.

When things quieted slightly, she said, "San Francisco might be too much for us, but if we can't manage it, we'll pick something smaller and work our way up."

Gratitude—a very unVampirelike emotion—drove me forward, and I hugged her. To her credit, she didn't stiffen or cringe or push me away. After a moment or two, she hugged me back. "Be careful," she spoke low. "The charms protecting those two are strong. It's why we failed."

I started to tell her Witch charms didn't work on Vampires, but then I remembered the ones Riteway and Hernandez had in their possession. They'd shielded them from Vampiric mesmerism. "Assuming they have charms, here's hoping they're not keyed to Vampires," I muttered.

Clive blasted into the room crowing as he waved a hand to wipe out his portal. "Kelpies are in!" he shouted.

Nick pounded him on the back. "Nice work. Ari and I are off to do a spot of hunting. Love to have you along, but daylight adds an extra layer of complexity, and—"

"It's okay, mate. I understand." Clive looked pleased with himself.

Meanwhile, Ruby and several others surged near. "Kelpies?" She quirked a dark brow. "Haven't seen one of them in forever."

"I had no idea they ever left the Old Country," Dee said.

"What exactly did you mean by 'Kelpies are in?'" Percy sidled near. "They're nasty pieces of work and on no one's side but their own."

I wanted to know too, but I could find out after the two cops were either dead or permanent idiots.

"Ready?" Nick asked.

"Never readier. Who do you want to go after first?"

"The man. His scent was more pronounced on the mages' clothing. Let's move outside."

Nick hooked an arm through mine. I steeled myself for the sting of sunlight as we walked out the front door. It was a miniscule price to pay. We were going hunting. For humans. My day couldn't get any better than that.

CHAPTER SIXTEEN, NICKOLAS

*W*ouldn't you know today lacked the thick layer of clouds typical for this part of the States. I tugged the hood from my jacket over my head, but I could still feel the bite of the sun. We had locations for the two failed assassination sites. I stopped long enough to sniff the air, hoping maybe I'd pick up enough to follow a scent track.

"What do you think?" Ariana asked softly. There were a few people about, all striding purposefully this way or that.

"I catch a whiff here and there, but it would be more efficient for us to go to his last-known location."

"Agreed." She untied a bandana from around her neck and turned it into a scarf. "Want to risk our alternate means of travel?"

Teleporting would be expedient, but it held risks, particularly in the middle of the day. We ran at least even odds of emerging in the middle of a crowd of people. We could ward ourselves. It would work—unless someone magical was close.

"Nick?"

"Eh. Thinking. It's a ways to our location, right?"

She nodded.

"Maybe driving would be a compromise."

"My car is at home, but we can go get it. Adds well over an hour to this project, and then we'll still have the second escaped cop to deal with."

"Sounding like another argument for a car. Is there one we could borrow that's closer?"

Ariana stopped walking, said, "That's brilliant," and turned back the way we'd come.

While her compliment pleased me, I scarcely had an opportunity to bask in warm fuzzies. My sideways slip into modern vernacular amused me. Meanwhile, Ariana was chattering up a storm with Dee. The necromancer Witch met us in front of the bar, a set of keys dangling from one hand.

"Do not blow my cover," she cautioned Ariana. "That vehicle is registered in my name. If it's implicated in a crime scene..."

She didn't have to spell it out any more clearly.

"I'll be careful," Ariana promised. "I'll park a few blocks away." She motioned to me, and we got into a smallish blue car.

When we pulled away from the curb, I couldn't even hear it running. "Why is it so quiet?" I asked.

"It's electric. Has a battery."

"So, no petrol?"

"Some electric cars don't use gasoline," she said, "but this is a hybrid version. It runs on both gas and a storage battery. How in the hell do you suppose Clive talked the Kelpies into helping out?"

I grinned as Lake Washington's shoreline slipped past. Soon we were on an enormous bridge that sat right on the water. I wondered what kept it from sinking, but that wasn't especially important. Hundreds of cars appeared to trust its integrity. Good enough for me.

"Clive could charm the scepter right out of a king's grasp," I told her. "He's hard to say no to when he wants something."

"On the one hand, I suppose I should be delighted to have help."

"And on the other?" I pressed.

"Yeah On the other hand, I don't have any confidence in Scottish water horses. Never have. It's kind of like sticking your hand into a pit of vipers and trusting them to keep a sketchy pledge not to poison you."

"I thought you said you hadn't run into them."

"I haven't," she agreed. "But I've read enough about them. They're never heroes. More like the stuff bad dreams are woven from."

"Kind of like us," I pointed out.

"Exactly," she replied. "That being said, we'll need an edge if we're going to take on the San Francisco task force. A major one. Something that makes whatever mages they've co-opted to do their bidding stop dead in their tracks."

"More Vampires would have the same effect," I pointed out.

Ariana laughed. "Not sure we carry quite that much clout."

"Aye, we do when we're sporting full fangs and there are a lot of us. Not many would take on a pack of Vampires."

"Now that you mention it"—Ariana turned off the freeway—"you're probably right. Clan Hawke wasn't much into warrior stuff. So long as we had a ready supply of human blood, no one left the seethe to do anything. Except Mistral. He left all the time, but his mission was recruiting new Vamps, not waging war." After a few more lefts and rights on city streets, she backed into a parking spot that looked too small, except she made it work.

"Once the dust settles, I need a car and driving lessons," I reminded her.

"We may not have the luxury of waiting for anything to die down. I have a feeling we'll be going balls out until this is over. But you can drive to our next location—once we're done here. It would be good for you to know how. In case something happens to me, someone needs to return Dee's car."

"Nothing will happen to you! Nothing." The words burst from me and mingled with a surge of protectiveness that would have flattened me if I'd been standing.

"You might be onto something. You saved me once. No one else I'd rather have my back. Come on." She got out of the car.

Her words touched whatever I had left for a heart. I shot out my door as if I'd been launched from a canon.

Streets were busier than they'd been in Kirkland, and we were surrounded by what appeared to be older buildings. The stench of our target was thick. Even a newly turned Vampire wouldn't have had any trouble following it. Hell, any dog worth his salt could have waltzed up to the cop.

"He's close," I said.

"Ya think?" Ariana's generous mouth twitched into a smile. "He stinks to high heaven. Fear sweat is the worst. He may have escaped, but not with either pride or dignity intact."

We walked briskly. Running would have drawn undue attention our way. As it was, no one paid us the slightest heed. I stuffed my hands into my pockets. Their backs were burning now we were outside. After about half a kilometer, we located the building. An old white clapboard house was set back from the street. Signs out front suggested it no longer served as a residence but as offices for two solicitors and a tax consultant.

"Interesting." Ariana kept walking past the house, but we'd slowed our pace considerably.

"What's interesting?"

"Either the cop knows one of the business owners, or he threw his authority around and claimed a right to hide out inside."

"Regardless, he's in the basement," I said quietly and scanned the place as unobtrusively as I could. "At least one other human is inside, and a few scents I can't quite identify."

"Not surprising," Ariana noted. "It's the middle of a workday." Her nostrils flared, and she drew her dark brows into a line. "Know what you mean about odd scents. It's like someone's concealing what they are and not quite pulling it off."

I glanced around. It appeared this had once been a neighborhood, but all the structures had been converted to accommodate one business or another, from a beauty shop to a place advertising psychic readings. I resisted a snort. I assumed that kind of shit had gone out with the 1800s. Prophecies can be dead-on accurate. For mages. Only charlatans profited from selling false hope—or false divination—to mortals. At least, that's how it was before I left Northern Italy.

Being warded would help us sneak around the back of the house, but we couldn't shimmer into nothingness. Too many people around. After a brief search, I spied what I was looking for. An alleyway running between two of the houses beckoned, and I set a path for it. Ariana understood. The feel of her magic wrapped around me before we'd taken twenty paces down the small side street.

The reek of our prey was so strong I didn't realize Conan had joined us until the wolf was almost fully corporeal. His ward was probably more bulletproof than ours. *'You're a welcome sight.*" I switched to telepathy so the sound of us talking wouldn't give anyone pause. It's weird to hear voices and not see who owns them.

"Reason we're here—" Ariana began.

Conan cut her off. *"I know. Talked with Ruby. Let's get this predicament taken care of."*

"He may have charms," Ariana warned.

"They don't affect me," the wolf reminded her.

We edged back toward the street; my gaze darted to all

sides. If anyone sensed our presence, they didn't offer obvious signs. A quick trip across an expanse of grass brought us around to the back of the three-story building. The house sat near the rear of the property. A fence that might have been two-and-a-half meters high circled the back part of the house. No lawn here. All the shrubs were dead. Someone had gone to a great deal of trouble to make the front of the house appear normal, but their attention to detail had fallen into serious decline. Perhaps it was why the fence was so high. To keep the neighboring property owner from peering over the top and complaining about slipshod maintenance.

"Something's not right," Ariana muttered and dragged her phone from a pocket. The backs of her hands were developing blisters. I'd have herded her beneath trees, except there weren't any.

"*Look here.*" Ariana thrust the phone toward me. Conan nosed it as he checked it out as well.

An image of a building blazoned with the same two solicitor names and the tax guy was displayed on her screen. Except it wasn't this building. "*I don't get it,*" I said.

"*The date is right here.*" Ariana pointed. "*Appears Jones, Jones, and Teegan moved into their new digs about six months back. This is where they used to be.*"

Conan woofed. Ariana shushed him.

"*This might be a place like that big fancy home not far from Ascent.*" I frowned, remembering the dark Witches and Sorcerers. "*Does this building sit atop a gateway between worlds?*"

"*Let's find out.*" Conan loped down a set of steps leading to a door recessed halfway below ground level.

My fangs snapped into place; Ariana's too. We stood right behind the wolf as he broke the lock with a shot of subtle magic. The hasp of a rusty padlock swung to one side; I reached over Conan's head to lever it out of its bracket and readied myself for battle.

Our target was here, but he wasn't alone. Aside from the second man I'd sensed, the others had to be mages of one variety or another because I couldn't quite pinpoint what they were. *"Kill first. Ask questions later,"* I said.

"Yeah. The Vampire motto." Ariana smirked back. *"I'd laugh, but I'm trying for stealth."*

The padlock might have been rusty, but someone had oiled the door hinges because it swung inward without a single squeak. The basement walls were probably concrete, but they'd been covered with something shiny. Easier to wipe down than nubby concrete. I didn't see any blood splatters, but I sure smelled them.

Conan was ahead of us; he stopped, ears pricked forward, tail held low. I caught a hint of Vampire over the blood odor but was certain I'd been mistaken. Other mages might have fallen so low as to aid mortals, but even the worst of us wouldn't make such a sophomoric error.

Or would we?

"Fuck!" Ariana shouted.

Three Vampires shot out of shadows and launched themselves at us. I've never fought my own kind before, but there's a first time for everything. At least I understood Vampire vulnerabilities. My assailant was a woman. Beautiful like all of us, her midnight hair swung around her in a shiny halo as she grappled with me, doing her damnedest to dig her fangs into my neck.

Fat fucking chance.

I swatted her head so hard with an open-handed slap, her neck made a snapping noise. Good. I hoped I'd broken it. Not that such a simple thing would finish her off, but it was a promising start. All that hair was useful. I dug a fist into it and twisted her head back farther still. Bones cracked against each other. While I had the upper hand, I plunged my fangs into her neck and drank as fast as I could. Normally, the only Vampire blood we drink is when we're turned, or during sex play. This wasn't play. I was engaged in a race against time. I had to empty her of blood before she sent magic to heal her busted neck.

I drank so fast, it threatened to come right back up.

No way in fuck would I let that happen.

Around me, the sounds of scuffling meant Conan and Ariana were engaged in lethal battles as well. I upped the ante, breaking more bones as I drank. The more damage I inflicted, the less chance Ms. Vampire would do aught but turn into a pile of moldy bones.

Maybe it was the power of suggestion, but the body in my arms suddenly changed. Instead of flesh, I held bones and sinews and a few frayed tendons. Good enough. I was done with her and tossed her to the floor. Given her advanced state of decomposition, she was one of the old ones. Why hadn't she been stronger?

Ariana grappled with a male half again as big as she was, but she was far more supple. I'd have given my left fang for a long blade. Instead, I threw myself atop the other Vampire and drove him to the floor. Rather than feeding, I dragged my fangs all the way across both sides of his neck until blood pumped out.

"Hold him down," Ariana cried.

"I'll do better than that," I told the woman I loved and drew my dirk from its sheath. It didn't have a whole lot of heft, so I added a shot of magic to its path and hewed through his neck the same way I'd have carved through a tough roast. The worst were the vertebrae. Ariana reached forward, grabbed two, and snapped them until the gray center of his spinal cord came into view.

Our victim had stopped bellowing a long time back.

"You can quit now," Ariana said.

I could, indeed. His flesh guttered like a candle in a pool of hot wax. He was considerably younger than the woman I'd ended.

"Get over here," Conan snarled.

I raced to where he held the third Vampire in place with paws on his shoulders and magical netting. "Why?" I shouted at the Vampire.

"Why else?" he tried for a jaunty smile but failed miserably. "We're half-starved. We needed blood."

Ha. So that was why we hadn't seen the officer who'd gone to ground here. He was sleeping off these three feeding from him.

"How many others like us shackled themselves to mortals?" Ariana asked and dropped a truth spell over him.

"Don't know."

"What clan are you?" I kicked him in the ribs.

"Ravnos. The best one, Vampire," he sneered.

"Done with him?" Conan inquired.

"Yeah," Ariana answered.

Bolts of something like lightning shot from Conan's front paws. The Vampire's back bowed. He bucked and heaved and bellowed, but it was short-lived. Where he'd been was a stack of messy bones.

"What in the fuck is going on out here?" a man's bleary voice sounded from behind us. His words were slurred as if he were drunk. No wonder. Being dinner for three Vampires would wipe anyone out.

"I've got this." Ariana's words dripped disgust. She took the dirk from my hand, raced forward, and ran it through the man's heart. His eyes widened in shock and disbelief. He hadn't understood anything—until it was too late.

"But it wasn't part of the deal," he gasped as blood bubbled from his mouth and ran down his chin.

"What deal?" I grabbed him by the arm to keep him from crumpling into a heap.

"You protect me. I help you."

"Who'd you bargain with?" Ariana shrieked, but it was hopeless. He was dead. "Fuck! Should have questioned him first."

I dragged my blade from the guy and wiped it on his pants before sheathing it. Ariana knelt on the floor, slurping blood from his open chest wound.

At least there hadn't been any channels to other worlds. Any open portals. Or any links to the ley-lines. Just perfidious Vampires selling the rest of us down the river. Fury ran through me, red-hot and forged by disbelief and outrage. How could they have?

Conan butted me in the side. I looked up in time to see another mortal, this one female, who looked just as dazed as the man had. I was so sated with blood, I wasn't as quick on the uptake as I might have been.

Until she fumbled yanking a gun from her belt.

This had to be the second cop who'd escaped our clutches. It figured they'd all know one another, working together and all. Conan executed a sideways leap and knocked her to the ground. I didn't waste time. For once, I didn't want any more blood, so I sliced neatly through her neck vessels with a fingernail I keep especially sharp for just that purpose.

Blood geysered, spraying everything nearby, including me. Once she was well on her way across the veil, I compared my memory of what she was supposed to smell like with the human sprawled in front of me and came up with a match. I hadn't picked up on her scent before because the man's had overpowered it by a factor of ten or better.

Ariana raised her bloody face and smiled. Blood dripped off her fangs, making her look deadly and dangerous and so stunning my chest felt tight. "Bingo," she said and fist-pumped the air. "We got 'em both."

She flowed to her feet and headed for a basin on the far side of the large room. The sound of running water told me she was cleaning herself up. It wasn't a bad idea.

"Thanks," I told Conan.

"None needed," the wolf said grimly. "We did a good day's work."

"Except for discovering Vampires are the same slimy traitors as the rest of magedom, we did," I answered him.

Ariana tossed me a wet towel. I swiped it across my face and hands before dropping it on the floor.

"Ready to go?" she asked.

I nodded. "We can ward ourselves and teleport back to Dee's car." I turned to Conan. "What'd you find out?"

"A lot," the wolf replied, "but it will keep until we get out of here."

"Damn it," Ariana muttered. "Did we just add a full-out war with Clan Ravnos to all our other problems?"

"Probably not," I told her. "I refuse to believe the entire clan has turned sour."

"Hope you're right." She tugged out her phone and shut her eyes for a moment. "Not quite sure how it happened, but it's nearly time to open the club."

"Time flies when you're having fun." Conan woofed at his own joke.

I drew a quick transport spell together. When the basement liquefied around us, I was glad to leave. For the first time, I understood what it had cost Percy to destroy other Sorcerers. I hadn't known these Vampires, but ending them was horrendous, an experience I didn't want to repeat but was afraid I'd end up duplicating anyway.

My casting was spot on, and we ended up smushed into Dee's car. Conan didn't exactly fit in the backseat. His legs and snout spilled into the front until he somehow shrank his bulk.

"Maybe we can hold off on that driving lesson for another day," Ariana said.

"Probably for the best," I replied. "I need to concentrate, and I'm still stunned any Vampire would turn traitor."

"Me too." Ariana started the engine and we rolled into the street. "What's wrong with animal blood? It's what we've been living on. Or morgues."

I didn't have an answer for her. But one revelation I did have was I'd stopped caring about Mistral. Ariana had crossed a line, but it no longer mattered to me. I'd been on the fence for so long, it was a relief to stop vacillating and spinning my wheels while I argued both sides of the point.

Now wasn't the time, but I needed to let Ariana know the ball was back on her side of the line. I hoped I hadn't hesitated for too long. By all the demons in the universe, I'd tried to kill her. She could well harbor concerns of her own.

Conan woofed. When I twisted to look at him, he was the size of a large dog. "Ready for more bad news?" His whiskers twitched.

"Sure. Why not?" Ariana shot back. "May as well get it all out on the table so we know what we're facing."

"Remember, I gave you a choice," the wolf growled. "One thing about my kind is we cannot lie. We can omit things and pervert them, but we're incapable of out-and-out untruths..."

CHAPTER SEVENTEEN, ARIANA

J did my damnedest to sweep everything else aside and home in on Conan and what he was saying. I should be in hog heaven. I'd just drowned myself in human blood. Never mind it hadn't come from a neck vessel. Blood was blood when it came down to it, and the woman's heart had stopped pumping.

I'd been smug, self-righteous even, about Vampires never walking the same path as dark Witches, Sorcerers, or Sidhe. Humble pie was a bitter pill. I still didn't see the attraction of becoming pawns and turning tricks for mortals. Why couldn't the Clan Ravnos Vamps have done the same thing as the rest of us? Gotten by on animal blood or morgue leavings? We weren't hurting for sustenance.

Pride was a sorry bedfellow if it meant kowtowing to humans. They answered to us. Not the other way round.

The Ravnos dicks aside, Nickolas had been a thing of beauty and grace when he was fighting. Even better, he'd looked like an avenging devil straight out of legends. I'd caught glimpses of him out of the corners of my eyes as he dispatched the hussy Vampire who'd launched herself at him. I'd smelled her interest. Fucking her would have been another way out—it would have bound him to her clan—but Nick had appeared oblivious to her charms. He'd killed quick, clean, sure. Vintage Vampire in action. I'd have loved to have focused all my attention on him, but I had issues of my own. My assailant could have cared less what sex I was. He was out to annihilate me, except his bulk made him simple enough to evade.

"My kinsmen want Earth to revert to an earlier time, one when its survival didn't hang by a thread," Conan was saying. "That story about Yggdrasil was true enough. The One Tree is bound to the fortunes of this world, but it's been dying for hundreds of years."

"Just like Earth," I said crisply. No reason to dance around the point.

"Actually faster, but that part isn't important," Conan retorted. He was sitting up in the backseat, looking rather like an oversized hunting dog. I'd never truly appreciated his infinite ability to alter his form until now.

"The quickest way to accomplish their goal," the wolf went on, "is to clear out vast segments of humans. A war against magic would do that, but the guardians had something quicker in mind."

"Oh really." Nick's words were laced with derision. Clearly, he wasn't any more impressed with Conan's kin than I was, but Moonglow had saved my life.

Because Conan asked her to, an inner voice reminded me.

"Their plan is to alter the composition of the atmosphere until it can't support human life. It's a fine line to maintain animals and wipe out mortals, but if anyone could pull that off, guardians can. The maneuver is more a matter of timing, actually. Animals can survive an atmospheric mix that is toxic to humans. The alteration wouldn't last more than, perhaps, five minutes, if that."

"Wait a second," I said as I guided us onto the freeway. The backs of my hands hurt from exposure to daylight. So did my head. "Why do they want us out of the picture?"

"Why else? So no one bears witness to their destruction. It will be major. Billions of dead mortals. No one left to deal with their remains. When I pointed that out to Fairclaw, he shrugged. Time is close to meaningless to us. I suppose he figured waiting out decomposition wouldn't be a problem. It would be a real boost for animals. Free food, and lots of it."

"So what they told us was true as far as it went," Nickolas said slowly.

"The part about us needing to step aside and let them pick up the reins?" I sought clarification.

"Aye. Having us mucking up the works engaging mortals in one skirmish after another won't generate nearly as many deaths as their plan."

"Ick," I muttered. "I'm a Vampire, and that's just disgusting even to me. I never wanted to get rid of mortals. Mostly, I want them to respect what I am and leave us be."

"I still don't understand," Nickolas said. "Not totally. That other world, the one with all the snow and silver in its core was the guardians' base. Why do they care two figs about Earth?"

"From their perspective, all worlds belong to them." Conan woofed to punctuate his statement.

"Being the source of all magic, and all that rot," Nick said sourly.

I shook my head. "I'm not sure I believe that. It's what they want us to think, but maybe it's just one more manipulation."

"It's true enough," Conan spoke up. "We were the first, but none of that is important. What do you want to do? We need a position before we talk with everyone else."

"They want to fight," Nickolas said. "Hell, Clive even rustled up the Kelpies."

"What?" For once, surprise rippled through Conan's tone. "The Scottish water horses?"

"The same," I said. "It wasn't my idea. Not sure what possessed Clive to rattle their cage, but here we are."

"What exactly did they say?" Conan pressed.

"We don't know," Nick replied. "We left before Clive could launch into what happened. He looked damned pleased with himself, though."

"That he did," I murmured, and then asked Conan, "Why is their offer to aid us important?"

"Some magical creatures sprang from a different line entirely," the wolf answered me. "To home in on it, the Celtic monsters are completely independent of anything linked to guardians."

I thought about it. "Alrighty. Beyond Kelpies, I can come

up with a couple of others. The Dearg-Due, and the Dullahan."

"This is taxing my memory," Nick said. Isn't the Dearg-Due a type of Irish Vampire?"

"Yeah, and the Dullahan is the headless Irish horseman," I replied. "Except the Dearg-Due isn't exactly a Vampire. Not in the same way we are."

"It's just one, right?" Nick persisted. "A woman who seduces men and then drains them?"

"Yes, but we're getting off track." Conan deepened his voice to make a point.

I quit scratching through my mental database for more monstrosities with roots in the British Isles.

"There is one advantage to the guardians' proposal," Conan went on. "We could leave and return once the worst of things was done."

"To cities littered with rotting corpses?" Nick's delivery was neutral, but his words weren't.

"Depends how long we remained off world," Conan replied.

"This isn't only our decision," I said as I drove toward *Ascent*. We were off the expressway and navigating city streets. It was rush hour, and traffic was doing its usual slow-and-go routine.

"No. Nor does everyone have to make the same decision," Conan said.

"Aye, but they almost have to," Nick spoke up. "If we remain, we need every mage for projects like the San Francisco one." He half-turned so he was looking at Conan.

"What do you know about Kelpies? Why would they have agreed to help so readily?"

"They're born warriors," Conan said. "I've never known them to turn down an opportunity for a good battle. You can't trust them, though. They'd as soon drill their way through our ranks as mortals. They can absorb power from other magic-wielders. It's something none of the rest of us can do."

It took all my self-control not to bring Dee's little car screeching to a stop. "Christ on a bloody, fucking crutch," I swore. "Of course they'd agree. Clive offered up a tempting hors d'oeuvres tray."

"Featuring Vampires, Sidhe, Fae, Witches, one and all," Nick said sourly.

"There is that aspect," Conan agreed, "but don't forget their asses are on the line too. If magic dies out—because mortals shanghai too many of us—Kelpies won't fare any better than the rest of us."

"They need us, but we can't trust them," I summarized the picture that was beginning to emerge.

"Exactly," Nick said. "They're using us, but we're doing the same in return. A bit of a mutual jerk-off."

"Just so long as they don't come first and decide we're expendable," I muttered and rounded the final corner to the club. Street parking wasn't happening, so I pulled into the alley and left the car in a No Parking zone.

As settled as we were likely to be, we walked into the club. Almost everyone was deep into getting the club ready to open. I thanked Dee, and returned her keys. Standing on a table was starting to feel like my go-to place, so I picked one, vaulted on top of it, and whistled. "Problem solved," I yelled to make certain everyone knew there were no more loose ends. Not from our last mission, anyway. Cheers rolled through the bar with shouts for details, but I shook my head. I was ashamed Vampires had sold themselves up the river for twenty pieces of silver—or in this instance, twenty drams of blood.

Conan, back to his usual size, leapt deftly up beside me. In fewer words than I'd have imagined possible, he sketched out the guardians' final solution to the human problem. "None of us have to do anything," he ended with, "but the choice is out there."

"It's a coward's road," Percy's deep voice rumbled. "Leave and return after someone else has done the dirty work."

"Besides," Ruby cut in, "it pains me to admit this, but not all mortals are bad enough to deserve to die. Lots of them, but certainly not every single soul."

And therein lay the biggest difference between Vampires and most of the other mages scattered through the room. They retained compassion. While I supposed I might have some, mine was more like sniffing fumes than full-blown empathy.

I cupped my hands around my mouth. "So, we fight?"

A deafening chorus of ayes and yesses filled my ears. When it died down, I asked, "San Francisco PTF, or a more modest goal?"

"We talked about that while you were gone." Percy strode closer. "I've been monitoring com channels from the Seattle group. They're shaken."

A grin stretched across my face. "They ought to be."

"At the moment, they're heavily into blame mode, as in whose fault this whole mess was," Percy went on.

"Did they come up with anything?" Nick was grinning too.

"Of course not, but they're still trying to find someone to hang out to dry." Percy cleared his throat. "Anyway, if we can even eliminate 75 percent of the San Fran bunch, I believe they'll back off for a while. Perhaps a long while." The big Sorcerer turned to Conan. "How will the other guardians take it if we don't follow their instructions?"

"It isn't as if they can turn all of you into toads for disobedience," Conan retorted. Dee, Dahlia, Zoe, and several other Witches began to laugh. Forcing enemies into unwelcome shapes was their bailiwick.

"No, but they can throw magic around and make our lives miserable," Ruby said.

"Or sabotage our next mission," Christa added.

"They wouldn't do that," Conan said. "In the dim reaches of their minds, even they understand we're all on the same team, even if they fancy themselves the leaders."

I nodded and reminded everyone, "Conan's mother leveraged magic to save my life. She didn't have to do it. Afterward, she was astonished she'd summoned power to help a Vampire, but she didn't walk away when I needed her."

"Will you tell them?" Nick asked Conan.

The wolf nodded. "I will."

"Let's do this," I said. "Percy, hang out a sign that says we'll be closed for a week after tonight. That will give us time to execute a plan." It killed me to shutter the club, but it couldn't be helped.

"Any whiff of us being behind Seattle's PTF problems?" Nick asked Percy.

"Not so far," the Sorcerer said. "Wiping out their computer records was a big help. There's nowhere for them to dig for possibilities."

Finally, a true plus to the digital age. We could have set fire to paper, but what Percy had done was infinitely quicker. No charred scraps to dredge through for clues, either. Once an electronic record was truly obliterated, there was no bringing it back.

"We'll finalize plans after closing tonight," I continued. "Who wants to make certain as many of the others as possible are here?"

"I will," Dahlia said. "I'll send a few Witches out trolling."

I didn't have anything further to say, so I jumped down. Everyone sprang into action doing last-minute things before Percy propped the front door open.

Conan loped to the bar and closed his jaws loosely around my lower arm. "You're needed in the storeroom."

I glanced around for Nick and Clive, but didn't see them. "What's up?" I asked the wolf.

A ruffling snort emerged from the back of his throat. It was noncommittal as hell, so I supposed I'd find out once I poked my nose in the back room. No one actually required my presence here. The harsh reality was I'd been absent for six weeks after Nick vanished. Part of that—maybe the first two weeks—I'd been recovering from my near brush with death. The next four were sheer indulgence on my part, and an unwillingness to face anyone.

Regardless, my friends had done a bang-up job keeping things rolling even when no one was sure if I'd ever return. They'd done it for me. And for themselves. Finding work as an immortal held a specific set of challenges. All of us lived on forged documents. They were great—so long as no one looked too closely, or researched our names, trying to match them up with phony birth certificates.

I strode briskly, following the wolf across the rear of the bar. The door to the storage room was ajar, so I shouldered through, kicking it shut behind us. My nostrils twitched, suddenly filled with the scents of the sea. And not just any sea. Born in the northlands, I'd recognize the North Sea any day.

On the heels of that revelation, a sharp hunch formed why Conan had fetched me. The back door that opened onto the alleyway stood open. The minute I walked through, Clive jumped in front of me. "Sorry, Ariana, but they said they needed to talk with you."

Nick flanked me, and I was pleased by his quiet, unstinting support.

I glanced Conan's way. "You could have given me fair warning."

"Why? What difference would it have made?"

Eh, the wolf had a point. The alley was deserted, but by design. The throb of powerful magic draped the length of it. I wondered what it looked like from the outside, but it didn't matter. The spell had the desired effect of keeping passersby away. The clip-clop of hooves grew louder. Yeah. That's right. Even in human form, they retained their horsey feet.

I turned toward the sound and deployed my psychic senses. Not that I needed them, but I didn't want to miss anything. Tonight was all about threes. We'd dispatched three of our own, and three Kelpies walked—pranced?—toward us. The men had long, shiny black hair that fell straight as a stick to waist level. Liquid dark eyes matched their hair. In their own way, they were as eerily beautiful as Vampires. Tall and muscular, they fairly screamed "bad boys." If it weren't for their feet, they'd have looked like a motorcycle gang with leather and chains and tatts and piercings.

I grabbed the point and hoped to hell I could hang on to it. "Thank you for offering to support our cause," I said, keeping to a formal tone.

"We are still deciding," the one in the middle observed. His voice was honeyed, low, mellifluous. Where I mesmerized with my eyes and spells, he clearly used voice tones.

"It's why we are here," the one on the left added. "To either sign on or leave."

I resisted rolling my eyes and muttering, "Duh." I wished I knew more, like where Clive had actually found this trio—and what exactly had passed between them. But I didn't feel like making small talk. Questions like, "Hey. Do you live around here?" weren't fruitful.

"We don't fraternize outside our own kind," the middle one said.

"No need to change that now." Conan punctuated his words with a low growl.

"We wish it were true, guardian," the righthand one said, "but we're just as besieged as the rest of you."

"How would you incorporate us?" Middle Kelpie was back.

"How many are you?" I answered his question with one of my own. "How long can you remain in your human forms?"

"Over a hundred of us are scattered along the Pacific Ocean's coastal area," he told me.

Nick whistled. "I had no idea you were so numerous."

Lefthand Kelpie brayed laughter. With it, the scents of brine intensified, and I noticed his teeth were equine as well. Broad and squared off. "Our company here is miniscule compared with who we left in the Old Country."

"And my second question?" I pressed.

"It varies, Vampire," the Kelpie said. "We're not so different from your people in that regard. The older ones can hold onto their human form for as much as a day. The younger ones, perhaps a couple of hours."

Younger ones? Kelpies reproduced? It was news to me, but I could live without the nitty-gritty details. How in the hell did they manage it in the absence of females? Or were the women hidden away similar to some obscure religious sect?

"Out of those hundred or so, how many are older?" Clive asked. His usual bravado was notably subdued. I got it. This was his brainchild. If it went south on us, he'd bear the brunt of the blame.

The Kelpies held a hushed conversation. I'd never heard their language before. It consisted of clicks, clacks, and the occasional whinny.

"Roughly three-quarters," Middle Kelpie said, followed by, "Now, will you answer my question?"

"I haven't really thought about it," I told him. "The nightclub"—I gestured behind me—"will be closed for the next week. We did a good job wiping out Seattle's Paranormal Task Force, and—"

"We know," Righthand Kelpie cut in. "We've been monitoring your progress."

Something about the way he said it, or maybe it was his tone, made the small hairs on the back of my neck stand on end.

"It's the only reason we're here," Middle Kelpie said. "We know you can deliver."

"Not exactly what you told me." Clive pursed his mouth into an annoyed expression. Fangs peeked out, which told me just how pissed he was.

Breath hissed from between Middle Kelpie's teeth. "And do you always tell the truth, Vampire? When you're bent on seducing—or draining—some prime piece of real estate?"

I chopped a hand downward. This wasn't the venue to get into a pissing contest about who had the moral high ground. I was pretty sure it wasn't Vampires, but neither was it Kelpies.

"Just making certain I have this right," I said. "You want to be on the winning side. Keeping magic alive in the world is an outcome worth crawling out of the woodwork—er the ocean—to accomplish?"

"More or less," Lefthand Kelpie said. "How would our skills be utilized?"

I had a feeling they wouldn't follow orders to save their asses. "You'd work within your own groups," I told them. "Just like most of the rest of us. So there would be a regiment of Kelpies. We'd position you for maximum effect. I'm fairly certain none of those PTF idiots have even heard about you, let alone seen one."

Middle Kelpie chuckled. It was the kind of noise Dracula might have made before he cut someone's head off and ate them. "Suits us fine. Even better would be a choice."

"As in?" Nick asked.

"Give us a couple of options and let us choose which is a better fit," the Kelpie said.

"Sure. Easily done," I agreed.

The darkness developed a shiny, liquid aspect, and the magic that had floated through the alley dissipated. The Kelpies left along with it, but in an odd way. One minute they were in front of me, the next there was no trace of them beyond a lingering salt smell. The whole episode was damned unnerving, and I consider myself fairly unflappable.

"Will they keep their word?" I asked Conan.

"I believe so," he said. "No percentage for them to set the rest of us up. They're self-serving—and not overly insightful —but even they know full well if they fuck us over they'll end facing all thousand plus of the San Francisco cops on their own."

"Bollocks. I'm sorry," Clive muttered.

"No need to be," Nick reassured him. "It's appearing this will work out."

"But they kind of used me."

"Eh, well we're using them right back." Nick's jaunty grin came out in force. "I call it a dynamic balance."

I didn't have anything even vaguely related to sanguine feelings about our brand-new allies. It was rather akin to saddling ourselves with a tank of piranhas. Or a nest of cobras. Plenty deadly, so long as we aimed their poison the right way—or their teeth.

The sound of music starting up wafted through the still-open back door. Meant we had customers. I turned and walked inside. If tonight was the last normal night for a while, I was determined to make the most of it.

"I'll be back later," Conan told me once I cleared the lintel.

I dug my fingers into his neck ruff. "If you miss us here, I'll be home for a little while after the meeting ends." The backs of my hands were healing, but still on the sore side. No matter what master plan we ended up launching after tonight's powwow, I wanted it to happen after the sun had set.

CHAPTER EIGHTEEN, NICKOLAS

The evening sped by. Coming face to face with Kelpies had been more unsettling than I'd imagined it would be. Most magical creatures, other than the dark mages, weren't especially evil. Kelpies held a chill edge that gave me pause. They didn't come in female versions, yet one had mentioned variations in power that were related to age, which suggested they reproduced. How in the hell did they make new Kelpies absent two sexes?

I'd expected the all-mage meeting to last a long while, but everyone was in full agreement on our next moves. About all we did was split into working groups and agree to meet east of San Francisco toward ten the following evening. Dahlia and her Witches had managed to scare up about 2000 of us. Guess they combed the woodwork, and mages emerged. Some causes are worth exposing what you are.

"That was easy," Ariana said after the group had dispersed.

I nodded. Almost too easy, but I didn't want to queer our chances by throwing doubts around.

"I'm going to our place," Clive told me. "See you later." Despite my reassurances, I could tell he still felt out of sorts. He'd believed he was in control—a very normal Vampiric assumption—when in fact the Kelpies had manipulated him for their own ends. Left to their own devices, I was fairly certain they wouldn't have reached out to us, but Clive luring them had provided an opportunity that proved too good to pass up.

"I might be there," I told him.

He clapped me across the back. "If not, I'll catch up with you before we leave for our journey south."

After he was gone, only Ariana and I remained. "If it wouldn't be an imposition, I'd like to come home with you for an hour or two," I told her. No reason to dress things up. I had things I wanted to say, and I preferred to do it somewhere other than the nightclub. I tossed in a time frame so she wouldn't worry about being stuck with me through what little remained of tonight and all the next day.

She angled a speculative look in my direction. "Um, sure. You're always welcome. Your spell or mine?"

The question made me laugh. "Always happy to ride on your coattails," I told her.

"At least you didn't call it my broomstick," she retorted.

"Ssht. Dee and Dahlia would take exception to that." I was still chuckling.

"Nah. They poke fun at themselves all the time."

The musky scent of Ariana's magic wrapped around me. Copper and heather and blood, her magic was as familiar as my own. Even though I'd finally laid my outrage over Mistral aside, it didn't mean whatever I managed to piece together by way of apologies and hopes would make a difference.

She and I had established détente. We were good work partners, exceptional at anticipating each other's moves. Maybe it was a place to begin: telling her I didn't want to jeopardize what we had, but I hoped for so much more. While I was considering how to couch what I wanted to say, the walls of her living room took shape around us.

"Would you like tea?" She arched a dark brow and bent to unlace her boots and lever them off.

"Sure. That would be lovely, but I can make it."

"Nah. I'm good." She walked toward the kitchen, leaving me with a view of the tantalizing swing of her hips. She was one fine-looking woman, but beauty alone doesn't sway me. If it did, I'd have bedded every Vamp in a fifty-league radius. Ariana was brilliant, courageous, and daring. She had every worthwhile Vampire trait while managing to hang onto the best of her human ones.

I was too wound up to sit, so I dug through some of the older scrolls in her expansive library.

"Looking for anything in particular?" she called from near the stove.

"Aye. Kelpies. First I knew they had a way of producing young."

Ariana made a snorting noise. "So I'm not the only one who stumbled over that little tidbit."

I was still sorting through scrolls. I'd never spent so much as a moment wondering where the hell Kelpies came from. Vampire history was clear. We all sprang from a cocky

Italian explorer, Ambrogio, who'd done a bang-up job pissing off some of the gods and goddesses.

Maybe because I wasn't invested in results, the current scroll had exactly what I was searching for. Penned by hand in archaic Gaelic, the words were faded in spots. So faded, I extrapolated to come up with meaning.

The enticing scents of mint and rosemary teased my nostrils as Ariana drew near bearing two steaming mugs—and a bottle of mead. "Find anything?"

"Aye."

She set the cups down on the coffee table. "Just aye, eh?"

"Hold on." I finished skimming the section and moved the scroll to the table where I unrolled it so both of us could read.

She sat to my left and asked, "Where do I begin?"

I pointed and kept reading. Nothing about the faded script scribbled in front of me made me feel any better about aligning ourselves with the Scottish water horses.

"Fuck," Ariana muttered. "Aw geez. This is worse than I imagined."

"Aye. It's worse than I envisioned too. Where do you suppose they keep the unfortunate women who produce their young?"

"They don't." Ariana bypassed her mug and went straight for the mead bottle, tipping it back.

"Well, they do for a little bit. They'd almost have to, otherwise who'd feed the babies?" I glanced back over what I'd read wondering if my translation had missed something.

She angled her index finger over one passage. "No. It says right here they cut the fetus out of the woman. Once they have the kid, they divvy up the hapless human and eat her."

I stared at the passage and made a few adjustments for badly faded words I'd misinterpreted, probably because the reality was grisly even for a Vampire. "Damn. How have they gotten away with it for all these years?"

Ariana shook her head. "Because the women vanish and are never heard from again. Their families probably assume they were kidnapped and murdered."

"Not so far from the truth," I muttered. "Except, no one would ever believe their assailants were Kelpies."

"Probably not," Ariana agreed. "Back in the day, I'm certain sprites and spirits drew blame. Like as not us too." She twisted to look at me, folding her arms beneath her breasts. "Was there something particular you had in mind when you said you wanted to come home with me?"

I let go of the scroll. Despite the age of the vellum, it snapped back into place handily. After picking up my mug, I angled my body so I faced her. Perhaps half a meter separated us. It would have been easy to scoot close, wrap my arms around her, and crush her lips against mine. Grabbing hold of my mug had been purposeful. It kept my hands occupied.

I owed her an explanation for my request. And then she could decide if we had a future together. Vampires didn't select mates; it wasn't part of who we were. On one level, I felt significantly out of my depth, but it wasn't a reason to back down now.

"Whenever I'm struggling for words"—her voice was

soft, encouraging—"I pick the simplest ones and spit them out."

Emotion surged, both welcome and unfamiliar. She recognized my inner conflict and was trying to make things easier for me.

"Thanks. I'm not sure when the transformation caught me up, but I don't care what occurred between you and Mistral. Not any longer. I only realized it earlier tonight when we were dispatching our kinsmen. That's a forbidden act as well, yet we didn't hesitate."

"Good thing." Ariana's voice vibrated with outrage. "Because they weren't playing by the rules, either."

"No they weren't, but this isn't about them. All they were was a catalyst that helped me understand I didn't care about Mistral's death. Not anymore. My reaction when you told me what you did was ridiculously overblown, but I couldn't have stopped it any more than I could have held back a thunderstorm."

She nodded solemnly, never breaking eye contact. "I understand. More than you think."

She hadn't thrown me out yet, so I forged ahead. "I recognize why you had to tell me. I'd have found out eventually. I'd have seen it in your mind in an unguarded moment."

"Exactly," she said. "And you'd have had the same reaction. Except it would have been worse because our relationship would have moved beyond what it is now. You'd have felt cheated. Betrayed. It would have been ugly."

Every word resonated deep within me; somewhere along the way, she'd come to know me well. Given I'd lost it to the extent I did, the level of my fury if I'd stumbled on the truth after we'd become lovers was unfathomable. "Before I go any further," I told her, "I want to stress how much I value working with you and sharing your company. No matter what else happens, I don't want to lose that part."

Her smile was soft and engaging. "No worries on that front. I value our...partnership too. We understand one another, and it runs deeper than both of us being Vampires."

"You're wise as well as beautiful."

She rolled her eyes. "Cut the crap. I'm not a mortal you need to seduce."

I set my cup on the table and extended a hand. She placed one of hers in it. I took it as a good sign. "First off, I meant every word. Second, I'm delighted you're not a mortal, but I'm guilty as charged on the seduction front." I paused and sucked in a totally unnecessary breath. "I love you, Ariana. It's unfamiliar territory for me. I remember being in love as a mortal, but never in this form."

She curled her fingers around mine and squeezed. "What I feel for you is different from what I felt for Mistral. I was a girl when he came into my life."

"You don't have to explain."

"But I want to. I want you to know because I love you too."

I pried the cup out of her other hand and threaded my arms around her. She'd just said she loved me. Sweet as honey and hot as fire, the words arrowed into my heart and soul. I'm not sure quite what I'd expected, but her forthright declaration touched me deeply.

"I didn't make a total botch of things that day I attacked

you?" I asked as I cradled her against me, reveling in the feel of her skin beneath my fingertips.

She snuggled close and hugged me back. Our knees knocked against each other. The position was awkward, but I didn't care in the least. The woman who meant everything to me was in my arms.

She'd said she loved me. I still couldn't quite believe that part.

"Of course, you didn't," she replied. "I thought I was the one who'd screwed the pooch. Since I didn't have much of a choice, when we were rolling around on the ground fighting, I figured I'd laid my soul bare for nothing.

"I thought long and hard before I confessed. It wasn't an easy choice. We could have remained friends and left it at that, except I was having a hell of a time holding a line."

"The line is definitely cracked," I murmured and stroked hair away from her face, tucking it behind an ear.

"Cracked in a good way," she said. "I had no idea you'd react so strongly, but after it happened, I understood it was how things had to play out."

"What did you think I'd do?"

She shrugged against me. "Walk away? Worst case, I thought you might call in reinforcements to hang me out to dry. It was why I made you swear to keep my secret." Leaning away, she stared straight into my eyes. "You're certain?"

I nodded. "Absolutely. I want you by my side forever, Ariana."

Her generous mouth formed a radiant smile. "You've just made me very happy."

"And you've illuminated my world. Now and always."

I didn't need words. Not anymore. Tilting her chin, I kissed her. She opened her mouth to mine, and our fangs dropped simultaneously. We were going to make love, but we were going to do this the Vampire way. Lust began in my toes and swept through me, igniting every cell with heat and hunger.

I teased her mouth with my tongue and sucked on hers when she swept it across my lips and into my mouth. With our lips still crushed together, I swung her legs straight so she sat across my lap. The press of her firm breasts with their pebbled nipples was a delight, and I jammed a hand between us to cup one of them.

She moaned, broke our kiss, and grazed my neck with the tip of a fang, the touch so sensual I almost couldn't contain the sensation. My cock was so erect it hurt. As I thought about it, I'd been hard ever since she'd offered understanding and acceptance for when I'd done my best to end her. I didn't deserve her forgiveness. Hell, I had yet to forgive myself.

I rolled and pinched her nipple between my thumb and forefinger. She writhed beneath my touch, the movement setting my nether regions on fire. Clothes were an impediment. I tried to reach the buttons of her blouse, but it was hopeless. She'd been working on dragging my shirt off my shoulders with similar results.

When she jammed a wrist against my mouth, I understood she'd opened a vein, and I slurped greedily, sucking down the taste of her blood like an exotic nectar. This ritual was unique to our kind, and it added a whole other layer to lovemaking. I offered my wrist, trusting her to help herself.

Ariana made little mewling noises as my blood flowed into her mouth. Everything else faded, lost to the beat of our ancient ritual. Beyond the night Roseann had turned me, I'd only done this a time or two, and always with her. I'd never felt close enough to any of the other females to want them anywhere near my blood.

Waves of eroticism crashed over me, receded, and built again. Ariana's other hand had closed over my cock, but both of us were too far gone to deal with the prosaics of zippers or buttons. She squeezed me through layers of fabric, and I longed for flesh-to-flesh contact.

Licking her wrist to seal the wound, I stood with her still cradled against my chest and still feeding from me. Crossing the house in a few strides, I pushed the bedroom door open and set her on her feet, prying my wrist away from her mouth so I'd have two hands to undress her.

Blood smeared across her blouse as I pushed it off her shoulders, and left crimson streaks on her the high, rounded mounds of her breasts. Blood is where we live. Looking at mine marking her pale flesh smote me. It was all I could do to fumble the button and zipper holding her trousers in place and push them down her legs. Good thing she'd gotten her complicated lace-up boots out of the way.

She stepped out of her pants and underthings and stood proud and naked in front of me. If I'd had any breath to steal, her nudity would have done the trick. I'd never viewed all of her before. She was even more spectacular than I'd imagined with her graceful shoulders, long shapely legs, and concave stomach nested between the finest set of flared hips I'd ever seen.

"You're stunning," I managed, coercing my uncooperative tongue to find words. I was still high on her blood.

"Bet you say that to all the girls," she purred, walked forward, and licked my neck.

"Nay. Only to you." I reached for my shirt, but she batted my hands away. Maybe she was better at undressing than me, but she had my shirt off and my slacks undone and partway down my legs before she made a clucking sound.

Taking a step back, she just looked at me for a long, sizzling moment. "Gods, you're the gorgeous one."

"Now who has a silver tongue?" I teased. If I'd had a normal circulatory system, I'd have blushed at the compliment. I wanted her to be just as smitten as me.

Something close to a deep throaty purr rolled from her before she said, "Shoes. You still have shoes on." Kneeling, she licked her way down my chest and stomach, blowing hot breath tantalizingly on my aching member.

I wanted her to take me in her mouth again. I wanted to bury myself in her body. And I wanted to do everything all at the same time. I backed toward the bed and perched on its edge while she removed my shoes and stockings and finished removing my trousers.

I reached for her shoulders intent on pulling her onto the bed with me, but she closed her mouth around one of my toes, licking and sucking. The sensation was so unusual and so sensual, I groaned with delight as she moved from toe to toe.

My cock stood out like a flag in a staunch breeze. I'd never been this hard for this long without release, and my balls ached. The sight of Ariana at my feet, dark hair spreading around her like a cloud was incredible. Knowing we were on the verge of finally joining our bodies—and our hearts and souls—was heady, intoxicating.

Finally, she slithered back up my body. This time, she swiped her tongue across the head of my cock. I might have yelped at the intensity of that quick, hard lick. I say might have because I was too lost in lusting after her to notice anything beyond her body's proximity to mine.

Blood smears painted her body and my own, adding macabre artwork to our passion. She pushed me onto my back and straddled me, sinking onto my cock in one fluid motion. The heat of her closing around me was powerful, too intense to wait, or for low-key lovemaking. I gripped her hips and drove myself upward into her. Lifting and lowering, I moved my shaft, making certain I maximized every centimeter. If we'd been mortal, we'd have been gasping and panting for breath. Above me, her breasts with their distended nipples bounced in time to our motion.

She splayed her hands across my chest, pinching my nipples, and balanced herself as she fucked me with abandon. We moved hard, fast, sure, knowing exactly what we wanted.

Each other.

I've never experienced anything like the depth of our coupling. It touched me on every level. My soul cried for her. My heart sang to my love. My mind was flooded with wonder she wanted me after I'd been such a jackass.

And then I stopped thinking about anything beyond the miracle of her vault snugged around me.

"Soon." She breathed the word into my mouth.

I was more than ready, and I took control. Pure male Vampire, I poured on magic and compulsion and said, "Come, darling. Come with me."

"Thought you'd never ask." Her generous mouth was swollen from our kisses and smeared with blood. An unbeatable combination, it drove me mad with desire.

I felt an orgasm rise from her belly, crest, and smash into her. The control I'd been hanging onto like a drowning man shattered. Jism shot from my balls and into her hot little body. We clung to one another, shuddering and grinding our bodies together for long moments as the spasms of delight settled.

Drawing her down, I turned us onto our sides, my cock still buried within her. "Forever," I told her. "This is forever."

Nuzzling my neck, she murmured, "I wouldn't have it any other way." She tightened her muscles around me. I flexed back.

"The day is young," I murmured.

"Does that mean I get a repeat performance?" she teased.

"It might be arranged," I teased back. I longed to tell her how much what we'd just done meant to me, but words were bound to fall short. In lieu of talking, I rolled us so she was on her back and closed my mouth over hers. We had hours before we had to make ourselves presentable, and I aimed to make good use of every single one of them.

After offering her my wrist, I began thrusting into her again. No longer in a hurry, I moved slowly, deliberately, determined to bring every erotic fantasy she'd ever had to life.

276

You've reached the end of *Cracked Line*. The Cataclysm series has one more book, *Broken Line*. Read on for a sample. Lots of irons in the fire for book four. Will the mages manage to corral humans who want them imprisoned—or dead? What happens when you ally yourself with Kelpies? Will Balor show back up? Nick and Ariana are brand new as a couple. Do they have the stuff to go the distance? While you're thinking about *Cracked Line*, please leave a review. Doesn't have to be fancy. A line or two will do. Thanks in advance.

BOOK DESCRIPTION, BROKEN LINE

In all my years as a Vampire, hundreds of them, I never imagined humans would be anything other than food.

Rich, pure, delectable blood. Prey that fought back never posed a problem. Mortals couldn't stand against those of us with supernatural ability. That world still exists, but it's taken a backseat to humans who've joined forces with turncoat mages. Mortals were never meant to wield power. Over the long haul, they're sure to be very sorry for the choices they've made.

Meanwhile, they're a huge pain in the rear and a threat to every type of mage, not just Vampires. Some days, I just want to go back to running my nightclub. *Ascent* is a "don't ask, don't tell" establishment. I never cared who frequented my bar, so long as they brought plenty of money and a powerful thirst for booze.

Maybe someday I'll be a humble innkeeper again, but it's

so far in the future I can't even think about it. Nope. For now, all I see is blood. Rivers of it, and not running down my gullet, either. On the plus side, I have good friends, powerful allies, and a Vampire who loves me.

We have to come through this unscathed. Have to. I'm Ariana Hawke, and I take care of what's mine.

BROKEN LINE, CHAPTER ONE, NICKOLAS

*B*riny ocean smells greeted me as our travel spell faded, spitting Ariana and me out a few kilometers east of San Francisco. I've never stopped missing the scent of the sea. It charmed its way into the core of my being during my years in Scotland before I was turned. Northern Italy—at least the part where Clan Giovanni's seethe was located—wasn't close enough to saltwater to carry that characteristic tang.

I still couldn't believe Ariana was mine. Truly mine for the rest of our immortal lives. The ramifications were staggering, and I wanted to spirit her away to a private spot, build us a magical tower, and retire there for the next couple of centuries. It might happen, but not anytime soon.

Not with a major war ahead of us. One where if we lost, we'd be in a world of hurt. These weren't run-of-the-mill mortals we faced, ones who'd learned what they knew about supernatural creatures from television and the Internet. Nay, we faced men and women who were part of a paranormal task force. While far from naïve, they didn't know as much as they thought they did about us. Hopefully, we could capitalize on their relative ignorance. A similar effort had gone well in Seattle, but San Francisco's squad was over ten times the size.

Even if there were 5000, we'd blast through their ranks. We had to. The early battles in any war are critical. I was a knight before I was a Vampire, it's how I know these things.

In a far more pleasurable vein, Ari and I had made love for hours, until it was time to meet up with everyone east of San Francisco. We could have kept going for days. Months. Sex with another Vampire is unbelievably erotic. It's not just the blood that's mixed in, but the entirety of the experience. We can push limits like no other magic-wielder. Just culling up memories of all the ways we'd pleasured one another made my cock shoot to attention. As if I hadn't come so many times I'd lost count.

Focus, an inner voice hissed.

I considered telling it I was smitten, and Ariana eclipsed everything, but the task that lay ahead was daunting. Indulging in lusty imaginings was counterproductive. I aimed to ensure she and I had all the years I planned on. For that to happen, we needed to get through the series of battles to come.

Not just this one, but all of the others that followed. I've always had a practical bent. I understood full well we'd be up to our fangs in conflict until mortals backed down. They'd made the mistake of their pathetically short lives when they got greedy and didn't want to share Earth with anyone magical.

That lesson should sink in damned quick, but I had a feeling it might take years and millions of dead before humans recognized their mistake. We'd lose mages along the way, but even one dead magic-wielder was unacceptable to my way of thinking. Strange I'd feel that way, since most mages view Vampires as one step up from pond scum.

Ariana glanced around, her blue eyes narrowed in thought. She's almost as tall as I am with a sinuously muscled frame, high cheekbones, a regal forehead, and full, sensual lips. Her waist-length black hair had been tucked into braids. Both of us wore dark clothing. We were warded, but eventually we'd drop our invisibility casting, and the fewer who saw us the better. We'd stood on the edge of a grassy verge. In the distance, a sign read Tilden Park, our agreed-upon meeting place.

"Appears we're early." Ariana ran her tongue over her lower lip. "Too bad. We could have snuck in one more—"

I captured her hand and placed it over the bulge in my pants. "Hush, darling. I'm having hell's own time as it is not dragging you into that thicket over there."

Silvery laughter rustled through my mind. "No one can see us. Why not right here?"

"Don't tempt me, wench."

More laughter as she wound her arms around me and crushed her mouth over mine. Licking, sucking, biting. The brush of her fang tips nearly did me in. For long moments, we lost ourselves in a hot, sweet kiss. The points of her nipples pushed against my chest, and where she straddled my thigh the heat from her seared me.

Before I gave in and shoved a hand between her legs, I dragged my mouth from hers. She nuzzled my neck and murmured, "Yeah. I get it. We're in a strange place, vulnerable as fuck. But damn it, Nick, you're hotter than a Times Square Rolex."

I'll be the first to admit modern terminology flummoxes me. Despite my cock beating like a second heart where it curved against my belly, I managed, "Huh? Times Square is in New York, and Rolex makes watches, but..."

After a final hip butt, she untangled her legs from mine. "Something stolen is said to be hot. People steal Rolexes all the time, and—"

"Got it." I grinned at her. Being with her, kissing, talking, fondling felt right, perfect, but we had to pay better attention. Mortals might not know we were here, but anyone magical would feel emanations from our spell—and from us.

Groups of people walked by, some with dogs on leads. Others sat at long tables chatting up a storm. "Maybe not the best place to have selected as a rendezvous spot," Ariana said softly.

I'd been thinking the same thing, once I wasn't transfixed by the wonder of her in my arms. Pheromones and the unique musk of sex clung to us. I was making a point to breathe just to keep savoring them. A uniformed guard, or maybe a policeman, rode through the various groups on a bicycle, stopping to talk with them. One by one, people rose and strolled toward the park gate where I'd seen the sign.

"Mmph. Must be closing time," I murmured.

"Makes sense," Ariana said. "They usually shut down public gathering spots at dusk."

A woman angled her head our way. She must have heard voices, but of course she couldn't see us. With a slight shrug, she hurried toward the entry point. Hooking a hand under Ariana's arm, I tugged gently and we hurried to where trees grew thickly uphill from our current location.

Before we got to the top of the hillock, I felt the distinctive bite of Witch and Sorcerer power and changed course to intercept it. Portals formed within a tangle of birch and aspen trees, disgorged mages, and were eradicated as soon as they'd done their job. Not everyone was warded, but I bit my tongue. These were allies, many of whom weren't overly fond of Vampires. I wouldn't make any friends by chiding them for being sloppy. Shifters and Sidhe joined the newly arrived.

Percy, a Sorcerer I worked with at Ariana's nightclub, *Ascent*, strode to us. Over two meters tall and built like a tank, he cut an imposing figure in his customary tartan, linen shirt, and sandals. Grey stubble was showing on his shaved head, cheeks, and chin. He nodded and ran shrewd blue eyes over the gathering crowd.

"I have the personnel info. Their system was eminently more hackable than Seattle's database," he said, not bothering with telepathy. No reason to since the park must have emptied of everyone but us by now.

Other mages drew near, forming a rough circle around us. I exchanged greetings with those I knew, as did Ariana.

"There you are, mate," Clive exclaimed. Another clan Giovanni Vampire, he'd come to the States with me a hundred years before. Blond, striking, and charming, he had a ready smile that concealed his fierce nature. He glanced from Ari to me, nostrils flaring. A knowing grin formed as he put two and two together.

"Congratulations," he said and pushed between us, wrapping an arm around my shoulder.

"He was worth waiting for." Ariana grinned back. Her words sent waves of delight coursing through me, and intensified the push-pull of wanting to ravish her and needing to sharpen my concentration and make certain I didn't miss anything on the eve of a major conflagration.

Leaning into her, I whispered, "Thank you."

"None needed," she whispered back. "What I said was true."

Clive rolled his eyes and made a snorting sound. "Not sure which is worse," he muttered, "the two of you lusting after each other or the two of you now you've gotten a taste of the merchandise."

Percy chuckled. "That's a good one, son. I'll have to remember it."

Clive was diplomatic and didn't mention he was a hell of a lot older than he looked. "Where's everyone else?" I asked after minutes ticked past and it became clear no one else was arriving.

"We talked about deployment through the day," Percy said without detailing exactly who "we" referred to. "What we came up with was if over 2000 of us aimed for Tilden Park, someone was sure to notice. Even having 500 of us here is risky. This region is thick with mages. With the current problems, they're bound to be on the lookout for alterations in the status quo."

"Point taken," Ariana replied. "Thanks for not chiding us for being absent from the war powwow, but are the others not coming?"

"They're nearby," Percy said, "in four groups about the size of this one. They already have their assigned targets. Once I've parceled out tasks here, we'll let them know and launch."

"Did we tap any local mages to help?" I asked.

Percy nodded. "We did, indeed, but only those I've known for a long while. Tough to know who to trust these days."

"No shit," Ariana growled. "Hard to say who's working for the other side."

"My concerns too," Percy concurred, and added, "Where's Conan?"

"Good question." Ariana gave a slight shrug. "Haven't seen him since before the club closed last night."

"I'm sure he'll show up." I raked a hand through hair that needed to be bound up and tucked out of the way. If anyone could take care of himself, it was Conan, a shapeshifting mage who usually favored his dire wolf form. Guardian magic was powerful, and Conan was heir apparent to his tribe.

"Not much we can do about it." Ariana looked straight at me. I knew her well enough to read concern in her finely honed features and blue eyes.

"Have you tried raising him with telepathy?" Percy pressed.

Ariana shook her head. "Didn't want to risk any more magic than was necessary to transport ourselves here."

"Good choice." Percy made come along gestures with both hands, and everyone pulled in close enough to listen.

Over the next quarter hour, he parceled out assignments. Because the San Francisco Paranormal Task Force was so big, we were working in pairs, not trios like we'd done in Seattle. Granted three of us to one cop had been major overkill in some instances, but not quite enough in others. Three of our targets had escaped and had to be run down.

It was when I'd discovered Vampires were as big a turncoats as other mages who'd sold themselves to mortals for devil-only-knew-what inducements. I could have lived out my years without that prime bit of knowledge. It made me ashamed.

Not much love lost between Vampires, particularly those from different clans, but I'd assumed we had a sense of decency and sufficient integrity not to sell out to mortals. Crap! They're food. We control them, not the other way round.

"Erm, I almost hate to ask," Clive spoke up, "but has anyone heard from the Kelpies?"

I'd been wondering the same thing myself, but I'd been content to let sleeping horses lie. The Scottish water horses were definitely a mixed bag. Stronger than fuck magically, they were dicey allies since none of us trusted them.

"Nope," Percy said. "I was getting around to asking you about them. You three were the last ones to talk with them. This isn't the type of undertaking where they can just pop in unannounced."

Interesting. Not much got past the big Sorcerer. He must have known about our chat in the alley behind *Ascent,* although this was the first he'd mentioned it.

"Oh, we can't, eh?" a strongly accented British voice inquired. Along with it the brine-smell of the nearby sea intensified tenfold.

"Well, I'll be damned. They were hiding." Ariana didn't even try for subtle.

"Poor choice of words, Vampire," the voice continued.

Kelpies swarmed downhill toward our group, hooves clattering against the rocky ground. Even in human form, they retained their horse's feet. Even though we numbered in the hundreds, and they were perhaps only twenty-five or so, the fine hairs on the back of my neck rose. Once upon a time, Ariana and I had a discussion about who inspired fear most effectively: us or them.

My vote went with Kelpies.

Ariana crossed her arms under her breasts. "If you don't like my word, Kelpie, pick another."

"We were observing," another of the Scottish water horses said. "Making certain we'd come to the proper decision."

Percy strode to the Kelpies, planting himself firmly in front of them. "And your choice was? I'm inquiring because I'm in charge of strategy, and we had one mapped out that will need some alterations if we're to include you."

I was trying to decide if any of the Kelpies were the ones we'd talked with behind *Ascent.* It was impossible to determine since they all looked alike with long, tangled black hair, dark eyes, and burly builds. Garbed in leather and chains and tatted up, they looked like a bad-boy motorcycle gang. An eerily beautiful motorcycle gang. They shared that otherworldly trait with Vampires.

One Kelpie took a step forward until scant centimeters separated him from Percy. The Sorcerer held his ground. "We shall assist," the Kelpie announced, "but we will do it in our own way."

"Which is?" Percy spun one hand in a circle.

"We will march on their offices and wreak havoc," the Kelpie replied. "You only selected officers; we will destroy everyone else. Including all their electronics."

Percy cocked his head to one side. "I'd been planning to finish sabotaging their databases, but that could work," he agreed.

"It will work," the Kelpie said. "Timing is essential. Your operation must be well in hand before ours begins."

I took a few steps until I stood next to Percy. "Forgive my ignorance of the extent of your power, but—"

"Nothing can harm us, Vampire," the Kelpie said. "Not lead. Not iron. Not silver. Our only weakness is a limit to how long we can remain human."

"Even that's not a weakness," another Kelpie snorted, and brine bubbled from his nose. "So what? We gallop back to the nearest water. Ought to scare a few mortals half to death."

"Where is the guardian?" The first Kelpie asked.

"Why does it matter?" Ariana skewered him with her direct gaze.

"We liked him," the Kelpie said. "Him joining forces

with Vampires went a long way toward validating yourselves in our eyes."

"Yeah? Well we love you right back," Ariana sneered.

Percy sent a pointed look skittering her way. "How will we communicate with you?" he asked the Kelpies. "Does telepathy work?"

The water horses dropped into their own language, a combination of clicks and clacks punctuated by the occasional whinny. They seemed to be arguing. It was hard to tell. Finally, the one who'd spoken first withdrew a polished piece of white quartz from a pocket. About the size of a chicken's egg, it was lit with a soft inner glow.

"Take this," he said. "When it is time, speak into the stone and say now."

Percy took it between two fingers as if he didn't trust its magic. I didn't blame him. "Just now?" he raised his bushy eyebrows. "Any particular language?"

"Aye, just the one word. Use whatever strikes your fancy, Sorcerer. We know them all," the Kelpie replied.

Just as they'd done on the first occasion I'd met with them, the group vanished in the time it took to blink my eyes shut. One moment they were there, the next the only evidence of their presence was hoof prints in the dirt. The brine smell remained, but it too was fading.

Percy stared at the glowing stone. "Seems too simple," he said.

"Do you suppose it's some kind of tracking device?" Ariana asked.

He shook his head. "I'd feel that kind of energy. This reminds me of the North Sea, all pounding water and storm-tossed waves." With a small shrug, he dropped it into a sporran wound around his waist by a leather cord.

"Best get moving," I said.

"Yeah, it's going to be a long ass night," Ariana muttered.

"Only if our prey eludes us," I replied. It wouldn't take long to kill one mortal, unless said mortal was armed with charms making him immune to Vampire persuasion.

Or had a sidearm loaded with silver bullets.

"I'm working with Clive," Dee called out. A necromancer Witch, she'd moved past her initial distaste for Vampires, but like I said Clive can be a charming fellow when he puts his mind to it.

Black hair in a geometric cut framed the Witch's stark cheekbones. Olive skin, black eyes, and pronounced bone structure confirmed her Indian heritage. Medium height, she was thin with ropy muscles that hinted she might be stronger than she appeared. Tonight, she wore her usual tattered jeans and a denim jacket.

"Sounds good to me." Clive trotted to her side. "We make a great team."

She smiled back. "We do all right together."

"Everyone ready to roll?" Percy asked.

Amid a sea of ayes and yesses, the teams teleported away. I set a spell in motion to take us closer to our assignment, one Thomas McMurdy, a deputy police chief in charge of the Paranormal Task Force.

"They assigned the head honcho to us," Ariana said.

"Means they trust us to not fuck it up," I told her.

"Then we'd better not. I'll manage our warding." Her

fangs dropped, making her so irresistible breath would have swooshed from me if I'd been the breathing type.

McMurdy was supposedly off duty, so I brought us out about half a kilometer from his home.

"Wow. Are you sure this is right?" Ariana craned her neck around taking in huge houses with extensive landscaping.

I'd memorized the address and rattled it off. Ariana dragged out her phone and tapped its display. "Yup. Right place."

"Why did you think it might not be?" I asked, wondering if she didn't trust my navigational ability—or my magic.

"Because cops don't make this kind of money," she replied. "Nowhere near it."

"Maybe he married into money," I suggested, relieved her concerns didn't revolve around incompetence on my part —and grateful I hadn't launched into a diatribe rebuking her for not believing in me.

"Possible, but my first instincts say he's on the take. Cops are in a unique position to make far more than their salaries on the side."

"That's the house." I pointed to a multi-story brick affair partway down the block. "Shall we sneak round the back and do some sleuthing before we barge inside?"

"Man after my own heart. Hang on a moment, I want to shore up my warding. In case he's playing host to mages—or has them on retainer as watchdogs."

I wrapped an arm around her shoulders. Once she nodded, we glided silently up the neighboring home's driveway, cutting across a short fence separating its backyard from McMurdy's. The portion of the house facing the street had been dark. Not so back here. Light flooded from several street level windows.

We settled between two large trees. Scanning through warding is a neat trick. I was just drilling a small hole in Ariana's protective layering when my nostrils filled with fur and wet rocks, the scents of guardian magic.

A large dire wolf padded toward us, his black and silver pelt glistening in muted light from a partial moon. *"You can't do this,"* Conan told us. *"A veritable army resides within."*

"We have to do something," Ariana replied in kind.

"We would have figured out McMurdy wasn't alone," I inserted, wanting to make certain Conan understood we were neither helpless nor stupid.

"Maybe yes, maybe no," Conan said. *"His bodyguards include a guardian."*

"What?" Ariana clapped a hand over her mouth. *"Sorry."*

"How is that possible?" I demanded.

"Long story," the wolf said. *"No time for it now, but I have an idea that I'm fairly certain will work."*

Ariana looped an arm around the wolf's neck and hugged him. *"Let's hear it,"* she told him. *"I want to get this show on the road."*

ABOUT THE AUTHOR

Ann Gimpel is a USA Today bestselling author. A lifelong aficionado of the unusual, she began writing speculative fiction a few years ago. Since then her short fiction has appeared in many webzines and anthologies. Her longer books run the gamut from urban fantasy to paranormal romance. Once upon a time, she nurtured clients. Now she nurtures dark, gritty fantasy stories that push hard against reality. When she's not writing, she's in the backcountry getting down and dirty with her camera. She's published over 75 books to date, with several more planned for 2020 and beyond. A husband, grown children, grandchildren, and wolf hybrids round out her family.

Keep up with her at www.anngimpel.com or http://anngimpel.blogspot.com

If you enjoyed what you read, get in line for special offers and pre-release special reads. Newsletter Signup!

SERIES

Alphas in the Wild

Hello Darkness

Alpine Attraction

A Run for Her Money

Fire Moon

Bitter Harvest

Deceived

Twisted

Abandoned

Betrayed

Redeemed

Cataclysm (coming spring and summer 2020)

Harsh Line

Warped Line

Cracked Line

Broken Line

Coven Enforcers

Blood and Magic

Blood and Sorcery

Blood and Illusion

Rebel Reaper

Untamed Reaper

GenTech Rebellion

Winning Glory

Honor Bound

Claiming Charity

Loving Hope

Keeping Faith

Ice Dragon

Feral Ice

Cursed Ice

Primal Ice

Rubicon International

Garen

Lars

Soul Dance

Tarnished Beginnings

Tarnished Legacy

Tarnished Prophecy

Tarnished Journey

Soul Storm

Dark Prophecy

Dark Pursuit

Dark Promise

Underground Heat

Roman's Gold

Wolf Born

Blood Bond

Wolf Clan Shifters

Alice's Alphas

Megan's Mates

Sophie's Shifters

Wylde Magick

Gemstone

Lion's Lair

Unbalanced

STANDALONE BOOKS

Branded, That Old Black Magic Romance (paranormal romance)

Edge of Night (short story collection, paranormal and horror)

Grit is a 4-Letter Word (nonfiction)

Heart's Flame (post-apocalyptic romance)

Icy Passage (science fiction romance)

Marked by Fortune (post-apocalyptic coming of age story)

Melis's Gambit (historical paranormal romance)

Midnight Magic (paranormal romance)

Red Dawn (post-apocalyptic paranormal romance)

Shadow Play (historical paranormal romance)

Shadows in Time (Highland time travel romance)

Since We Fell (contemporary romance)

Warin's War (paranormal romance)